The Master of Misrule

The Master of Misrule

LAURA POWELL

ALFRED A. KNOPF 🐎 NEW YORK

THIS IS A BORZOI BOOK PUBLISHED BY ALFRED A. KNOPF

All rights reserved. Published in the United States by Alfred A. Knopf, an imprint of Random House Children's Books, a division of Random House, Inc., New York. Originally published in paperback in Great Britain by Orchard Books, a division of Hachette Children's Books, a Hachette Livre UK Company, London, in 2010.

Knopf, Borzoi Books, and the colophon are registered trademarks of Random House, Inc.

Visit us on the Web! randomhouse.com/teens

Educators and librarians, for a variety of teaching tools, visit us at randomhouse.com/teachers

Library of Congress Cataloging-in-Publication Data
Powell, Laura.
Master of Misrule / Laura Powell. — 1st American ed.
p. cm.
Sequel to: The Game of Triumphs.
Summary: The Game of Triumphs lies in ruins, but Cat and her friends must enter the Arcanum once again to usurp the Master of Misrule, a corrupt leader who threatens to unleash the power of the game into London and the world at large.
ISBN 978-0-375-86588-6 (trade) — ISBN 978-0-375-96588-3 (lib. bdg.) — ISBN 978-0-375-89784-9 (ebook) — ISBN 978-0-375-86566-4 (tr. pbk.)
[1. Supernatural—Fiction. 2. Role playing—Fiction. 3. Games—Fiction. 4. Tarot—Fiction. 5. Space and time—Fiction. 6. London (England)—Fiction. 7. England—Fiction.] I. Title.
PZ7.P87757Mas 2012
[Fic]—dc23
2011021135

The text of this book is set in 12-point Bembo.

Printed in the United States of America
June 2012
10 9 8 7 6 5 4 3 2 1

First American Edition

To Lucy
"For there is no friend like a sister."
—Christina Rossetti

The Game of Triumphs

Cat was an ordinary London teenager until a chance encounter led her to the Game. After that, nothing would ever be the same.

The Game of Triumphs had existed since ancient times, but it was known only to a select few. Based on the lore of Tarot, the Game took place in an alternate world called the Arcanum. The players were divided among four courts—Swords, Wands, Cups and Pentacles—and each court had its own master. Under the rule of these kings and queens, everyday men and women took on the role of knights, competing for marvelous rewards. Fame, wealth, love, inspiration—no prize was too great. To win, each knight must venture into the Arcanum and complete a series of moves determined by a hand of cards. The Arcanum could be dangerous and unpredictable, but the prizes were worth dying for—and many players did.

Cat needed the Arcanum to solve the mystery of her parents' death. But the Game was invitation-only, and because Cat stumbled into it by accident, she was allowed only to watch—able to see the possibilities, but not to compete for her own prize.

So Cat teamed up with three other watchers who were equally desperate to play: Flora, Blaine and Toby. Together they fought to change the rules, depose the kings and queens, and make the Game open to all.

Their guide was the Hanged Man—a prisoner who could only be freed by their success. And succeed they did. The Game would never be the same. It was time for Cat and her companions to claim their prizes. Or so they thought. . . .

Those spacious regions where our fancies roam,
Pain'd by the past, expecting ills to come,
In some dread moment, by the fates assign'd,
Shall pass away, nor leave a rack behind;
And Time's revolving wheels shall lose at last
The speed that spins the future and the past;
And, sovereign of an undisputed throne,
Awful eternity shall reign alone.

—Petrarch, *Triumph of Eternity*

CARDS PLAYED IN THE GAME OF TRIUMPHS

The Greater Arcana
(Triumph Cards and Their Prizes)

ETERNITY

Victory

FAME

Fame

THE SUN

Beauty

THE MOON

Inspiration

THE STAR

Health

THE TOWER

Destruction

Hedonism

Reconciliation

Death

Sacrifice

Strength

*Can be played to
win a new card*

Time

Justice

Heroism

Love

Wisdom

THE EMPEROR

Leadership

THE EMPRESS

Wealth

THE HIGH PRIESTESS

Prophecy

THE MAGICIAN

Charisma

THE FOOL

*Represents chancers
in the Game*

The Lesser Arcana
(Court Cards)

King of Cups
Queen of Cups
Knight of Cups
Knave of Cups
Ace of Cups   *Root of Water*
Two of Cups   *Reign of Love*
Three of Cups   *Reign of Abundance*
Four of Cups   *Reign of Blended Pleasure*
Five of Cups   *Reign of Lost Pleasure*
Six of Cups   *Reign of Past Pleasure*
Seven of Cups   *Reign of Illusionary Success*
Eight of Cups   *Reign of Abandoned Success*
Nine of Cups   *Reign of Material Happiness*
Ten of Cups   *Reign of Perfected Success*

King of Pentacles
Queen of Pentacles
Knight of Pentacles
Knave of Pentacles
Ace of Pentacles   *Root of Earth*
Two of Pentacles   *Reign of Change*
Three of Pentacles   *Reign of Material Works*
Four of Pentacles   *Reign of Possession*
Five of Pentacles   *Reign of Material Trouble*
Six of Pentacles   *Reign of Material Success*
Seven of Pentacles   *Reign of Success Unfulfilled*
Eight of Pentacles   *Reign of Prudence*
Nine of Pentacles   *Reign of Sheltered Luxury*
Ten of Pentacles   *Reign of Wealth*

King of Swords	
Queen of Swords	
Knight of Swords	
Knave of Swords	
Ace of Swords	*Root of Air*
Two of Swords	*Reign of Peace Restored*
Three of Swords	*Reign of Sorrow*
Four of Swords	*Reign of Rest from Strife*
Five of Swords	*Reign of Defeat*
Six of Swords	*Reign of Earned Success*
Seven of Swords	*Reign of Futility*
Eight of Swords	*Reign of Shortened Force*
Nine of Swords	*Reign of Despair*
Ten of Swords	*Reign of Ruin*
King of Wands	
Queen of Wands	
Knight of Wands	
Knave of Wands	
Ace of Wands	*Root of Fire*
Two of Wands	*Reign of Dominion*
Three of Wands	*Reign of Established Strength*
Four of Wands	*Reign of Perfected Work*
Five of Wands	*Reign of Strife*
Six of Wands	*Reign of Victory*
Seven of Wands	*Reign of Valor*
Eight of Wands	*Reign of Swiftness*
Nine of Wands	*Reign of Great Strength*
Ten of Wands	*Reign of Oppression*

THE HANGED MAN

PROLOGUE

THE POSTCARD OR FLYER was lying trampled on the ground, and the woman wouldn't have noticed it if it wasn't for the silver trim glinting up at her. It was late evening and she was trying to get across town to pick up her children from their father's. Public transport was minimal on Boxing Day, and she had grown cold and tired waiting for the bus. In an otherwise dreary street, the card was an unlikely touch of glamour. There was a picture on the back, of a glittering blue circle or wheel on a black background. On the reverse side was a silver embossed coin, and written in ornate curly script:

The Triumph Lottery of Luck.

Heads You Win,
Tails You Lose.

Some advertising campaign, the woman thought. A new book or computer game. Or else it's for one of those online gambling sites. She stroked the embossed coin and found that the silver flaked off easily, as on a scratchcard. A little icon of a man's face, laughing, was revealed underneath: There was no real information, though—no telephone hotline or website, no PO box to write to with her winning claim.

But she put the card in her bag nonetheless. You never knew, did you?

CHAPTER ONE

CAT WAS STANDING UNDER THE STATUE of Eros in Piccadilly Circus. The post-Christmas sales were in full swing, and the damp sidewalks were teeming with bargain hunters. Illuminated billboards shimmered under a leaden sky. HEADS YOU WIN, their flashing words promised, TAILS YOU LOSE.

Behind her, winged Eros hovered, forever drawing back his bow. His body was slick from rain. The trickling of the fountain below the statue should have been a soothing noise, yet it set Cat's teeth on edge. Her eyes smarted at the neon signs. Every nerve jangled as she clutched the coin in her palm. Her other hand held a card with a picture of a stern-faced woman bearing a sword and scales. It was called the Triumph of Justice.

The card was Cat's next move in an ancient and infinite game of chance. Once she tossed her coin, London would vanish, to be replaced by the landscape of a world just the other side of our own. The Arcanum. It was the Game's board, and those who took their cards onto it would find their illustrations brought to strange and dangerous life.

Cat had played many cards and won many moves. Yet the fear that bit into her heart was sharper than ever before. Come on, she cajoled herself. One last time. Clenching her teeth, she tossed the coin into the air and straightened out her right hand. Its palm bore the scar of a four-spoked wheel: the emblem of Lady Fortune. All players in the Game of Triumphs carried her mark. When the coin landed on the wheel, the silvery scar on Cat's palm and the disc of metal merged briefly into one.

She raised her head to see where the coin had taken her. Nowhere.

London sprawled around her in all its damp, dirty splendor. The same shoppers and tourists thronged the pavements; the same buses and cars thronged the roads. The fountain trickled and adverts flashed just as they always had. The only difference Cat could find was on her playing card. The illustration of the Triumph of Justice had vanished, replaced by a dark horseman.

And then, through the splashing of the water, the buzzing of the crowd and the grind of the traffic, Cat heard a new sound. A heavy clip-clop.

An armored figure on horseback was approaching from Lower Regent Street, weaving through the traffic with unhurried ease.

The horse was pearly white, with a flowing mane and

tail. Its rider was clad in shining dark armor, and carried a banner of a white flower. Both should have belonged to a scene of romance, of faraway chivalry. As they drew nearer to the junction, they seemed to grow in stature, or else the scene around them began to recede. Clip-clop, clip-clop, rang out the hooves, as steady as the beat of a heart.

The horseman was only twenty paces or so from her now. Stuck fast to where she stood, Cat felt sweat beading clammily at the back of her neck.

Now other people were beginning to turn and look. Some pointed and exclaimed, applauding; others jeered, though their laughter had an uncertain note. Sickness rose in Cat's throat as the knight lifted one gauntleted hand to open his visor. She knew what was coming; she had seen the card. . . .

There was no face: only empty sockets and the pale gleam of bone.

The Triumph of Death.

A woman to Cat's left began to scream. The skeleton knight grinned; the sound of screaming spread. On and on, a high, shrilling note that split the air . . .

Cat woke up sweating; her throat felt like sandpaper.

She couldn't find the switch for the blaring alarm, and in the end it only shut up when she knocked it off the table. Bel yelled something indistinguishable from the kitchen.

"Sorry," Cat croaked in reply. She sat hunched over herself, clutching her pillow like a little kid with a teddy bear. It was all she could do not to ask her aunt to come to her and help chase the bad dream away.

It had been like this the whole night long, and the previous night, too. Dream after dream, seething with menace, and though she had woken up after several of them, this had been the only one she could distinctly remember.

Cat stumbled out of bed toward a flap of peeling wallpaper in the corner of her tiny room, behind which a card was hidden. Thank God. The Triumph of Justice was still there, still safe, its illustration as vivid as it had always been. I've already won the Game, she told herself; it can't hurt me anymore. All I have to do is claim my prize.

It was the lure of fabulous rewards that led players to the Game. The same cards that came to life as ordeals in the Arcanum could also be enjoyed as prizes—"triumphs"—in the ordinary world. Some players joined the Game in search of Strength or Fame; others, Justice; still more, Love. Yet these were only a few of the desires and transformations to be won.

Cat's wish was intimately connected to the Game. Surviving its moves had been hard enough. Far harder, though, was the discovery that her parents had not died in a car accident twelve years before, as she'd been told, but had been murdered by someone in search of an invitation to the Arcanum.

First the Game had orphaned Cat, then it had claimed her as a player. And finally it had seduced her, with the promise of a prize that would give her everything she craved: disclosure, judgment and punishment.

Cat had been given her reward two days ago, on Boxing Day. The Triumph of Justice had all the answers, all her hopes for retribution, yet she still had not gone into the Arcanum to claim it. She could not shake off her nightmares' sense of dread.

But enough was enough. Cat was sure that Toby, Flora and Blaine weren't letting themselves be spooked by a few bad dreams. They were probably already reveling in their success, busy getting on with their new, brighter lives.

I'll make my move today, she decided. No more excuses. I just need to get this over and done with, and then I'll be free of it. I'll be free of everything.

Bel was doing the ironing, singing lustily but with little tune. "I hope you're a bit more bright-eyed this morning," she said as Cat came into the kitchen. "You must've had a good twelve hours' nap."

She gave her niece a swift sidelong appraisal. Lately, she'd often shot Cat worried little glances when she thought she wasn't looking. Though neither of them talked about it directly, Bel had been given to understand that Cat was having a hard time dealing with the true circumstances of her parents' deaths. Bel knew nothing about the Game's involvement, of course, but she blamed herself for making up the car accident story in the first place. It had been her attempt to protect Cat from the official account of the killings: a robbery gone wrong.

Cat tried to grin. "Got to make the most of my lie-ins before school starts."

Her aunt's nervous sympathy made her feel faintly ashamed, as if she was getting it on false pretenses. Cat was three when her parents died, Bel nineteen, and it had been just the two of them ever since. They'd never gone in for the touchy-feely stuff, and they could be tough with each other if needs be, but that's why it worked. Theirs was a partnership against the world.

Bel didn't look entirely convinced by Cat's grin, but she returned to her singing anyway. She was about to start a new job at Alliette's, a posh casino off Trafalgar Square, and was already fizzing with anticipation.

"Look," she said, breaking off midchorus to gesture at the window. "It's that boy again."

"What do you mean?" Cat was listlessly pushing corn-flakes round the bowl.

"I first saw him yesterday afternoon. Skulking around outside, watching our door. And now he's back."

Cat got up to stand by the kitchen window, from where she could see a tall figure slouched against the lamppost across the road. In his shapeless, dull-colored clothes, he looked like what he was: a street kid. It was Blaine.

"I passed him on my way out earlier. Must be one of our friendly neighborhood thugs." Bel's tone wasn't entirely disapproving, though. Blaine had cut his hair since Cat had last seen him, so its former dishevelment was now a close-cropped brown fuzz. Even from here, she could see how it made the angles in his face more prominent, his eyes more deeply shadowed.

"It's OK," said Cat. "I know him."

Bel was half entertained, half suspicious. "Oho! Do you, now?"

"Yeah. He's, uh, a mate of some girl in school. He lent me a CD the other day. He's probably just here to get it back."

"Well, you be careful. He looks more the type to be grabbing handbags than sharing music."

As if he'd heard her, Blaine looked up into the window and straight at Cat, who raised a hand in greeting.

"I'm going down."

"Not in those pajamas, you're not—"

But Cat was already hurrying between bathroom and bedroom, pulling on clothes. As she tugged a brush through the sleep tangles in her strong black hair, she caught her eye in the mirror and scowled. She was always pale, but this morning she looked positively ashen. Ferociously, she scrubbed her cheeks with a washcloth, hoping to bring a bit of color to her face.

Five minutes later, she was outside. The last time she and Blaine had seen each other was in Mercury Square, outside the ancient house where our world and the Game's converged. There, at their shared moment of crisis and victory, Fortune's Wheel had spun a new fate, and the Arcanum had whirled around them. Now they nodded in awkward greeting, hunched against the cold, as pedestrians and traffic clogged the street.

"How are you?" Cat finally asked when it became apparent he wasn't going to start the conversation.

"Not bad."

Not good, either, she thought. He looked as tired and drawn as she did.

Blaine coughed—a wet, rasping sound. "I've been waiting for you."

"So I heard. You could've just, y'know, rung the bell."

"I got the impression that redhead wouldn't give me much of a welcome."

"Nah, you'd have been fine. Bel's a softy."

"She's your aunt, right? You don't look much alike."

This wasn't strictly true. They had the same gray eyes, the same stubborn mouths and the same tilt to their chins. But Bel, with her swaggering brightness and brashness, was—at a superficial level, at least—everything Cat was not. Blaine considered her again, straight-faced. "Wouldn't like to mess with either of you, though."

Aware that Bel probably had them under surveillance, Cat cleared her throat. "D'you, um, want to go sit down somewhere?" Whatever it was Blaine wanted to talk to her about, she had a feeling this wasn't a social call.

He gave a half nod of agreement and they walked down the street, in the direction of Soho Square. Even though most of the businesses were closed for the Christmas break, the neighborhood still had an air of prosperous bustle. The first time Cat had wandered into the square and seen the gardener's dainty half-timbered cottage through the trees, she had thought the place looked like something from a fairy tale. Of course, that was before she had fallen into a whacked-out fantasy of her own.

The two of them sat on a damp bench and watched the pigeons squabble over crumbs. They didn't know each other well enough for the silence to be comfortable, and Cat found herself wishing that the others were here. Clever, twitchy Toby, not as much of a geek as he pretended to be ... Prim and pretty Flora, with her sweet smile and nerves of steel ... Thrown together in the Arcanum, four strangers—and rival players—had become allies in a common cause. Yet even now, there was so much the other three didn't know about her. Or she about them, for that matter.

Cat and Blaine's silence stretched on. Greg, Bel's on/off boyfriend, had told Cat that one of the benches here was engraved with the lyrics from a song:

ONE DAY I'LL BE WAITING THERE
NO EMPTY BENCH IN SOHO SQUARE

The words kept running through her head, over and over.

Blaine coughed, interrupting the silence. "Have you been to Temple House since ... everything?" he asked.

Temple House, in Mercury Square, was the headquarters of the Game Masters. It wasn't far from here, but Cat would have been quite happy never to set foot in it again. She shook her head.

"And you haven't gone to the Arcanum to take your prize." He made this sound self-evident. "The Triumph of Justice."

"No. . . . Not yet. It's just . . . well, it's such a big step, and I guess I haven't felt ready for it. The thing is—I haven't been sleeping and . . ." She trailed off, realizing how lame that sounded. "Never mind. You haven't claimed your prize yet, either, have you?"

"Oh, I've cashed my card in, all right."

Cat's sense of foreboding increased. Blaine didn't have the look of someone who'd just won their heart's desire.

He had pushed up one sleeve and was tracing the line of a ragged scar along the outside of his right arm. Cat knew that the injury had been done to him by his stepfather.

"Blaine, your prize was meant to represent your stepdad, wasn't it? The Knight of Wands."

"Yeah." His tone was reluctant. "I knew he was hiding out in the Arcanum. Biding his time, making his plans. . . . Getting ready for a big comeback, with prizes galore. And I couldn't let that happen." Blaine touched the scar again.

"So I went into the Arcanum to look for him. Move after move, card after card. I'd almost given up when you met me. And then—well, everything changed, didn't it?" He was speaking quickly and angrily now. "The three of you seemed to have it sorted. You gave me all that motivational stuff about cutting the Hanged Man loose, and kicking out the kings and queens, bringing on our very own revolution. . . . You had me convinced, so I played along. There we were, the heroes, the winners, freeing the Game, saving the day. Just like we'd been promised.

"Then yesterday, I decided to make good on those promises. I'd been told the knight I was looking for was still in the Arcanum, and the Knight of Wands card would take me to him. So I rolled my die, and I entered the move."

"What happened?"

"*Nothing* happened. He wasn't there."

Absurdly, Cat's first reaction was to think of the song on the bench, its wistful promise that one day, the waiting would be over. "But—but there must've been something. Or someone. Or some kind of—"

"There was *nothing*," he said again, with a kind of smothered violence. For a moment, he looked at her as if he hated her, and she thought he was going to get up and leave. He rubbed his hands over his face, swearing under his breath. But when he spoke again, his voice was calmer.

"Afterward, I went back to Temple House, looking for answers, explanations, clues. Christ, I don't know. Anyway, it's been trashed."

"Trashed? Like how? I mean, I've seen it derelict before. Because the thing about Temple House is that it does change inside—"

"This is different. It's been wrecked, deliberately. And there's something else."

He coughed again, then drew out a card from his pocket. It was trimmed with silver and illustrated with a four-spoked blue wheel on a black background.

Cat frowned as she read the words on the other side.

Heads You Win,
Tails You Lose.

A few silvery specks clung to an icon of a curling forked tail.

"I think it's a kind of posh scratchcard," said Blaine. "But the tail was already uncovered when I found it."

"In your last trip to the Arcanum?"

"No. That's the strange part. It was lying in the street outside a supermarket this morning, and it wasn't the only one."

"It's part of some marketing promotion, then, and the similarities with Arcanum stuff are just a coincidence. It *has* to be." The emphasis sounded hollow and unconvincing, even to Cat. "Cards from the Game might turn up randomly, but they're incredibly rare. They aren't scattered around for anyone and everyone to pick up. It doesn't make sense."

Blaine took back the card. "Maybe not. But I don't believe in coincidence. Something's wrong with our prizes, and something weird is going on in the Game."

Cat remembered her dream. The skeletal knight and the billboards that shimmered behind him.

Heads You Win, Tails You Lose. . . .

Perhaps it had been a warning. Her prize would not bring Justice, but destruction: the Triumph of Death. And though she realized that everything Blaine was telling her meant that her hopes were ruined, that all their struggles had come to nothing, she didn't yet feel the outrage that was due her. Instead, a kind of numb exhaustion seeped through her veins.

She drew a sharp, effortful breath. "So we've been cheated."

"Yeah."

"Either the Hanged Man didn't have the power to give us real prizes, or he was never going to reward us in the first place. They were just bait so we'd do whatever it took to set him free."

"Yeah." Blaine's cough rattled. "It wasn't just about our prizes, though, was it? We released him so he'd make the Game fair and kick out the Game Masters. These scratch-cards are making me wonder what he's put in their place."

"The Lord of Misrule . . ."

"What?"

"That's what the Hanged Man called himself, remember? After he came and took charge. Lord of Misrule."

A card has two faces, he'd told them, *a die has four or six, and a man, even more. . . .* Cat thought of the blue fire in his eyes, how his smile had slanted when he made his promise of freedom and revelry.

"It's hard to imagine that the Arcanum could get any

15

crazier," she said. "But if the Game's been messed with . . . Bloody hell! And what about Toby and Flora? Have they already tried to play their cards, or—"

Her senses, blunted by shock, now began to spark with alarm. Suddenly things were rushing forward again. She got out her cell phone. She tried Flora, then Toby. Nobody picked up.

CHAPTER TWO

THIS IS THE FIRST DAY of my new life, thought Toby. He gazed solemnly at the poster over his bed, a print of one of Escher's surreal labyrinths. It seemed to him that his face—imperfectly reflected in the glass—had a new maturity. The freckles were less noticeable; the sandy color of his hair appeared to have darkened. Even the line of his jaw looked more determined.

And no wonder. Hadn't he taken on the Game of Triumphs and won? He, a Fool, had proved himself a champion.

Toby's gaze moved to the gaming table, where miniature knights and goblins were lined up on a plaster battleground. The figurines were childish, but the self-conscious irony with which he'd arranged them was even more so. In one impatient movement, he sent them tumbling to the floor, and reached for Malory's *Le morte d'Arthur* from the shelf above.

A photograph and a playing card had been tucked into the pages at the back. The playing card was called the Chariot, the seventh triumph of the Greater Arcana—the hero's triumph. It depicted an armored warrior standing beneath a canopy of stars on a chariot drawn by sphinxes. *Yours is the card that rewards all risks,* the Hanged Man had said to Toby. *The Chariot is the hero's prize. I know you will be worthy of it.*

The photograph showed the cast from a sixth-grade production of *A Midsummer Night's Dream.* The girl third from the left at the front had played Helena. She was slim and curly-haired and (though you couldn't tell from the snapshot) had a smattering of freckles on her nose. Her expression brimmed with suppressed laughter. Toby preferred to think of her this way rather than as she looked the last time he saw her. Then her face had been ice white, her forehead bloodied, as she staggered away from a falling tower. . . .

For in spite of everything Toby had witnessed in the Arcanum, his first glimpse of the Game was still the most potent.

Every detail of that summer's night was pin sharp in his memory. The dusty grass of the school playing fields . . . The hot black air and thunder of falling stone . . . It had, literally, changed his world.

And so the other three chancers' attitude to the Game— a mixture of fear and hostility—was something Toby found hard to understand. Of course the Arcanum was a danger-ous place. Of course the risks were high. But as Toby closed the door to his building behind him and contemplated the drab London morning he was about to spin out of joint, it seemed to him that he was the only one of them who truly grasped the Game's possibilities for greatness.

Toby pictured the Arcanum as a giant chessboard, with each move taking place on a different square. What lay in wait in the square depended on the card a player had been dealt. First, though, you had to get onto the board—and that meant throwing a coin.

Coins were found at the Arcanum's thresholds. But the four chancers each possessed a triangular metal die that could create a threshold whenever and wherever they chose.

As soon as Toby rolled the die, the wheel-scar on his palm began to prickle, letting him know that a threshold was near. He found its sign, another wheel, worked into the hubcap of a van parked down the road. With a tremor of excitement, Toby ran his finger along the lines of the raised chrome circle and its four spokes. As soon as he'd done so, the matching mark on his hand emerged and solidified into a coin. It was as dark and gleaming as the die.

A slow grin spread across his face. This was it. He threw the coin into the air, feeling the print of the wheel throb as his hand opened to receive it. The next second, the coin had vanished, the scar had faded and Toby was standing in the Arcanum.

The gray dawn he'd left had given way to a pitch-black night of pouring rain. Otherwise, the van with the wheel in its hubcap was unchanged, and so were the physical structures of his street. This wasn't so unusual, since every move in the Arcanum bore a resemblance to its threshold's location in the ordinary world. Sometimes this could be seen only in the line of a wall or the print of a paving stone; at others, the new landscape would be an embellished copy of the old one. But although Toby's surroundings were familiar, all the windows were dark and there was no sign of life in any part of the cityscape around him.

In seconds, Toby's hair was plastered down over his head, and his tweed jacket had become heavy and sodden. He curled his hand protectively over the card in his pocket. A row of streetlamps lit up, as if to suggest his route.

Toby hastened through the deluge to the end of his road and then around the corner, in what he thought was the direction of the nearest tube station. He soon realized, however, that the lights were guiding him toward another local landmark.

A glossy new shopping center had been opened that autumn with much fanfare. And here it was again, brought to new life in the Arcanum. Just as on the home side of the threshold, its sprawling glass walls were shiny with light, and piped Muzak floated out from a row of revolving doors. But here the building marked the end of the city, for there was nothing beyond it except pavement, stretching endlessly into the pouring rain.

Toby surveyed it with dismay. Of all the possible settings for his triumph, this had to be one of the least appropriate. He knew that the Arcanum brought cards to life in all manner of ways, most of them unexpected, yet he had nonetheless imagined a battlefield or king's castle, somewhere inspired by the plains of Troy, the halls of Camelot. Instead, he got . . . a *shopping mall*?

"I've already won," he said aloud as rivulets of water ran down his face and into his eyes. "I'm here to take my prize. That's all that matters."

He saw a figure within, moving toward the entrance of the building. He stiffened his back, ready to face whatever was expected of him.

"Hello, Toby. It's been a while."

It was Mia. She was standing underneath an umbrella as the mechanized doors purred round behind her.

"Uh, y-you r-remember me. . . ." The moment was both overwhelming and ridiculous. *He* was ridiculous. A drowned rat, shivering on the pavement.

"How could I forget?" She hadn't taken her eyes off his face. "Come inside."

Toby followed her into the glossy atrium. Two escalators hummed softly in the background while the rain hissed on the domed roof. In the center of the hall was a fake-marble fountain, over which giant silver-and-crimson baubles had been suspended. Swags of plastic holly and ivy hung from the rails of the first-floor gallery, while the piped music played a souped-up version of "White Christmas."

Mia drifted in the direction of the escalators, past shops that displayed nothing but bare shelves, blank signs and stripped mannequins. Toby's leaky sneakers squeaked horribly on the floor. He cast around, desperately, for something to say.

"So," Mia said at last. "How have you been?"

"Good, thanks. Yeah, good. I mean, there's obviously been a lot to, y'know, get my, um, head around."

They had reached a seating area by an empty food stand. A faint scent of syrup and coffee lingered in the air. Mia pulled out a chair and patted the table in front of her invitingly. "Don't be shy."

Toby wasn't delusional. He would never have expected Mia to fall to his feet in gratitude or greet his arrival with cries of joy. She was three years—and several social leagues—above him in school. He knew, too, that his involvement in her move had been more accidental than heroic. But nonetheless, since it was his intervention that had saved her, Toby had felt that if they were ever to meet within the Arcanum, there would be an implicit acknowledgment of the bond between them. Mia's casual manner put all this in doubt.

Part of the problem was the setting, he thought aggrievedly. It was like a parody of some lame high school comedy, when the geek and the prom queen hooked up by a soda fountain.

"I expect you've got some questions for me," she said.

Yes. What am I doing here? What are you doing here? And where is my prize?

But in the face of her cool amusement, he couldn't launch into any of these. "Um, I suppose I always wondered why . . . you . . . how you—"

"How I joined the Game?"

Toby nodded. It was a place to start.

"There's not much to tell, really. I found a Triumph of Eternity card in the school chapel, in one of the hymnals. There was an invitation to Temple House on the back: *Throw the coin, turn the card,* it said. And then, written in gold ink, *What will you play for?*" Mia's expression turned dreamy at the memory.

"So what did you choose?"

It was the wrong thing to say. "That's private," she said austerely.

"Right. Sorry."

She waited for a while before going on. "I knew right from the start the invitation wasn't a hoax, that it was meant to be.... It was like I'd found something I'd been searching for my whole life without realizing it."

"Same here! Same *exactly*. But, uh, the thing is, you weren't the only person at school who was in the Game, were you?"

"No." Mia touched her hand to her forehead. The skin around the scar there still had a new, pinkish look. "I knew pretty quickly that Mr. Marlow was in it as well. You get an instinct for other players. Later, I saw him at one of the gatherings at Temple House. But though we never acknowledged each other as knights, the thrill of the Game was always between us ... part burden, part privilege. Our secret.

"And then it turned out we were going for the same prize, at the same time. We were evenly matched, too: each with a complete round behind us. The fifth and final move in a round is always the triumph you want to win. So the

Game Masters told us we had to compete within the same card. Winner takes all."

"Like a duel," breathed Toby. "You went to the threshold in the school clock tower, ready to play the move, but Marlow tried to knock you out before you could even enter the Arcanum. And when I came and pulled him off you, he tried to wipe you out with his ace instead! What a dirty trick."

Mia shot him a swift look. "How did you know we were there, anyhow?"

"I overheard you arranging to meet. Of course, I didn't know about the Game. I assumed it was something to do with the Chameleons."

"The Chameleons? Oh . . . that silly secret society."

He winced. Once upon a time, that "silly" society had meant everything to Toby. It had been his creation, his vision, and it had been stolen from him.

Although Toby was not a natural loner, at boarding school he had found himself treated like one. Forced to hide out in quiet corners, he had spent a lot of time in accidental eavesdropping. That was how, in the library one lunchtime, he'd overheard a group of seniors talking about their legacy for the final year. They wanted to do something for the school to remember them by. They should form a secret society, they decided, but what for?

It was at that point that Toby had popped up from behind a bookshelf. "The society could be about dares," he said.

The older kids had stared at him with a mixture of pity

and contempt. The ringleader, Seth, had sneered. But Toby made them listen. "Most dares are for short-term stunts, to do something silly or dangerous. What if you drew straws to actually change people, to upset the natural order of things?"

"How d'you mean?" Seth asked.

"Like, how about a dare for two completely incompatible people to start dating? Or a dare for a player on a sports team to start losing games? Or for one of the prefects to start breaking the rules? Think how it would shake this place up!"

And he was right. The society, and the games they played, became a runaway success. A success that Toby was given no credit for.

"I thought if I followed you that night," he explained to Mia, "the Chameleons might let me join them."

Finally, he was able to tell her his side of the story. He had stopped fretting about his prize. The only thing that mattered now was Mia, listening to him intently with her chin propped on her hands.

"I'm just glad I could, you know, help out," he finished.

She screwed up her mouth in an odd little smile. "You did more than that. You changed my fate."

"Well, you're safe from Mr. Marlow now. You won."

"Not quite. I never got the chance to play that final move, you see. To win my triumph, I would have to start a whole new round. And there's not much chance of that. The old ways of winning are gone."

"Gone?"

"Gone, changed, lost." Mia leaned across the table. Under the intensity of her gaze, he felt his own begin to waver. "And all because of *you*."

Then she suddenly rose to her feet, her voice brightly social. "Come on. I've got something to show you."

This time she led him to the back of the mall, past more empty shop fronts and through several sets of swinging doors, until they were outside the delivery entrance to the building.

The concrete plain spread out ahead of them, as far as the eye could see, but in contrast to the bareness inside the mall, their immediate vicinity was crowded with abandoned merchandise and discarded window displays. It was half dump, half depot. Wide-screen televisions, still in their boxes, were piled up alongside limbless mannequins and banners proclaiming SALE! SALE! SALE! A huge Christmas tree, its needles soft and brown among shreds of tinsel, was propped up inside a Dumpster. For a nasty moment, Toby thought there was a body lying among the trash bags, until he realized it was the life-sized Santa mannequin from the mall's grotto, lying facedown with one plastic arm drunkenly outstretched.

Mia moved among stacks of boxed microwaves and coffeemakers, designer sofas and racks of men's suits, all waterlogged. The rain had slackened, and she didn't seem to think her umbrella was necessary, even though she was wearing only a cotton tea dress over leggings and worn-down ballet flats. Toby was shivering in the drizzle.

When he caught up with her, she was standing by

a larger version of the gaming table in his room. This one's terrain was much more intricate, however: a chaotic hodge-podge of model mountains, forests, rivers, towns and plains, each of which, though beautifully detailed, had been built to a different scale. The figures, too, were of contrasting shapes and sizes, and although he saw a couple of knights and goblins that could have come from his collection, there were also old-fashioned lead soldiers, Lego men and the kind of plastic animals sold with toy zoos. All were hopelessly entangled in the landscape and with each other, for the display was in even greater disarray than his one at home.

Mia swept her arm over the table in an oddly formal gesture. "Behold, our Field of Play."

"Is this . . . is this supposed to be . . . the Arcanum?"

"And look at the state of it," she said severely. For it was true that, quite apart from the strewn figures, the miniature landscape was badly chipped and cracked, its painted details streaky with rain. One of the legs was wonky, so that the table tilted dangerously. "Look what you've done."

"I don't understand you. The Arcanum has been set free. Not . . . *broken*."

"Free! What does *free* mean?"

"That the Game is fair for the first time. The kings and queens have been kicked out, along with their stupid rules."

"So who is going to be umpire?"

"Well, the man I—we—released, the Hanged Man—"

"The Lord of Misrule."

"Yes," Toby said uncomfortably. "If that's what he's calling himself now. But he's not a tyrant like the old kings and queens. He's more of a new, improved Game Master. A Master of Misrule—without any of the point scoring and punishments."

"He's not interested in dealing cards and awarding prizes, either, let alone fair play. And where does that leave all the other knights adrift in the Arcanum?"

"They'll be free to do what they want. Everyone in the Game is."

"Everyone and anyone," Mia echoed. Her face was bleak. "Heads to win, tails to lose. Yes . . . we won't be the chosen few for much longer, Toby. The Game is growing, finding new players, and the old rules and boundaries are falling away."

"The rules were wrong," he said stubbornly.

"The rules imposed limits. Some of those limits weren't there to constrain but to protect."

Before he could respond, Mia had shaken her head impatiently and moved on.

He found her waiting for him behind the Dumpster with the Christmas tree.

Another prop from Santa's grotto was there: a red sleigh, festooned with tinsel and drawn by two white fiberglass reindeer. Mia was enthroned in the sleigh, lolling against its high back.

She turned to survey him, eyebrows raised. "Well, I suppose it would be more impressive with sphinxes."

Toby took out his card, and looked from the tacky novelty carriage to the warrior's chariot, the winged creatures at his reins, the canopy of stars. From inside the mall, "Jingle Bells" was playing. The song floated through in snatches, jumbled as the figures on the toy landscape.

Dashing through—
—open sleigh—
Oh, what fun it is to ride—
Oh, what fun—
Laughing all the way—

If this is the punch line, then I am the joke, thought Toby. And he flushed red with shame and bitterness.

"Tell me, Toby, what did you imagine your reward would be?" Mia asked him, leaning down from the chariot to reach for his card.

But the truth was, he'd never thought very hard about how the abstract qualities of his triumph would translate into real life. The most he'd come up with was a soft-focus vision of himself striding through moves in the Arcanum, rescuing damsels in distress, making judgments, completing quests. . . .

"Heroism isn't much good in the ordinary world," she said, as if she'd read his mind. "Not the kind you're thinking of, at any rate. Not these days."

"I guess not." He hung his head.

"The Game needs it, though. In fact, you could say that heroism is one of the few prizes that work best in the Arcanum rather than outside of it."

At this he looked up, newly hopeful. Mia was sitting straight and proud now, as the tinsel garlands at her back quivered in the night breeze.

"This is an empty move, Toby. The Charioteer has abandoned his chariot. The boundaries between the moves are breaking down, and with them the Arcanum. So if you want to keep playing, you're going to have to put the Game to rights first. You'll soon see how corrupted it has become . . . and then you'll have to *fight* for it, you hear?"

"Yes. Whatever needs to be done, I'll do it. I swear."

She nodded. "I believe in you." Mischief hovered at the corners of her mouth again. "Though I'm sorry about the sphinxes."

"Oh, this version's more festive." Confidence was suddenly bubbling inside him, and he realized that he wouldn't want to change anything—not the mocking Christmas jingle, or the shopping mall, or even those absurd reindeer. Everything was as it should be. Because although the Game worked in crooked ways, his faith in it had been proved right. What should have been an appalling blow—he'd been cheated and exploited, disaster had struck—had instead given him new strength and purpose.

Toby, the hero, had a wrong to right.

CHAPTER THREE

FLORA'S CELL PHONE BEGAN to ring. Insistently. She looked at the screen and saw that it was Cat.

"Aren't you going to answer it?" Charlie asked.

"No. It won't be anything important." She shrugged sweetly at him, though what she really wanted to do was stamp the phone into silence beneath her heel. Flora had already had an incoherent voice mail from Toby, rambling on about quests and sacred duties and Saving the Game. And now this. Why couldn't these people just leave her *alone*? Of course, that was unfair of her—unkind, too—but knowing she was being unreasonable only made everything more frustrating.

Part of the frustration was at being at this stupid benefit luncheon, the latest in the round of seasonal parties. Her parents avoided being left to their own company as much as possible, and it seemed her every moment had been taken up by some enforced festive gathering since . . . well, since the events of Boxing Day. She felt another jab of anger.

"Flo, are you all right? You're looking a little stressed out." Charlie was leaning over her solicitously.

"Oh, it's just the post-Christmas grumps. Mince pie withdrawal syndrome." Remembering where she was—who she had to be—Flora twirled a strand of honey-blond hair and sparkled up at him in her best party manner.

Charlie grinned back, a little sheepishly. He was a nice boy, she thought, as if considering someone much younger and not particularly connected to her. If she'd been in a better mood, she would have acknowledged that it was a nice party, too. The Avoncourts' large drawing room was filled with the contented hum of people relaxing into well-established social routines. From where she was standing, she could see Georgia and Tilly, two of her best friends from school, gossiping in a corner. Her father was holding court on the other side of the room, where he was laughing at something Lady Swinton had said, all crinkly-eyed amusement and easy charm. And there was Mummy, with a glass in her hand—of course—but, thankfully, without that over-bright, brittle look that meant danger. Perhaps today was going to be one of her mother's good days, when the drink worked its old magic of making the world a kinder place.

Flora's phone beeped. Cat had left a message. She ignored it and forced herself to look as if she was paying attention to whatever Charlie was saying. She wondered what Georgia and Tilly were giggling about. It might well be to do with her; she and Charlie had kissed on a couple of occasions, one fairly recently, and it was becoming harder to ignore the expectation building within their group.

Well, it made sense. They had known each other forever; in fact, his older brother, Will, had been friends with Grace, and was one of the few people outside the family who—very occasionally—still visited her. Moreover, they shared the same kind of unassuming good looks, both being blue-eyed and fair, and he was popular in the same steady, unshowy way that she was popular. Two sides of the same coin, Flora thought with black humor. Because of course she and Charlie were nothing alike. How could they be? Neither he nor anybody else here could possibly imagine the things she had seen, and what she had done.

But if the secret of the Game was lonely, it could be exhilarating, too. Sometimes, when she was with the others in the school common room, or at their favorite coffee shop, she would be laughing at the jokes, joining in with the stories, and still feel the tug of her other life, like a dark ripple through her veins. Then she would look at Charlie, or Georgia, or whoever it was, and think with a disdainful thrill, You don't know me at all.

Right at the moment, her sense of displacement was excruciating. Grace was waiting. Grace! Her sister, the miracle, the prize that would make their family whole again. The only thing Flora needed to do was to bring her home. For what felt like the hundred thousandth time, her hand moved to touch the card in her pocket. The Eight of Swords depicted a young woman, bound and blindfolded, inside a cage of swords. A cliff-top castle loomed behind her. It was the same card Grace had been holding when her ten-year-old sister had found her in her scarlet evening gown, splayed across the snow. That first card had been taken away from Flora, but this one was new, and hers to play.

And with each further delay, it became harder not to twist her bland smile into a snarl, to keep from screaming curses in the midst of this complacent crowd, to stop herself kicking and scratching until she drew blood, lashing out at anyone who got in her way. . . .

She took a deep breath.

"Charlie," she said after patiently waiting for the end of a rugby match anecdote, "I'm frightfully sorry but I'm afraid I'm going to have to take off. I've started to get a splitting headache."

Of course he was the perfect gentleman, and offered to make her excuses to the relevant friends and family without even having to be asked. The Avoncourts were neighbors, only five minutes down the road from Flora's house, and so she felt quite able to turn down his proposal to walk her home. His kindness made her feel both undeserving and exasperated.

No sooner had Flora left the house than her phone began to ring. Again, she ignored it. "What does everyone *want* from me?" she said aloud. The more quickly she walked, the more quickly their faces seemed to crowd around. She thought of her mother after she'd come back from visiting Grace, and how she'd never asked Flora anything or even said a word, but after reapplying her lipstick with a hand that trembled, she'd topped up the glass by her side. She thought of the look her mother had exchanged with her father: his contempt, her appeal, their shared helplessness. She thought of Charlie, so considerate and so clueless, and, like everybody else, wanting what she couldn't give. . . .

By the time Flora reached the end of her street, she was practically running. She forced herself to slow down and breathe normally. It was important to be calm. She had plenty of time. Her parents were bound to stay at the Avoncourts' for a good while yet, as it was their last social engagement before they left for a New Year's skiing party tomorrow. Flora wasn't going, pleading the pressures of coursework and plans with friends. Of course, the trip would be off as soon as they got the phone call from the clinic, but— No, don't think ahead, she told herself with a kind of panic. The swell of expectation was almost too much to bear.

The Seaton home was part of a row of tall white Regency mansions that backed onto one of London's loveliest parks. When Flora let herself into the house, she could hear Mina, the housekeeper, moving about upstairs, but she didn't stop to say hello. Instead, she walked—neat, calm, purposeful— straight through the ground floor to the garden, and the door in the wall that opened directly onto the park.

It was a dank, raw day, and there weren't many people

about, just a few dog walkers and, in the distance, a half-hearted football game. Near the main gates, three teenage boys were bickering over something.

"I'm telling you, if it comes up tails, you're *doomed*," one of them was saying. "Some random disaster hits you out of nowhere and—*bam!*"

"Yeah," said his mate. "And if you win heads, it's the opposite. Like having all your Christmases come at once."

"You two'ud believe any old crap," the other boy jeered. "Everyone knows those rumors are a windup. It's just some dumb publicity stunt."

"So why haven't you scratched your coin off, then?"

"'Cause I'm not bothered."

"No, 'cause you're chicken."

"Screw you—"

Idiots, thought Flora, walking briskly by. She was headed toward a summerhouse set on a small hill. In warmer weather, there were often people relaxing on its steps, but today she had it to herself. It was designed like a miniature classical temple, and there was the sign of the wheel worked into the base of one of its columns.

Flora had no need to use a die to play her card. The threshold to Grace's last move was already in place, and had been ever since the winter's night five years ago when her sister had used it to enter the Arcanum and had never come back. Or rather, only part of her had come back: the inanimate doll in the hospital bed, as much a captive as the prisoner on the card. But Flora knew that the real Grace—the living, laughing Grace—was somewhere in the Arcanum still. And it was this hope that kept Flora returning to the Game, as if each new move she entered would bring a fresh clue, another chance.

But today was different. Today, she would go into the Eight of Swords and find her sister waiting. That was the promise.

Flora bent to sketch the lines of the wheel, the coin heavy in her palm. When she tossed it, it felt as if her heart was leaping into the air along with the metal, up and up, so that the whole world seemed to be soaring with her. . . .

Because as soon as the scene flipped sides to the Arcanum, she knew that everything was going to be all right. It was as if she'd stepped back in time to that snowy evening five years before.

The Arcanum's landscapes were frequently silent and lifeless, but here the city's lights glittered above and behind the fringe of trees, and traffic still purred at the park's rim. She could even hear a distant echo of the football game. And, most wonderful of all, there was a skein of embroidery silk looped around one of the summerhouse's columns. It was red, just like the thread she had found tied to Grace's finger, and snaked invitingly down the slope from the column and along the line of a path.

Flora touched the card in her pocket, with its picture of the caged woman and the castle behind. "Grace," she said aloud. "Grace, I'm coming."

The snow was several inches deep and as immaculate as sugar frosting. As she took the thin red thread in her hand and followed it across the folds of glistening white, the sense of familiarity receded until, a little after leaving the park's main thoroughfare, Flora looked behind her and saw that the city's rooftops had vanished from behind the trees, along with the traffic's hum. She was in a landscape of rolling hills and tree-furred hollows.

It was bitterly cold. She was wearing a wool coat and scarf, but she'd forgotten her gloves, and her shoes were unsuited to wading through snow. The drifts were getting deeper, and new flakes were already beginning to spiral through the darkening sky.

I'm coming.

I'm coming.

She reached the foot of a steep hill. Through the lace of trees above, there were windows shining, warm as syrup, and she saw a house of high gray walls and wide lawns. It was Grace's clinic, an old country mansion that had been converted into a center for long-term care. Here in the Arcanum, it was larger and grander than on the other side of the threshold, its roof higgledy-piggledy with new slopes and turrets. Moreover, it was blazing with light, every chimney smoking, every door flung open in welcome.

The embroidery silk was still in her hand, a fragile scarlet filament winding through the white-dappled dark. Flora began to stumble up the hill. Her feet were numb and clumsy; her eyes watered and cheeks stung. It didn't matter. She drew in jubilant gulps of icy black air, laughing giddily as she slipped and scrambled through the drifts and along the tunnel of trees leading up to the house. Grace was inside, talking, dancing, sparkling. . . . Grace was waiting at the end of this thread. Above her head, branches creaked under their burden of ice.

The smell of the clinic, a mixture of expensive flowers and antiseptic, was as familiar to Flora as that of her mother's perfume or the school dining hall, and she automatically braced herself for it as she went through the main entrance. But the building had reverted to its plush country house interior and all its hospital trappings were gone. Furthermore, it seemed that she had arrived at the late, disorderly stages of a black-tie ball.

The crowd was grandly dressed, yet in a state of considerable dishevelment. The women's hair straggled around their faces and their lavish makeup was smeared. The men weren't much better: flushed and moist-looking, with ties and collars askew. People were greeting each other with bellowing enthusiasm, bawling jokes and waving their glasses so wildly that the drink sprayed everywhere.

Flora hovered at the edge of the crowd, with a backward look at the silk strand zigzagging down the steps. She was used to the Arcanum's crowds; in fact, there was a pleasurable recklessness in being swept up in gatherings conjured by the Game. Afterward, she would tell herself that none of it mattered because it was all illusion anyway.

This was different, because every guest was someone she recognized. Among the baying throng she could see her hairdresser, several teachers and the priest from their local church, St. Bernadine's. And all the people who had been at the Avoncourts' were here, in a kind of grotesque parody of the party she'd left behind.

The Arcanum version of Charlie was leaning lecherously over the Arcanum version of Georgia, who was looking up at him with an inane grin, her dress falling off her shoulders. His handsome brother, Will, was downing shots alongside Mrs. Avoncourt as they coughed and spluttered and shook with mirth. Lady Swinton was pawing greedily at a man in a white cravat. Then she realized it was her father.

Of course it wasn't really him. None of these people truly existed. They were phantoms conjured by the Game. But it was horrible, just the same. All those familiar faces turned ugly and foolish, with slurring mouths and glassy eyes . . . eyes that slid over her without acknowledgment or recognition.

Meanwhile, the fires roared in the grates and the party roared through the rooms. The clinic's staff break room had been set up with an extravagant buffet. Tumbled piles of shrimp lay on wilting lettuce leaves; haunches of meat squatted on silver platters between mashed-up trifles and sweating wedges of cheese. Just looking at it made her feel queasy, and she longed to be rid of the place, so that it was just her and Grace, walking home through the clean, cold silence of the hills.

But Flora had to find her first. She struggled on through the mêlée, trying to concentrate on the thread she still followed, trying to ignore the damp heat of her coat and the chafing of her shoes. She took comfort in the thought that Grace had been due to attend a ball on the night of her "accident." This setting was, in a skewed sort of way, appropriate. It was surely part of re-creating the conditions for her sister's return.

Her resolve wavered when she caught sight of her mother by a window in the larger of two reception rooms. She couldn't bear the thought of looking into her mother's face, blurred by drink, and being met with only blankness. It was too close to the reality on the other side of the threshold. In her anxiety to avoid the moment, Flora turned away. It was then that she saw her.

A slope of white neck. A loop of golden hair. The scooped back of a scarlet gown.

Grace.

Grace.

She was weaving her way through the throng, untouched by the mayhem all around. Flora, however, couldn't move. She was rooted to the spot, though shaking so violently it seemed impossible that the whole building wasn't trembling with her. The far side of the room opened onto a small stairwell. When Grace reached it, she looked over her shoulder and smiled at Flora. It was the first time Flora had seen her sister's eyes open or her face mobile in five years. The smile was one of serene welcome. Then Grace turned her back, and glided on.

Flora found she was clutching the thread so tightly it cut into her palm. She was terrified she'd drop it, that the silk would fray or snap beneath somebody's heel before she could catch up with her sister. She called Grace's name but her voice was immediately swallowed up by the din. Finally, she began to push against the barrier of hot, obstinate flesh until she was kicking and struggling, shouting obscenities. . . .

At last, she fought her way to the stairwell, just in time to see Grace disappear through a set of doors on the second floor. It was a relief to close them behind her and shut out the sights and sounds of the party. She was now in an area of the building that was completely unfamiliar to her, either because she had never ventured this far in her visits to the clinic or, more likely, because she had reached a part that was entirely constructed by the Arcanum.

Flora padded down a long, curved corridor whose carpeting was so thick that she strained to hear Grace's footsteps ahead. Still, she had the thread to guide her and, just occasionally, a flicker of scarlet skirts disappearing round the corner. It must be that Grace couldn't stop or slow down because she was leading her somewhere, somewhere they would both be safe.

She came to another corner and another staircase. It was steep and spiraling. Up she went, higher and higher, until she felt dizzy from all the turning and her heart banged in her ribs. She couldn't hear the party any longer, but there was another sound: a whirring and clacking. . . .

Something had happened to the embroidery silk. As she climbed the stairs, it darkened in color, from red to burgundy to a kind of burnt maroon. It felt thicker and more fibrous, too. By the time she reached the top of the stairs, the line of thread running through the gap between the door and the floor was black. And the whirring noise was much louder. As she opened the door, the whirring noise intensified.

The turret room was small and bare. In front of the window, three women were grouped around a spinning wheel. The youngest, who didn't look much older than Flora, was turning a crank to keep the wheel in motion. A woman of her mother's age was feeding raw yarn into the spindle, while an old lady wound the spun thread into little bundles. In spite of the antiquated nature of their task, they looked as if they belonged to the party downstairs. All three were identically dolled up in black cocktail dresses, lipstick and pearls.

Flora took all of this in without really registering it. The only thing she could think about was the fact that Grace was not there.

"Where's my sister?"

"I'm afraid you've taken a wrong turn," the spindle-woman replied coolly.

The girl turning the wheel smirked into her sleeve.

Whirr, whirr, clack, clack.

"The thread led me here. There must be a reason for it," Flora said, taking care to keep the tremor from her voice.

"Then I'm sure you'll find it," the old lady said peaceably as she straightened one of the bundles on her lap. Her face was creased like rumpled tissue paper, but in spite of her age, she was upright and trim and wore the same cosmetic flourishes as her younger counterparts. Their lips were painted in a crimson Cupid's bow, their faces powdered white, their eyebrows penciled in a thin black arch, and each wore her white-blond hair coiled high. All three were regarding her with their heads slightly tilted to one side, mouths pursed, an identical glint in their bright black eyes. As if, Flora thought uneasily, she was being measured for something.

She pushed the disquiet away and reached for the card, holding it up in front of her. "The reason is my sister. I'm here to take her out of this move. It's my prize, and I have the right to claim it."

"Do you indeed?" said the young girl sharply. "And how many wrongs has it taken to win this 'right'?"

"Hush now, Skuld." The old lady turned to Flora. "You'll have to excuse my sister—she can be a little quick-tempered at times."

"Your *sister*?"

"Well, of course, dear. Can't you see the resemblance? Three sisters as like as three peas in a pod!"

Skuld's lip curled. "There's small wonder she's unobservant, Urd. Why, I don't think the girl even realizes what she has done."

Flora returned her stare. "So tell me."

But it was the woman at the spindle who replied. "You plucked your prize from the ashes of Yggdrasil," she said without taking her eyes off the yarn. "And Yggdrasil is the tree from which our wheel was made."

The wheel was about five feet tall and crafted of dark polished wood. It had many more spokes than the emblem of Fortune's Wheel and seemed an ordinary wool-spinning mechanism. As Flora looked closer, she saw that the thread she had been following was attached to one of the little black bundles at the old woman's feet, and that these were actually a kind of doll, made by winding layers of thread around a stick man of bent wire. She thought of the trussed-up figure in the Eight of Swords, and was afraid.

Flora stepped back toward the door, and this time, she took care to keep her tone conciliatory. "I'm very sorry the tree was destroyed."

"Oh, Yggdrasil's roots go deep and it has many saplings," said the old lady. "It will seed again. But the Game is a different matter: you tried to cut it down, and now it grows crooked. . . . Verdandi, is the yarn ready yet?"

"A full skein," the middle sister replied with satisfaction. "Smooth and strong. It'll do nicely."

For the next few moments, the three women were preoccupied with the business of removing the bobbin from the spindle, unwinding the spun thread and setting up the wheel again. Flora felt herself forgotten.

"Please," she said, "I don't want to disturb you, and I apologize if I've done something wrong, or made things . . . crooked. But if you could—please—if you could just tell me where my sister has gone?"

Verdandi glanced at her indifferently. "As I said before, you took a wrong turn. You climbed up our stairs while she went down them. She won't have gone far."

"But before you leave," said the old woman, "you'll need to take this."

Urd picked up one of the little manikins. It was the one attached to the black thread that still lay across the floor, the thread that turned scarlet on the stairs and that Flora had followed for so far and so long.

"Skuld, the scissors, please."

The younger woman took a pair of silver shears and severed the thread. The blades made a crisp swishing sound.

"Here you are, my dear," Urd said, holding out the doll. "It's what you came for. Though I'm afraid we'll need to have that pretty card in return."

The manikin was no bigger than the palm of her hand, a crude thing of coarse black wool. Flora was still holding the Eight of Swords, and for a few moments she hovered in indecision, looking from the doll to the blindfolded woman on the card and back again. Meanwhile, the wheel had been set in motion again; the whirring and clacking sound, though soothing in itself, made it difficult to think.

"Is this thing . . . is it . . . *her*?"

"Take Dolly home with your sister, dear. It's only as far as the threshold in the park," Urd replied. "Just a hop, skip and a jump away!"

The three sisters pursed their crimson lips, arched their high black eyebrows and nodded their pale heads. The difference in age between them was less noticeable, though whether this was because Skuld was looking older, or Urd younger, was impossible to say. Verdandi put out a hand for the card.

Flora passed over the Eight of Swords, then reached for the manikin.

"Aah!"

She had pricked her finger on a tiny spike of wire that was sticking out of the thread. A fat, shining bead of blood trembled on her fingertip before dropping onto the doll. As one, the sisters let out a long, soft sigh of pleasure and release.

Whirr, whirr, clack, clack.

The room spun and blurred, as if Flora was a spoke on the wheel. And her head was still spinning as she watched the doll maker take out two long silver pins from her hair and begin to twist them into a little stick figure.

Slowly, deliberately, smiling all the while, Urd knotted a new piece of thread to one end of the wire. . . .

She looked up directly at Flora and her smile widened. And then it hit her: "The new doll is me," Flora whispered, and flung herself out of the room and down the stairs.

Even in the midst of her helter-skelter descent, Flora found time to think. There were several layers of wool on the doll she clutched. It would take time to finish the binding on a new one. She would just have to find Grace, take her and the doll to the threshold and then—

Was she imagining it, or were her legs already beginning to move more sluggishly?

At least she didn't have to fight her way through the party again, for when she reached the bottom of the spiral staircase, it was to find that the entire laughing, drinking, shouting crowd had fallen asleep. Every room was filled with inert bodies collapsed on chairs, slumped against walls or tangled on the floor in snoring heaps, snail trails of drool around their chins. The air was stale with the fumes of alcohol and sour breath. In her rush, Flora trampled over limp hands and tripped over unprotected heads. They were the hands of her friends, the heads of people she knew and loved, but she had to tell herself that it wasn't real and didn't matter, that nothing mattered except to keep moving while she still could. "Grace," she shouted. "GRACE! Where are you?"

Verdandi had spoken the truth. Grace was indeed downstairs. And she was not asleep—or not yet. She was propped against the doorway of the larger reception room, eyes closed, and humming a snatch of lullaby.

"Oh, Grace!" Flora flung her arms around her sister, her face hot and wet with tears. "Thank God! I'm so sorry—everything's gone wrong—we have to—"

"Hello, Flo-Flo. I didn't know you'd been invited," Grace replied sleepily. "Isn't it a lovely party?"

"*No.* It's not what you think it is. That's why we have to leave, Grace. We have to leave *now.* The Spinners—"

"Did they make you a doll, too?"

"Yes. And I've got yours. Come on, we've got to go."

Grace's forehead creased in thought. "If the Spinners are binding a doll, then you haven't got much time," she said. "It only takes seven layers." She seemed to be trying to remember something, but then she yawned, and the dozy blankness returned. "Funny . . . you look different, Flo. How have you grown so tall?"

"Never mind that." She tried to drag Grace to her feet,

but her sister sagged limply, and smiled her vacant smile. Flora's own body felt unnaturally clumsy.

"What's *wrong* with you?" she cried furiously. "I'm here to take you home, out of this. Out of the Eight of Swords."

"The Eight of Swords," Grace repeated vaguely. "Oh yes ... You helped me home before, I remember. When you gave me a thread and I used it in the maze."

"Maze? What maze?"

"I'm not exactly sure. . . . There were briars, I think. . . . Or were they swords? A maze of briars with the Spinners in the center. Yes. But my thread broke, and by the time I found it again, it was too late." She nodded and smiled, proud at having worked it out, then closed her drooping eyes.

Flora shook her roughly. "But you must have escaped the maze. You reached the threshold. You got out of the Arcanum."

"Ah, but not before the Spinners had tied the last knot. That's when I woke up here, you see. . . . Such a lovely party . . ."

"No—don't you dare go to sleep. *Grace!*"

"Mmm?"

To her shame, Flora found she was crying again. She was now too weak to push, let alone carry, her sister, and the longer she stayed, and the more layers of thread the Spinners bound around the wire manikin, the worse it would become. "How do I get you out of this place?"

"You take the dolly, of course," Grace replied serenely. "Over the threshold in the park. I have to stay at the party.

Don't worry, it's quite nice here—except when I'm back among the briars, of course. And sometimes I'm asleep in a strange bed and can hear all sorts of people talking. . . . Even you, occasionally." She stretched a little and looked at Flora with hazy, heavy-lidded eyes. "You know the trick, don't you, Flo?"

"The trick with the doll?" Flora gave her sister's shoulders another shake. "GRACE! What trick?"

"The trick . . . The trick with the maze."

A brief struggle showed in her face, and suddenly Grace was staring at Flora with wakeful and desperate eyes. It was like watching somebody come out of water after being submerged almost to the point of drowning. *"Every turn is left,"* Grace gasped. Her face was white and taut, and her voice hoarse with effort. *"Remember that. Remember."*

"I—I will. I promise. Grace, you must— NO! Don't go to sleep—no—please—"

But Grace was already closing her eyes and sinking down on the floor of the hall. "There's no more time, Flo-Flo," she mumbled. "The binding's half done. You have to . . . you have to . . . run. . . ."

Flora hesitated for one long, agonizing moment, then clambered to her feet. Her tongue felt hard and clumsy but she managed to speak through her tears.

"This isn't over. Next time you wake up, you're going to be home. I swear it."

"Such a lovely party," Grace murmured, lost to dream.

❧

Somehow, Flora made it out of the main entrance of the house, lurched across the lawn, down the avenue and into the open countryside beyond. There was no doubt that her body was slowing down, its intricate mesh of nerves and muscles starting to stiffen.

Thank God—the clump of trees that marked the beginning of the park was in sight. It had stopped snowing while she was in the house and the sky was clear. A minute or so later, she could even see the dome of the summerhouse glinting in the moonlight.

Breathing hard, Flora tottered toward its steps. It was then that the smooth white expanse immediately in front of her became oddly speckled. Something was rising up from under the snow—little black shoots and buds. . . .

The briars were growing.

At first the shoots were so small that they looked like flecks of soot on the snow. But quickly, very quickly, they knotted themselves into spreading snarls of spikes. Sharp black spikes that thrust wickedly against the soft white— dark tangles that grew so thickly and so fast that in moments there was an impenetrable circular hedge, nearly seven feet high, around the threshold.

Flora's first instinct was to push her way through the thicket, but she was immediately forced back, her arms and wrists scored with dozens of bloody scratch marks. With horror, she saw that each thorn was in fact a tiny, glinting sword.

In her desperation she began casting about for a fallen

branch, or even a stone, to fight her way through. It was then that she spotted a small gap in the hedge a few yards to the right. There was an increasing time delay in moving her limbs, as if the signals from her brain were slowing to a crawl, but she managed to squeeze clumsily past. "Oh God," she said aloud as she found herself in a narrow, winding lane between the hedge and another wall of briar-swords. "It's the maze."

The snow on the ground gnawed icily into her wet feet. Her eyes watered. The scratches on her arms stung. But she welcomed the pain and the cold: they were signs of life. It's not over till it's over, she told herself grimly as she dragged her body along the twisting path. *Every turn is left,* Grace had said. Her sister had given her the key to the maze, and her only hope of reaching the threshold.

It was a simple trick, really. One of those things that should be easy when you know how. But as Flora's progress became limited to a cramped hobble, even her thought processes started to stultify. There were moments when she began to forget what she was supposed to be doing, what the point of all this wearisome movement was. It seemed as if she had been wandering in the web of briars forever—that this was the only world there was, and all that she had ever known. She didn't care even when the thorns caught her clothes and tore her skin. They had stopped hurting now. When she couldn't recall if she had gone left at the last turning or not, it didn't seem to particularly matter. Nor did the little bundle of wire and thread that she was for some reason cradling to her chest.

White snow, black thorn, red blood. Turn and turn again. Except that sometimes it was the ground that was powdered black, the sky a scalding white, with black blood on the red thorns. Was she in a maze of briars or a cage of swords? Turn and turn again. . . .

It was when Flora rounded the last corner out of the maze that disaster struck. At the sight of the threshold, her senses recovered a little, and she was able to lurch forward on a brief energy surge. But her balance was gone and she fell stiffly to the ground. She tried to put out her hands to steady herself, and the doll tumbled from her weak grasp, becoming snagged on the briars at the base of the thicket. When she tugged at it, the wool only became more deeply ensnared.

Her fingers were too clumsy to untangle the thread, her hands too feeble to free the doll from the piercings of countless tiny black swords. She knew that this was a dreadful thing, a calamity, but as the swaddling lethargy increased its hold on her, she could barely remember why. And the more she plucked at the doll, the more hopelessly snarled its threads became, until it no longer resembled a manikin, just an untidy nest of black wool in a bramble hedge.

Flora tried to call out to her sister, but she couldn't open her mouth properly and the words emerged as a whimper. More than anything, she wanted to lie down in the white softness, let darkness and stillness bind themselves into every fiber of her being, cocooning her in peace. But the thought of Grace pushed her onward, even though she had only the faintest memory of her now. And so, just as her sister had done five years before, Flora began to crawl toward the summerhouse, inch by hopeless inch.

And when her nearly rigid fingers traced the sign of the threshold, and the Arcanum coin emerged from her palm, she could no longer remember her own name, let alone Grace's, or why, with the last spark of sense left in her, she felt compelled to jerk the coin into the freezing air.

THE HIGH PRIEST

CHAPTER FOUR

THE NEXT MORNING, CAT, Blaine and Toby met by the stump of the apple tree in Mercury Square. It was hard to reconcile their drab surroundings with the transformations they had witnessed three nights ago. For the apple tree that used to grow in the neglected garden was also Yggdrasil, a double of the tree on which the Hanged Man had been imprisoned, deep in the catacombs below Temple House. The chancers had used four aces to fell it, unleashing the forces of earth, air, fire and water, and toppling the power of the kings and queens. . . .

Their victory already seemed long ago.

To her surprise, Toby greeted Cat with a hug. Even more to her surprise, she found that she didn't mind. Blaine got a hearty handshake. Afterward, they stood around feeling uncomfortable. This was not the kind of reunion anyone had expected. There was no good news to celebrate, no nostalgia to indulge in. And where was Flora?

While they were waiting, Toby told them, again, about his encounter with Mia. He'd phoned Cat as soon as he left the Arcanum but his excited ramblings had been almost too much to take in. It was not a whole lot easier now.

Spread on the bench in front of them was an article from London's tabloid newspaper.

A LOTTERY FOR LUCK?
CITY GRIPPED BY MYSTERIOUS
SCRATCHCARD CRAZE

Londoners are baffled by a set of scratch-cards distributed by an unknown organization, bearing only the words "The Triumph Lottery of Luck. Heads You Win, Tails You Lose." Upon scratching off the silver coin embossed on the card, either a man's head or a forked tail is revealed. No prizes are offered and no company details shown.

But what appears to be a teaser for an ad campaign is fast gaining notoriety as a game of allegedly supernatural dimensions. The recipients of a "head" card are adamant that extraordinary good fortune has immediately followed their win, whereas those finding a "tail" claim to have suffered a series of bizarre mishaps.

Dr. Craig Mills, 31, found a so-called triumph card in his supermarket trolley.

Moments after scraping the coin to reveal a "head," he decided to purchase a EuroLotto scratchcard—and found himself £75,000 richer. Meanwhile, beautician Jane Cornwell, 23, suffered a road accident, in which she broke both legs, not more than five minutes after finding a "tail."

Mere coincidence, one might say. But a growing number of people are reporting similar experiences. Since Boxing Day evening, when the cards first appeared, a number have already been featured on an Internet auction site, where—in spite of the risk of finding an ill-omened "tail"—they are attracting bids running into thousands of pounds from all over the world.

One thing's for sure. Someone, somewhere, has created an epic new urban legend.

For Professor Pamela Coleman's examination of mind suggestion, mass hysteria and the Gambler's Fallacy, turn to page 7.

Full interviews with Ms. Cornwell and Dr. Mills, page 15.

"A Game of Triumphs marketing blitz." Cat shook her head in disbelief. "This is insane."

"Yeah, right. One big mass-hysterical joke," said Blaine sardonically.

"But what does it *mean*?"

The three of them had already talked this over at length without reaching any conclusion. They found it was easier to focus on the mysterious scratchcards than what might have gone wrong in the Game, and what it had cost them. A part of Cat still refused to believe in their failure. Toby kept banging on about how the Arcanum was "broken." What did that mean anyway? Broken things could be mended. There must be a way of putting things right. There *must*.

"I wonder where Flora's got to," Toby said impatiently. "Did she mention anything about her card or her prize, Cat, when she texted you last night?"

"No. All she said was that she'd got my messages and would be here."

"Then she's already been in the Arcanum?"

"I suppose so. I don't know."

"But—"

"Toby."

They relapsed into silence, except for the rasping of Blaine's cough. Cat tried not to let it get to her, but the sound grated on her nerves. It had got worse since yesterday.

Twenty minutes after the agreed meeting time, Flora walked through the gap in the railings on the garden's north side. The others were shocked by her appearance. It wasn't just the scratches on her face and the crisscrossing cuts all over her hands. Her skin was pallid and she wore a fixed, glassy stare. None of them had ever seen her outside the Arcanum looking less than immaculately groomed, but today her long hair was straggly and unbrushed, and her shirt appeared to have been pulled straight from the laundry basket.

"You've played your card," Blaine stated.

Flora nodded. She didn't volunteer any further information. Cat, who was the only one who knew the full story of Flora's sister, found she couldn't work up the courage to mention Grace, and shifted awkwardly on her feet.

"Like I said in my voice mail last night, we think . . . we think something's wrong with our prizes. That we were cheated," she said.

"Why's that?" Flora asked dully.

Since Cat hadn't yet tried to claim her prize, she didn't really feel in a position to present the case. However, as neither Toby nor Blaine appeared ready to contribute, she pressed on. "Well, the four of us were promised that the cards we won would give us something we'd been searching for in the Arcanum. Except it turns out that nobody who's played their card has actually been awarded anything." Toby tried to cut in at this point, but she continued, speaking over him. "It's starting to look like the whole prize offer was bait so we'd set the Hanged Man free to mess up the Game. And, er, there's this, too—"

She passed the newspaper article to Flora, who skimmed it listlessly. Afterward she let the paper drop to the ground. "I don't know about the scratchcards," she said. "I don't know about the cheating. All I know is that I failed."

"Our cards weren't tests for passing or failing. They were supposed to be rewards," said Blaine with the barely suppressed violence Cat remembered from their last meeting.

Flora turned to him slowly. "Then what happened to yours?"

"Not much. My prize was the Knight of Wands. The card should have taken me to whichever move my stepfather was in, but there was nobody there."

"I found who I was looking for," Flora said painfully. "I—I even held her in my arms. All I had to do, the *only thing,* was to get that doll and take it across the threshold. . . ." She swallowed. "As it turned out, I nearly didn't come back myself."

The other three waited. Finally, and with laborious reluctance, Flora recounted what had happened in the Eight of Swords: the Spinners and the doll, the sleeping girl and the maze.

"So you see," she finished, looking down at the scratch marks on her hands, "I did have the opportunity to save my sister. Only I got everything wrong."

Blaine shook his head. "It's not your fault. The Arcanum's bust. Whatever you did, however you played, the outcome would have been the same."

"Well, *my* wish was granted," said Toby tactlessly. He had drunk in Flora's story with rapt attention and shining eyes. "I wanted more adventure and now it looks like I've got it."

Cat snorted. "The only thing you got from the Chariot were murky warnings about the Game in meltdown, and how it's all our fault."

"Hey, I was given a *quest.* And anyway, what do you know about it? *You* haven't even played your card."

For a moment, the other three looked at her with resentment. They were all aware that for as long as her reward stayed unclaimed and unspent, Cat still had her chance of victory. It might turn out differently—better—for her.

Cat lifted her chin. "Seems to me that none of us here knows much about anything. In which case, it's time we went to HQ and looked for answers."

The first time Cat had seen Temple House, it had been on the night of a Lottery and a prizegiving. New to the Game, she had watched as a knight was allotted a new card to play, chosen at random by the spinning of a wheel. She had had no idea of the risk the knight had taken, nor had she understood what it meant when another player was awarded the triumph she'd won. But even without knowing what was at stake, Cat had felt the intoxicating luster of the place.

Then, and at every other formal gathering required by the Game, the house transformed into a grand old manor, glowing with opulent silks and polished wood. There had been a glow, too, surrounding the guests who cooed and applauded as the champagne bubbled and the wheel spun. At such times, the atmosphere was something between an exclusive cocktail party and a ceremony of state.

At all other times, however, the house had had the look and feel of a place that had been derelict for years. The windows were imprisoned behind heavy shutters, the rooms smelled of mold and much of the furniture was either missing or covered in dusty sheets. Yet neither these scenes of abandonment nor Blaine's warnings prepared her for the wreckage that awaited them.

As they approached the building, their feet crunched on crumbs of glass. All the ground-floor windows had been smashed. The shutters had been torn from their hinges, and the missing panes boarded up with cheap plasterboard. There were signs that someone had attempted to kick the front door in, too; its solid oak bulk had survived the attempt, although the bolt to lock it had been wrenched out of place. When Blaine shoved his shoulder against the door, it scraped open with a protesting groan.

"Welcome to the House of Horror," Toby said in sepulchral tones.

Once inside, they had to sidestep a huge iron candelabra that had crashed onto the black-and-white marble that checkered the floor. Entangled in the wreck of iron were the remnants of the gold brocade curtain that usually hung between the doorway and the hall. All surfaces were covered in a litter of smashed glasses, empty bottles and torn-up books.

Even though Blaine had told her what to expect, Cat was surprised by how shaken she was. Temple House was the heart of the Game—the place where the Lotteries were held, prizes given, forfeits allocated and judgments made. It was where the knights sweated as the wheel spun and the kings and queens flaunted their power. And yet it was also the threshold of all thresholds, the axis of the Arcanum. It should have been sacred ground.

"Who would *do* this?" Flora asked.

Nobody answered, but all were thinking of the man who now called himself Master of Misrule.

"Come on," said Toby. "We might as well have a poke around upstairs."

The four of them trudged up the grand sweep of the staircase and along the first-floor landing. The crimson silk lining the walls of the music room was ripped and stained; someone had taken an ax to the grand piano. The library next door was no better. Somberly, they contemplated the rows of wrecked bookshelves.

"What was that?" Cat asked suddenly.

"What?" said Blaine.

"I heard a noise from outside."

The door across the hallway led to a picture gallery that ran the length of the building, and had been closed when they'd climbed the stairs. Now it was propped open by a stack of broken chairs, to allow the person inside the room to sweep a heap of rubbish out onto the landing.

As soon as they saw the stiff, elderly figure, they relaxed slightly. It was the doorkeeper who supervised admittance to Temple House and presided over its ceremonies. His old-fashioned black-and-gold uniform—like those worn by concierges at hotels—was as crisp as ever, and he wielded the broom vigorously, his mouth puckered with distaste.

The distaste increased when he looked up and saw the huddle of chancers staring at him. With a jab of his broom, he thrust the pile of rubbish in the direction of their feet, and went back into the gallery, shaking his head.

There was no other lead, so they shuffled along behind him. Even after the destruction they'd already witnessed, it was a shock to see the pictures on the wall. The centuries-old paintings of the triumphs had been slashed and spattered with red paint.

The doorkeeper surveyed their stunned faces. "It's what you wanted, isn't it?" he remarked, his voice heavy with contempt.

"No!" Toby protested. "Of course we didn't. None of us ever imagined anything like this."

"You wanted your prizes, though. You wanted to win at whatever cost."

"The Game charges a high price," said Flora quietly.

He turned to look at her. His face was shrunken and lined, with colorless, cloudy eyes. "So do all things worth having. Everyone who plays for a triumph does so by choice."

"We've heard that argument before," Cat said. "All those sermons about how the Game helps us change fate, find a fortune . . ."

"Yeah," Blaine put in. "Funny how there're never any speeches about the losers. It seems like even mentioning failure's against your rules."

"And it seems that you would rather live with no rules than with rules you dislike," the man replied. "You would choose anarchy over authority."

"Every time," Blaine answered defiantly.

The doorkeeper let his broom fall with a clatter. "But you are not the only ones who must live with that choice. You had *no right* to make it." Gently, he placed his hand on the torn canvas of Fortune's Wheel, as if soothing a human hurt. "The man you set loose was imprisoned for a purpose.

Misrule is anchored at the heart of the Game, but it must not be unleashed on it. You have seen the damage he has wreaked on my temple, and the Arcanum will fare no better."

"There must be something we can do. To help reverse the damage to the Game, I mean," Toby said.

"So this time you're the Game's champions? How noble spirited!" The doorkeeper snorted. "No, you have discovered that prizes won by crooked means are awarded crookedly also. And so your gamble has failed, and you wish to change your luck. That is why you came here, to pick over the ruin of my temple. For I know very well what you're after."

He leveled an accusing stare at each of them in turn.

He pointed to Flora. "The sleeping girl," he pronounced. The finger moved to Blaine. "The man who made you bleed." It swung round to Cat. "And the one who stole your family." Last, he turned to Toby. "As for you ... Hmm. You, perhaps, are a different case. Still, there are no desires that the Game hasn't already uncovered, no needs that it hasn't been asked to satisfy. And I have witnessed them all."

"How come you know so much about us anyway?" Blaine asked grudgingly.

The old man looked offended. "It is the High Priest's business to know about everyone who enters my temple," he said, drawing himself up to his full height.

"No *way*! As in *the* High Priest? From the Greater Arcana cards?" Toby cut in.

The old man nodded curtly and continued. "I am the guardian of the Game's most sacred ground, the celebrant of its rituals and the keeper of its thresholds. I have known every king and queen who has ruled the Game, every knight who has gambled on it and every knave who has served it. I have known every chancer, too, though I never thought I would—"

"Live to see the day when oiks like us managed to spoil everyone's fun," Blaine finished. "No wonder you're peeved." He broke into a cough, looking at the man through watering eyes. "The thing is, how do we know you're telling us the truth? Any bunch of thugs could have got in here and trashed the place. And even if Mr. Misrule is responsible, I'm not sure that's proof he's any worse a Game Master than the others. Maybe nobody ever wins this Game of yours. Maybe it's always going to be a con, whoever's in charge."

This time, the man spoke calmly. "The Game has its traps, and the Arcanum its deceits. That is the gamble. Yet the principle behind our gamble is that a prize won fairly does not fail. Until now, every knight who has been awarded a triumph has been granted his wish.

"As for our new master of revels . . . The Arcanum grows too small for him, and his gambling lust has spread beyond the thresholds' bounds. I will show you Misrule's work, and where his Lottery will lead. Perhaps then you will begin to understand the ruin you have caused."

❧

They followed the doorkeeper—or High Priest, as they were learning to think of him—to the stairs at the end of the hall, which led up to a pair of doors inlaid with a design of interlocking wheels in black and gold. Behind the doors was a mirrored ballroom that took up the entire second floor.

It seemed the marauders' energy had flagged by the time they reached this final room, for the place was not as wrecked as the rest of the house. Most of the mirrors, although badly cracked, still lined the walls; the sparkle of light on their webs of shattered glass was oddly beautiful. Fists or weapons of some kind had left silvery starbursts at the point of impact, from which the fissures rippled outward like the rings after a stone is thrown into water.

For a few moments, the four chancers just stood, blinking. The disorientating effect of standing among so many mirrors was intensified by the fretwork of glimmering scars, in which things were both reflected and fragmented. The High Priest stood within the doorway, his hands clasped tight, murmuring nameless words under his breath and watching the chancers watch the walls.

Theirs were not the only images in the glass. As they looked, they began to see other figures moving across the gleaming surfaces, in a shifting reflection of scenes and people who were not there.

Gradually, they realized that they were watching the destruction of Temple House.

They saw a bearded man take an ax to the piano in the music room. A woman gleefully put her cigarette lighter to a silk wall hanging. A pack of youths rampaged through the bookshelves in the library. Another group hurled crystal champagne flutes down the stairs.

And in every splintered view, every jigsaw glimpse, there was a man with flowing white hair and hot blue eyes, whose face was neither old nor young, and whose smile was at one moment innocently bright and the next a crooked grin. There was no sound at first, but his head was thrown back in laughter as he urged the mob on.

Finally, the view of Temple House fractured and slid apart until there was only one image, everywhere. The Master of Misrule.

He had cast off the plain, dark clothes they had first seen him in for motley-colored robes, and he stood, arms outstretched, in the center of a wheel of blue fire. As the wheel spun and sparked, cards flew out from its axis and into the wind its whirling raised.

Before long the cascade of cards grew so frenzied it was as if the mirrors were filled with static. Yet when the fuzz and crackle cleared, the scenes revealed were remarkable only in their ordinariness. Pubs and offices, supermarkets and railway stations. There were cards there, too, though— glinting silvery blue on black, rich with possibility. . . . An allure that only grew stronger as people picked them up from pavements and doormats, or shook them out from magazines.

The chancers watched as a series of silver coins was scratched away and a sequence of laughing heads and forked tails was revealed. At first, the recipients responded with nothing stronger than a baffled smile or shrug. But soon their reactions grew more extreme. Winners punched the air in triumph. Losers recoiled, grew pale. Banner posters and billboards proclaimed:

Join the Lottery of Luck!
Prizes for All!

And it was the image of the cards that flashed around the mirrors now: reproduced in newsprint, beamed through airwaves, projected onto screens.

A burning wheel towered over a city skyline. This was the chancers' own London, free of the transformations and exaggerations of the Arcanum—except for that circle of azure flame. Beneath it, a crowd swelled. Every age, every profession, every kind of person was there. Some looked merely curious, but many bore the flush of desperation or greed.

The wheel spun to the sound of fairground jingles. Once again a wild wind blew, sending sparks and cards flying. These had no lettering or silver coins on them: their illustrations belonged to the Game of Triumphs deck. Nevertheless, the crowd surged to catch them, leaping and stumbling, trampling over each other in their lust to win.

The scene changed.

A gray morning. Quiet streets, tense faces.

The Day of the Lottery.

Let me be lucky. . . .

Be lucky, people murmured to themselves, whether fearful or excited or resigned, as they waited to receive their fate. Thick, gilt-trimmed cards that appeared out of nowhere to lie on doormats and desks, in handbags and briefcases, the folds of a newspaper or coat.

Many of the cards were blank except for a single line.

Your Fortune Is Unchanged!

Others bore pictures that the chancers recognized: illustrations of violence and transformation, fantasy and horror. But these cards did not need to be taken into the Arcanum for the experiences they depicted to come true.

Justice. Two of Swords.

Six of Wands. Love.

Death.

Their images came thicker and faster in the mirrors. Sometimes they were the flat illustrations from the cards; sometimes it was like looking into the Arcanum itself. Soon the glass was a kaleidoscope of moving color: rainbows and starbursts and shivers of light, all breaking, sliding, slithering into one another.

Until the mirrors returned to Misrule and his wheel.

The sun shone cold and black in a crimson sky, and skeleton trees grew root-first from rocks that writhed and squirmed. A ruined city sprawled around. The river that ran through it did not flow with water, but with yellow sand.

Snakes swam through the air, and birds dragged themselves across the ground with leaden wings.

Dead leaves twirled in the wind that whipped around the wheel and out of the mirrors, tangling the chancers' hair and tugging at their clothes. The leaves blew around them also—except they were not leaves, but the charred remains of triumph cards.

The Master of Misrule looked straight into their eyes. This time, they could hear his laughter. The wheel's blue flames burned cold as ice, and its reflection whirled on every side, so that they seemed locked in a prism of freezing fire. The light grew fiercer, whiter, spitting and hissing from each frosted shard of glass, until at last there was a mind-shattering crash as the mirrors fell to the floor, and the room plunged into darkness.

In the sudden silence, the four chancers could hear the laboring of their breath. The High Priest, meanwhile, was swaying with exhaustion. When he spoke again, they could see the effort it took to hold himself upright.

"Your city is the first to come under Misrule's spell, but it will not be the last. Already, you have seen his calling cards appear on your streets. Soon he will enslave chance to his will, corrupting its powers so that it is no longer one force among the many in men's lives, but the *only one*. Do you see, now, what you have done?"

All around them were scraps of burned cards and jagged heaps of glass. Cat's face swam out at her from one of the bigger pieces.

71

"Nobody wants a load of flying snakes and skeleton trees," Cat said, more aggressively than she felt. "But I don't see how all that doomsday stuff can come out of a few scratchcards."

"Then you should have paid more attention." The old man scowled. "To play even one of those scratchcards is to disturb the natural balance of luck in the world. With every head or tail that is uncovered, the more power Misrule gains. When he is ready, he will launch his Lottery, and deal the first round of fates from his wheel.

"You know the cards in the triumph deck, and how one card's lot has a thousand variations. At first, perhaps, the changes in fortune may be simple, and small. Some players might uncover a secret. Others might go on a journey or meet a stranger. Many will find new hope. Still more, sudden loss. As you saw, a number of cards will be blank. But whoever is dealt a new fate shall not escape it.

"For as Misrule's Lottery increases its grip, the nature of the cards will change. They will take on the Game's powers to summon angels and demons, resurrect the dead, create new gods. They shall burn towers and drown cities. Men will walk through their own pasts and see their most monstrous dreams made flesh.

"Human life is already erratic and perilous, threatened by crisis on every side. How many rounds of the Lottery will be played, how many different destinies will each man endure, before your civilization becomes as broken as my temple and as anarchic as the Arcanum? It will not be long, I think, before ruin takes hold."

There was a shaky silence.

Flora raised her bowed head. "Very well," she said quietly. "Tell us what we have to do."

The High Priest seemed to have aged since they had entered the ballroom, for his face was more heavily lined, with an unhealthy green tint. "Tomorrow I will deal you a new round of cards," he said, "and we will see what hope is left in the Arcanum. But tonight . . . tonight my strength is done. I want you gone from my temple."

"Can't we first—"

His eyes flashed. "What, you think it is an easy thing, to conjure visions in the scrying-glass? I summoned ghosts and demons for you, the image of Misrule himself! It was too much for the mirrors and nearly too much for me. No, I want you gone. Leave me, leave this place."

"But we'll come back tomorrow," Toby insisted. "Us four will come back, OK, and you'll show us what to do?"

"Regrettably, there is no other choice," the Priest replied sourly as he picked up his broom.

CHAPTER FIVE

USUALLY, WHEN THE CHANCERS left Temple House or a move within the Arcanum, they found that little time had passed on the other side of the threshold. But although it seemed like they couldn't have been in the house for more than an hour, they stepped out to discover that night was drawing in.

The four of them stood on the pavement in a disconsolate huddle.

"The King of Swords warned me that the Hanged Man's card used to be called the Traitor," Cat said at last. "At the time, I just thought he was trying to pull a fast one on me. D'you think we can believe what we saw of Misrule? Can we trust the Priest?"

Flora roused herself a little. "Unfortunately, it seems to fit with what we already know, and I don't just mean the scratchcards. When I was . . . was in Grace's move, they—the Spinners, that is—said we'd done a great wrong. They accused me of making the Game 'crooked.' "

"Exactly," said Toby solemnly. "And Mia herself showed me what a mess the Arcanum was in."

"It's not the Arcanum's welfare we have to worry about," Blaine said grimly. He coughed, and the noise echoed hollowly round the square.

Flora winced. "God, you sound awful."

"Sounds worse than it is. I think it's the damp."

"You're still staying in that basement place, aren't you?" Cat asked.

"The squat, you mean," Toby muttered.

Blaine shrugged.

"Well, no wonder you're ill," said Flora. She looked better than she had earlier: the dull, fixed look had gone from her eyes. Flora was beginning to accept that, perhaps, the disaster of the Eight of Swords had not been her fault. On one level, she recognized that the stakes they were now playing for were so high that all other concerns were meaningless. Yet as long as Flora could still play the Game, she reasoned, Grace still had a chance.

She smoothed down her hair. "I think you should come home with me," she announced.

"What?"

"I think you should stay with me until you're better. My parents went abroad this morning and I've got the house to myself. There's heaps of room."

Blaine half laughed. "I'm sure there is. Very kind of you and all that, but I'm fine where I am. I know how to look after myself."

"I'm not offering out of *charity*," Flora said stiffly. "I don't know exactly what we've got ourselves into, but however this crisis develops, we're going to have to go back into the Arcanum to deal with it. In which case, each of us needs to be as strong and resilient as we possibly can. And, frankly, if you're camping out in some squalid underground hole, you're going to get worse, not better, and won't be good for anything."

"She's right," Cat said, though she sounded reluctant about it.

Blaine didn't say anything at first. A chill wind sent cigarette butts and newspapers scuffling down the pavement, and he stooped over in another coughing fit. Finally, he straightened up and looked at Flora. "OK, fine. Whatever. I'll crash at yours."

In the brief time it took for Blaine to get his belongings from the squat, Flora had plenty of opportunity for second thoughts. They had said goodbye to the other two soon after leaving Mercury Square, and Flora agreed to wait for him at the top of Langdon Street. She disliked Soho at the best of times, and tonight its boozy garishness scraped at every frayed nerve. At the end of the road, a bus was pulling up to its stop. The advertising banner between the upper and lower decks was a swirl of silver, black and glitzy blue, and proclaimed:

The Triumph Lottery— Coming Soon!

Flora bit her lip. How had everything got so hideously out of control? Her invitation to Blaine already seemed nonsensical. She and Blaine had never had anything to say to each other. In ordinary circumstances they would never have anything to do with each other. This was also true of her and Cat and, to a lesser extent, Toby, too, but the hostility between her and Blaine had been mutual and instinctive from the start. Of course, after everything they'd been through in the Arcanum—where, arguably, she owed him her life—their antagonism had been left behind. In some ways Blaine knew her better than Georgia or Tilly or Charlie ever could. They were partners of a sort, she supposed, but that didn't make them friends.

It's going to be a disaster, she thought. And what on earth will I tell Mina?

Mina, the Seatons' housekeeper, was meant to be keeping an eye on Flora over the rest of the holiday. Her parents had left to catch their flight early that morning but she hadn't got up to see them go. She hadn't seen them the evening before, either. After she had dragged her battered and frozen body back from the Eight of Swords, she had managed to shut herself in her bedroom before they returned from the Avoncourts'. Flora got migraines occasionally, so her parents knew from experience to leave her alone in a darkened room. They had exchanged commiserations through the door, and left her to it.

But Mina had caught her on the way out that morning. She had responded to Flora's appearance with dismay, looking only partially placated by her story of getting on the wrong side of a cat. Tonight Mina was staying with her daughter in Willesden, so that was all right. But what about tomorrow? The arrival of Blaine would be a lot more difficult to explain than a few scratch marks.

And of course, while all these worries were running through her mind, Flora knew that none of it really mattered, that it was all just padding against other, real, unbearable things. At the edge of every thought was Grace and the cage of briar-swords, and layered over this anguish was the new one of Misrule's wheel of flame, the trials that must lie ahead. But she couldn't think of any of that now, mustn't think about it, or else it would be like sinking into the snow again, not into peaceful oblivion, but cold and pain, where the black bonds tightened and tightened. . . .

"Oh, there you are," she said brightly when Blaine appeared at the corner. "Good to see you're traveling light."

"That's kind of the point when you live on the streets."

Yes, no doubt about it: this was going to be a disaster.

Only a few streets away, Cat was passing a corner store when her palm prickled, letting her know that a threshold had appeared close by. She didn't think she would ever be able to wholly ignore the Arcanum's call, to go past a threshold without feeling an itch to see what lay on the other side. This time, she wondered if some knight had already used it to play their card, and what Misrule's disorder might cost them in the Game.

But it wasn't just the Game's other players who were at terrible risk. It was everyone going about their business around her, unaware that all their hopes and fears and plans for the future were about to be gambled away.

On impulse, Cat veered off her way home and began walking in the direction of Trafalgar Square instead. Bel had been in training at Alliette's today, and should be finishing around now. Though Bel wasn't big on coddling, her self-assurance was the generous kind, and comforting in itself. She had a way of dismissing difficulties with a snap of her fingers and flounce of her hair; just by being with her, Cat felt the world's rough edges smoothed out.

Alliette's was a very different affair to the Palais Luxe, the distinctly unpalatial casino opposite their flat. It was a Georgian town house with awnings in black and green, and a concierge almost as stately as the High Priest. Bel had enjoyed describing its glories to Cat; apparently, the splendor of the décor was outshone only by that of the clientele. "Royalty, too!" she'd said gleefully. "Well, once or twice. And mostly the foreign sort."

Cat went round to the staff entrance. Bel was just leaving, in the company of a muscular bartender. She was doing her special laugh and shaking out her hair in a way that would have been sure to make Greg, her most recent boyfriend, look even more doleful than usual. Cat quite liked Greg, with his kind, drooping face and disreputable store of local knowledge, but it was starting to look as if Bel had moved on. Bel had a low boredom threshold—it was the same with men as with jobs and places. They had spent the last twelve years moving back and forth around the country, often for no reason other than Bel "getting the itches."

"The sad fact is," Bel was saying to her friend, "part of me still believes that round one of these corners, I'll find a street paved with gold."

He laughed. "Every immigrant's dream."

"And it's high time I woke up from it. Specially since here and now's my second attempt at surviving this city."

"So what happened the first time around?"

"Trouble, that's what."

"Man trouble?"

Bel matched his flirtatious tone. "Is there any other kind?" Then, turning, she saw Cat. She looked startled. "Puss-cat! What are you doing here?"

"I was just, y'know, passing. Thought I'd walk you home."

Brief introductions were made, goodbyes said. Cat and Bel sauntered along St. James's and toward Trafalgar Square.

"You never told me you'd lived in London before."

"Didn't I? There's nothing much to tell."

"But you've never even mentioned it."

"Yeah, well." Bel cleared her throat self-consciously. "Attempt number one didn't count for much. Ran out of money, options, mates. Trouble, like I said. So this time around I wanted a whole new start." She aimed a playful kick at a pigeon. "And I've got one, haven't I? Now that I'm at Alliette's, me and you are on the up. We play our cards right, and there's no one and nothing to stop us. Gold pavements all the way!"

Cat was still frowning.

"Cheer up," said Bel. "You look like one of those gamblers who've won a tenner and dropped a grand. And speaking of gamblers, you know anything about this triumph card gimmick?"

Cat's body tensed. "The scratchcards?"

"That's right."

"Nope," she answered, trying to keep her tone light. "You haven't found one, have you?"

"Fat chance. Andy in accounts has a friend whose wife did, though. She got her hands on a heads card. Just lying in the back of a taxi, it was. Now, she was on her way to the hospital to have a mole taken off her back. It'd gone cancerous, you see. But when she took her clothing off in the surgery—what do you think happened?" Bel smacked her red lips in relish. "The sodding mole had only gone and vanished! Not so much as a freckle left, never mind a cancer cell."

"Impressive," Cat managed to say. "All the same, if you found one of those scratchcards, you wouldn't . . . play it, would you?"

"Depends how lucky I felt at the time. I've still got hopes of winning a head, and seeing the man of my dreams walk through the door."

"Don't joke. What if you got a snake's tail instead? Something really bad might happen—like a road accident or a mugging. Even a heart attack."

Bel came to an abrupt halt. "Hey," she said. "What's all this? You don't actually believe this scratchcard crap, do you?"

"You're the one who brought up the miracle mole."

"I was only messing with you! You know how these stories get blown out of proportion. Like urban legends." She took another look at Cat's face. "All right. Doesn't matter. If it'll make you feel any better, I promise to stay away from the scratchcards."

"You swear?"

"Cross my heart and hope to die." Bel put on her special saintly expression, hands clasped in prayer. "Mind you," she added, a little regretfully, "luck's one of those things everyone wants and no one can buy. It's a good notion for a lottery."

Later in the evening, Bel announced she was going out dancing, with instructions to Cat to tell Greg, if he called, that she was working at Alliette's. As soon as she was alone, Cat fetched the Triumph of Justice from its hiding place. She spent a long time watching how its pearly sheen glowed in the dark. In light of the others' experiences, she had to tell herself that playing it could end only in disappointment or deceit. She would not risk throwing her die and bringing the card to life across the threshold. But she would carry it with her into the Arcanum tomorrow nonetheless. It was her stake in the Game, and she wasn't ready to give it up.

Afterward, she watched a trashy cop show and went to bed early. She left the light on in the hall and the TV still on in the kitchen, so that its babble would numb her mind. She was afraid of what she might dream.

When Toby returned home, he found his parents writing notes at either end of the dining room table. They could almost have been twins, with their crooked spectacles and short, rumpled hair, their identical frowns of concentration. As the only child of two writers, Toby had always known that his parents led other lives in worlds of their own making. Watching them now, however, he was conscious of his superiority. After all, no imaginary world could compete with the one *he* was a flesh-and-blood hero of.

And now he wasn't just a champion of the Arcanum. He was a defender of humankind!

"I'll be in my room," he announced. "I've got stuff to do."

His father grunted. His mother waved a vague hand. They both went back to their footnotes.

Toby, meanwhile, went to stare once more at the Escher print above his bed. He looked at his wavering reflection and thought of the visions in the mirrors, and the Lottery of Luck, and a certain neat irony in the order of things. He thought of school.

The secret society had worked out even better than Toby had hoped. As the Chameleons' dares increased in frequency and boldness, he waited for his membership invitation to arrive.

Two weeks passed. Very well, thought Toby. If the

Chameleons wouldn't come to him, then he would go to the Chameleons. He would start with their leader, Seth. Seth was swarthy and sulky-looking, claimed to write poetry and was known to do drugs. But Toby told himself he wasn't frightened of him.

So he tracked Seth down to the clock tower, late one Sunday evening. The place had been off-limits for years, and the school caretaker spent much of his time chasing people out of it. However, successive generations of students always found new ways in. In the candlelit gloom of the ground-floor room, various demigods of the upper school were lounging and smoking.

"It's a squirt," Seth drawled, glancing up from the joint he was rolling. *Squirts* was upper-school slang for the junior years. "Come to eavesdrop again. What do you want, squirt?"

Toby gulped. "I, uh, wanted to talk to you. About the Chameleons."

Seth widened his eyes theatrically. "*Nobody* talks about the Chameleons. It's the rules."

"And what would you know about them anyway?" asked one of the demigods, to widespread sniggers.

"Look," said Toby, trying to shut out the others and focus on Seth, "I don't mind that the dares and stuff were my idea; in fact, I think it's great you're making such a success of it. I'm not here to ask for credit. I just wanted to, well, you know . . . help out. Participate."

More laughter, and louder this time. Seth waved a hand for quiet.

"How could someone like *you* possibly help someone like *me*?" he asked. He sounded genuinely perplexed.

"Erm, I think that's already been demonstrated, hasn't it? Because my idea—"

"Listen, squirt," Seth said in the patient tones used to address children or imbeciles. "It doesn't matter how many ideas you had or have, or even how good they are. The fact is, you're not the kind of person who will ever be able to make anything of them. Because other people won't be interested, so long as the ideas come from you."

"But I can—"

"No, squirt, you can't. Now piss off." Seth threw a beer bottle top at his head. Toby yelped, more from surprise than discomfort. Soon everyone in the room was throwing things and jeering, their grinning faces luridly distorted in the shadows. He fled.

Then came the second conversation that Toby shouldn't have heard but acted on anyway: Mia's whispered argument with Mr. Marlow—those tantalizing hints about midnight duels, and the Game, and playing fair. . . . Yet whenever Toby looked back to the moment he decided to follow Mia to the clock tower, he found he couldn't remember what he'd actually planned to do. Was it simply to spy on the Chameleons' secrets? Or was it a last-ditch attempt to redeem himself, this time appealing to Mia for support? It made little difference, of course, for in the tower his whole life was divided into before and after the Game, and everything beforehand became vague and insubstantial.

Yet the memory of Seth's words still stung. It wasn't so

much the humiliation that hurt, but the injustice. His powerlessness still astonished him.

Former powerlessness, that is. Thanks to the Game of Triumphs, Toby reminded himself, he had a quest now. A quest and a destiny.

CHAPTER SIX

A NOISY PACK OF TOURISTS got between Flora and Blaine during the bus ride home, so both were free to sit in their separate silences. Silently, she indicated their stop; silently, the two of them made their way alongside the park and turned into the row of mansions, with their ranks of pillars and porticoes.

Flora led the way into the house with a nonchalance she did not feel. The interior was adorned in "pearl," "chiffon," "jasmine" and "mist"—all subtle variations on white, and chosen to provide a restful backdrop for Mr. Seaton's collection of Chinese porcelain and Mrs. Seaton's inherited antiques. None of the lights could be turned to anything stronger than a flattering glow, which gave the impression that everyone who entered the house had been discreetly airbrushed.

"Nice place," said Blaine, and Flora—braced for something awkward or snide—found herself smiling at him in relief.

She took him to the smallest of the three guest bedrooms. The décor was a little chintzy, perhaps, with its lace curtains and embroidered bedspread, but it felt less like a hotel room than the others, and was slightly out of the way at the top of the house.

"Here we are! Whew—sorry about all the stairs. Now then, your bathroom is through that door. There should be towels and so on already laid out. My room's back on the first landing, second from the left, if you, um, you know, need anything. I'll be in the kitchen for now. It's in the basement. So whenever you're ready to eat, come down and we can fix something up. Otherwise, I'll leave you to get settled. Unless there's anything else you . . . ?"

Blaine bounced his grubby duffel bag against a leg. He looked too big, too dark, altogether too male for that dainty room.

"Actually, I could do with using a washing machine."

"Of course. I mean, yes, that's no problem. I'll show you the utility room. Do you need a change of clothes? Because I'm sure my dad's—"

His mouth twisted in amusement. "No, I think I can manage." Then he noticed her discomfited expression. "Thanks, though."

He came down to the kitchen about twenty minutes later, in a clean if fraying T-shirt, and still damp from the shower.

Flora heard the cough before she heard his footsteps on the stairs.

Mina had prepared a casserole, more than enough for two, and Flora put it on the Aga cooker to warm. The rich, soothing smell filled the kitchen. Flora had turned the radio on low and begun to chop vegetables while she waited. There had also been time to change her rumpled top, wash her face and put up her hair. She felt much better after doing this.

"Oh, hello, there you are. Is that the washing? Good. The utility room's just through here. Let me show you."

In theory, Flora did know how to use the washer and dryer, but since Mina was in charge of the laundry, she had no practical experience in getting them to work. Talking a little too much, a little too quickly, she showed him where the array of detergents was kept, and what she hoped was the right sequence of buttons. She was careful not to look as he put his shabby bundle into the machine.

Things went more easily after this. The kitchen, with its old oak table and cream walls, was cozier than the rest of the house, and the rhythmic gurgles of the washing machine were friendly sounds, mingling with the quiet chatter of the radio. Flora heaped two bowls with casserole and brought the vegetables, bread and cheese to the table. Salt and pepper, butter, a water jug. Plus a bottle of cough syrup she'd found in the medicine cabinet.

Blaine accepted his bowl without comment and they passed the dishes between them silently. Oddly, this didn't feel awkward. As soon as Flora began to eat, she realized she was ravenous. She hadn't eaten anything since a few canapés at the Avoncourts' party.

"My mum's always wanted one of those," Blaine said out of nowhere. He nodded toward the glossy cream Aga.

"Really? Well, they *are* lovely, even if they are old-fashioned. And ours can be tricky to cook on; we usually end up using the electric stove."

She spoke to cover her surprise. It was the first personal information he'd ever volunteered. "Where's your mother now?" she heard herself asking.

"She's ill."

"Oh." She looked down into her water glass. "Mine drinks."

She watched Blaine butter another piece of bread. Newly washed, his skin still had a worn, grayish look, especially around the eyes. Not that he looked frail, of course—with his light brown hair cropped, the bones of his face seemed harder, and he had bulk as well as height. Or rather, he had the frame for sturdiness; it stopped him from appearing too obviously thin.

Normal small talk wasn't an option, which left the Arcanum and its attendant traumas the only topic they had in common. But Flora discovered she wanted them to keep talking anyway.

She leaned forward a little. "Blaine, what was it really like when you played your Knight of Wands?"

Blaine didn't look up from his food. "It took me to a place full of tombs. There were statues of knights on them, but the man I was looking for wasn't there. Not in a grave, nor out of one."

"So . . . what do you want from him?"

He took a slow sip of water. Carefully, he put his fork down on the table. His jaw had tightened. Still, he didn't seem properly angry. More like he was bracing himself for something.

He was just about to speak when the doorbell rang.

Flora went to answer the door feeling exasperated and apprehensive in equal measure. It was nine-thirty at night, for goodness' sake. She hoped it wasn't some busybody neighbor, coming to check up on her because her parents were away.

"Hello, honeybun."

Charlie was standing on one of the lower steps, grinning up at her from under his mop of fair hair.

"Well, um, hello to you, too. This is a . . . surprise."

"A nice one, I hope."

"Of course. It's just that I . . ."

"I've been over at Rory's. Bit of an impromptu party going on."

Yes, she thought. His cheeks were a telltale pink, and he was speaking more loudly than usual.

"Anyhow, I wasn't really up for it, so I thought I'd swing by on the way home to see how you're doing, since you're all on your lonesome. Did your folks get off all right?"

"Absolutely. Daddy left a voice mail to say everything

was fine. Listen, it's awfully sweet of you to come round, but—"

Somehow, he was swinging confidently past her into the hall. "I hope Mina's stocked up on the munchies. I'm absolutely *starving*."

Flora hastened after him. "Wait, Charlie. The thing is, it's not really a good time—"

Too late: he was already thumping down the stairs to the kitchen. "Hello, hello," she could hear Charlie saying genially. "Who's this?"

Flora counted to ten, squared her shoulders and went down to join the fray. Charlie was lounging against the Aga, looking exaggeratedly relaxed, as he assessed Blaine—his tattered clothes and bare feet. The dirty duffel bag propped against the door to the utility room.

"Blaine—this is a friend of mine, Charlie. Charlie, this is Blaine."

Blaine gave a brief nod of acknowledgment. Then he went back to his food.

"Blaine's visiting London for a few days. On, erm, work experience," Flora said overbrightly. She began to twirl her hair. "Anyway, he's had an absolute *nightmare* with the organization he's with. There was the most frightful mix-up with the accommodation—you wouldn't believe! So he's staying here for a night or two while they sort everything out."

"I see. And you two know each other from . . . ?"

"St. Bernadine's," Flora said before the silence went on

for too long. "It's a church outreach program. The work experience, I mean. They, um, help coordinate it."

Charlie was still smiling. "So you're going to be a priest, Blaine? Or a choirboy?"

Blaine made a hacking, hawking noise in his throat, as if he was about to spit, and reached for the water jug.

"Mmm. That'll be 'no comment,' then.... And how do your parents—" But as Charlie turned to Flora, he did a double take. "God, Flo, what on earth have you done to your face?"

"Oh." Her hands flew defensively to her cheek. In the dimness of the hall and stairs, her scratches had been hardly noticeable. But she had just moved under one of the spotlights and the marks were now obvious. "Nothing. Just this stray cat I tried to make friends with, till it went all psychokitty on me."

"That's the thing about you, Flo: you're a soft touch for any old stray." He looked more closely at her. "Hey, your hands are all cut up, too."

"No, they're fine, honestly. It looks worse than it is."

"Let me have a look. Don't be shy—I've got the healing touch, you know. Magic fingers!"

"Charlie, don't, no—"

Charlie reached for her wrists and she backed away, laughing nervously. They had a breathless little mock tussle by the dresser, and she found she was looking over at Blaine, as if in appeal.

He got to his feet with a noisy scraping of the chair.

"I'm beat. If it's OK with you, I think I'll head for bed." Blaine took his plates to the sink and ran some water over them. Then he looked sidelong at Charlie. "Got a lot of praying to do."

In silence, the other two listened to his feet going up the stairs.

"Well," said Charlie, "I hope you're not going to wake up tomorrow and find all the silver's missing."

"Don't be silly." Flora set about stacking the dishwasher to cover her confusion.

"C'mon—a church outreach program?"

"That's right."

"He doesn't look like a good Catholic schoolboy to me. But I'm not sure how much of a good Catholic schoolgirl you are, either."

She whirled round on her heel. "Exactly what do you mean by that?"

"Nothing. Sorry. Bloody hell." Charlie rubbed his hands over his face and through his hair, frowning. "It's just that . . . OK, sometimes, Flo, I get the feeling there's all this deep stuff going on with you that no one knows about. Maybe it's to do with the way you just . . . disappear . . . every so often. It's as if you completely drop off the planet. And then when I see you afterward, it seems you're, I don't know, *going through the motions.* Like there's a part of you that's not really there, and that maybe it's the most important part. The part none of us ever gets to see."

Flora realized she was holding her breath. Charlie was more observant—unnervingly so—than she had given him credit for. "Perhaps you're right," she said carefully, despising herself. "The truth is, there are days when I need to disappear for my own sanity. Because there are some things you can't share with other people, however much you want to. Deeply personal, painful things—things that belong in families."

Charlie looked abashed, as she had meant him to. There was a pact among Flora's friends never to mention Grace, or Mrs. Seaton's little weakness. Nobody was quite certain how this agreement had come about, but all were sure it was with Flora's approval.

"Of course," he said. "Of course you're right. I'm being insensitive, and I'm sorry. Will you forgive me?"

"Always." She smiled up at him in guilt and relief.

"Just remember," he told her as she walked him to the door, "if you ever have anything you want to share, anything at all, I'm here for you. I know how lame this sounds, but . . . honestly, Flo, there's no part of you I wouldn't like."

After Charlie had gone and she had cleared away the rest of the supper things, Flora went to sit in Grace's bedroom. Most of Grace's things had long since been packed away, but a representative selection of books and posters stayed. To a casual visitor, it looked as if the Seatons' eldest daughter had gone away to university. Flora sat on the bed and looked from the bookcase—where *Little House on the Prairie* rested against *The Bell Jar*—to a Man Ray print on the wall. She closed her eyes and breathed deeply, trying to bring back the image of Grace working at her desk—the warm halo of light around her bent head, how her frown of concentration lifted into a welcoming smile when she saw her little sister at the door. But the picture wouldn't come. Instead, Grace's face was obscured by a tangle of black wool and briar-swords.

Flora's whole body ached with exhaustion. Now that she was alone in the silence, the creeping coldness had returned. She went and ran a bath, as scalding hot as she could bear, but even when her flinching pink flesh was totally submerged, she couldn't stop shivering. She lay in the steaming water and sobbed, and sobbed.

CHAPTER SEVEN

BLAINE HEARD FLORA CRYING as he went downstairs to collect his laundry. The sound was muffled and rhythmic, an almost mechanical keening, and was as familiar to him as other household noises, like a vacuum cleaner or radio.

He was tired but not sleepy. The house was too silent, the bed too soft; his limbs sank into it without relaxing, as if they didn't quite trust that the cushioning wasn't about to give way. How many weeks since he had last slept in a proper bed? Over a month, he thought—not since that emergency shelter in Holloway. There had been a couple of hostels before that, interspersed with night buses and train stations, a park bench on one or two fraught occasions.

Mostly, though, Blaine had been lucky. He looked older than he was: big enough and tough enough to more or less be left alone.

As he moved his clean clothes to the tumble dryer and watched them slump round and round in the hot air, he felt some of the tension leave his shoulders. You couldn't cadge for money or get odd jobs—packing up market stalls, washing dishes—if you stank or turned up in rags. Thinking of this, he decided that he'd probably been too quick to turn down Flora's offer of clothes.

He sat down against the wall and reached for his bag. There was a leather notebook concealed inside the lining. Its cover was stained and worn. Though he had first read it with confusion and loathing, its pages had become so well known to him that their familiarity was almost comforting.

The first page was a rough sketch of the card known to Blaine as the Triumph of Eternity. It was this card that gave a knight admittance to the Game. A dancing figure hovered above the earth, encircled by a serpent biting its own tail. The four corners of the drawing each contained a little wheel with a smudgy face in its center. Underneath the picture, someone had written in a neat, cramped hand, *Dancer = hermaphrodite. Is this significant? NB Vision of the Wheels. Ezekiel 10.* At the bottom of the page, written larger for emphasis, was *TEMPLE HSE. MERCURY SQ.*

The rest of the book was filled with more jottings and diagrams. Images of Death, the Devil and the Tower featured heavily, interspersed with notes on the ancient Egyptian *Book of the Dead* and the black magic practices of an occult society called the Hermetic Order of the Golden Dawn.

Blaine traced one of the bloodstains on the book's cover. He looked without really seeing at the tight, neat script inside, and thought of the first time he'd seen this handwriting.

My dear Helen, the card on the mantelpiece had read, *I hope you don't mind me writing to thank you for such a delightful evening....* Even as a small boy, Blaine had known that Helen wasn't like other mothers. She laughed louder than most people and cried more, too. As for other people's fathers, that was something Blaine didn't really think about. His own had left when he was a baby, or perhaps even before he was born. Blaine's grandmother looked after them both. Helen, she said, was too easily hurt by the world.

The trouble came when Blaine turned twelve, and his grandmother died. After the funeral, Helen shut herself in her bedroom for weeks. She didn't dress or wash and barely seemed to eat. Meanwhile, Blaine did his best to look after the house and do the shopping and cleaning, as his grandmother had taught him to.

After a while, Helen got better. She went back to giving piano lessons in their tiny sitting room and seemed to enjoy it. She started seeing friends again, too. Then one of their neighbors, Liz the nurse, invited Helen to a party. It was there that Helen met Arthur White.

Arthur taught Latin and history at a private girls' school. He wasn't bad-looking, except for his small, pale eyes and prissy mouth, but he had the air of someone much older than his forty-something years. Two days after meeting

Helen, he invited her to a piano recital. It was after that evening that Arthur sent the thank-you card. And it seemed that it was only a few weeks later that Helen, starry-eyed as a schoolgirl, announced that they were going to get married.

Even before they'd got to the registry office, Arthur had organized the sale of Helen's cottage, and she and Blaine moved into his respectably ugly place on the other side of town. Blaine had to change schools as well.

Meanwhile, Helen stopped giving piano lessons. Arthur said that she wasn't good at teaching, that it made her tired and tense, and she agreed with him. Because she had always been nervous of things like bank accounts and insurance and bills, he took care of this, giving her a small allowance every week.

They never went out or invited people round. Blaine's mother only seemed properly aware of him when she got in a muddle with her household chores. Then she would cry and beg for help, but guiltily, because Arthur had told her Blaine was not allowed to interfere. If Blaine did, or if Arthur was particularly displeased with him, then Arthur would hit him.

It was generally in places that didn't show, and if Helen noticed the marks, Blaine would shrug and say he'd been in a fight. *Boys will be boys,* Arthur would say, smiling his small, prim smile across the table.

Blaine tried not to react, but as time went on, the hatred that pulsed inside him grew too big and bloody to control.

He began staying out late to avoid going home. In a run-down seaside town, and a school full of wrong crowds, there was plenty of opportunity for trouble. He got suspended from school, and had some run-ins with the police.

Arthur was very forgiving of Helen. Her son's criminality wasn't necessarily her fault, he told her. Some boys just went bad. Helen might shake her head a little but she wouldn't deny it.

As time went on, Blaine saw that he had two options: persuade Helen to leave Arthur, or force Arthur to treat both of them better. Either way, he needed some kind of leverage. Blaine would try and keep a record of when Arthur hit him. But he also needed something that couldn't be explained away by a household mishap or the rough-and-tumble of school.

Arthur controlled the purse strings as tightly as everything else, but what if there was more to this than miserliness? Blaine had begun to wonder about the money from the sale of Helen's cottage, and what had happened to the savings his grandmother had left him.

And so one evening, after Arthur had left for a PTA meeting and Helen had taken some sleeping pills and gone to bed, Blaine used his newfound criminal skills to pick the lock on his stepfather's study.

He started with the filing cabinet, pulling out papers at random. He was just about to replace a file of insurance forms when his eye was caught by something colorful tucked into a plastic wallet at the back. It was a card with an illustration of a dancing figure encircled by a snake on one side and writing on the reverse:

The Arcanum
Temple House, Mercury Square

Admits One

Throw the coin, turn the card.
What will you play for?

It bore a little icon of a four-spoked wheel.

Blaine didn't quite know why the card seemed so sinister, but its careful placement in the insurance folder suggested it was important. He flipped rapidly through the remaining files in the drawer and found a leather notebook concealed within a file of old payslips. It opened onto a page of devil drawings and pentagrams.

"Well, well," came a voice from the door. "So it's breaking and entering now. You're turning into quite the career criminal."

Arthur had returned early. His entrance had been deliberately quiet, for Blaine had not heard the front door close and Arthur hadn't switched on the light in the hallway.

"What's this?" Blaine demanded, holding out the book and the card.

"Nothing that concerns you."

"It does if it's some kind of Satanist crap. Are you dragging my mum into a cult, along with everything else?"

"You have no right to be in here. Give me that card."

"Not till you tell me what it's about." Blaine was almost sixteen now; for the first time, he realized he was bigger and stronger than his stepfather.

Arthur smiled contemptuously. "You couldn't possibly begin to understand. This is your last warning. *Give it up.*"

And he took out a knife.

Instantly, everything was catapulted out of place. Arthur's blade was long and serrated, and Blaine recognized it from the kitchen drawer, but it was nonetheless absurd, a theatrical prop.

"What the hell are you doing?" he managed to ask.

"Protecting my home." Arthur's tone was as quiet and reasonable as ever, though there was sweat on his brow.

"It's my home, too. Jesus—you're deranged. You—"

But Arthur was advancing across the room, with the knife held before him. "Give me the card."

Blaine swore, and grasped it tighter.

Then Arthur slashed at his bare arm, the one that was holding the book and card against his chest. Blood ran, shockingly warm and bright, all along Blaine's arm and into his hand, so that his fingers were slippery with it. He heard the thump as the book hit the floor.

The next moment Arthur was on him, clutching for the card, clammy and panting. Blaine threw his weight against Arthur, slamming him into the wall, and made for the door.

Before he could reach it, Arthur lunged at him again, slashing with the knife. Blaine tripped over himself and stumbled to the floor, but he grabbed at Arthur's legs and brought him crashing down with him. The knife fell, too, was scrabbled for by Arthur, snatched away by Blaine and, between the two of them, kicked across the room. Blaine hardly knew why he was so desperate not to give the card up, but as Arthur clawed savagely at his hand, he forgot about trying to regain the knife or making his escape. Keeping the card from Arthur became all that mattered.

There was a slow ripping sound. Arthur gave a strangled cry. He had the card, but Blaine had torn off the top left corner. This time, it was Arthur's body that slackened in shock.

Blaine saw that he had the advantage now. Hot with hate, he drove his fist into Arthur's face, and when the prissy mouth gave a grunt of pain, a flash of joy sparked through him. As Arthur flailed and writhed beneath him, Blaine gripped him by his hair and smashed his head against the side of the filing cabinet.

Something plucked at his shirt. He twitched his shoulders impatiently. Then he heard his name.

Helen was standing over them, white-faced and making hiccupping little screams. Blaine found he couldn't speak. He and Arthur were both spattered in blood—Blaine's blood, mostly—and he knew his face was still suffused with the violence he'd inflicted.

He got up and released Arthur; there was nothing else he could do. For a few moments Arthur lay where he was, groaning, before he dragged himself up by the corner of the desk, and stayed huddled there in a defensive crouch.

"You see now, don't you, Helen?" he choked out. "You see what your son has done to me."

Helen had her hands crammed against her mouth. A low moan forced its way through them.

"Yes," said Arthur. He dabbed at the blood on his face, and when he spoke again, his voice was cracked but calm. "He broke into my room. He lay in wait for me with that knife. You saw him attack me with your own eyes. He is a monster, Helen."

Blaine swayed on his feet. He looked at Helen to try and get past the glaze of sleep and pills and horror in her eyes. "Mum," he said. "Please . . ."

But Helen shrank from him, and screwed her eyes tight shut. So he limped past her into the hall, pausing only to pick up the fallen notebook. He left the house and didn't look back.

Because he couldn't think of anywhere else to go, Blaine made his way to their old neighborhood and their old neighbor: Liz the nurse.

"I'm B-Blaine," he stammered out. "Helen's son? We used to live round here." Dizziness swilled through his head. "There was a—my stepfather tried—I couldn't . . . I didn't know what to do. . . ."

Once she'd got over her initial shock, Liz said she was taking him to the hospital. At that point he tried to leave, saying that he couldn't get anyone official involved, that the doctors would call the police, and his stepfather, and then—

In the end, his desperation must have persuaded her, for she made a phone call and another woman arrived—a doctor, he supposed—who stitched up his arm and gave him a shot of something, shaking her head and tutting all the while.

From there on, everything mercifully dissolved into blackness.

The next afternoon, Liz took Blaine to the police station and waited while he made a statement about the fight in the study. For some reason, though, he couldn't quite bring himself to show them the torn piece of card in his pocket. The day after that, Saturday, Liz went to see Helen. She was away for a long time, and when she came back, her face was grim. "Your stepfather's gone," she told him. "Apparently, the police came round yesterday evening. Asked some questions, took a look round Arthur's study. They wanted to know about your grandmother's trust fund, too. He got very upset, Helen said. Afterward he tore off in the car."

Blaine didn't read too much into this. Arthur hadn't even been gone twenty-four hours.

"How's Mum? Does she want to see me?"

"I'm sorry." Liz couldn't quite meet his eye. "She says . . . well, she says that she's afraid of you, Blaine."

She had brought back a bag of his things. She told him a woman from social services would be visiting, but that he'd be staying with her for "the meantime." Neither of them wanted to look too closely at what that meant.

Later, Blaine went to Arthur's house. The blinds were drawn and the place looked lifeless; Helen must have shut herself away in the bedroom. He didn't want her to see him lurking and get scared, so he stayed in the bus shelter on the other side of the street. He had no plans. He just wanted to be close by.

He got out Arthur's notebook to have another look at the drawing of the card he'd found, and the reference to TEMPLE HSE. MERCURY SQ., the address he remembered from the back of the invitation. The more he stared at it, the more mysterious it seemed.

A dark car purred along the road and pulled in a little way down from the bus stop. A man got out and walked up to Arthur's front door. He rang the bell repeatedly, hung about on the doorstep for a while and peered into the ground-floor windows.

Blaine watched this with some interest. Arthur didn't have many visitors; Helen, none. The man had noticed him watching, and came over to where Blaine was sitting. "I'm after Arthur Wh-white," he said. "I don't suppose you know him?"

The man wore an expensive-looking coat and had a hooked, handsome face, with silvering hair. Blaine wondered if he had something to do with the school where Arthur taught—a governor, perhaps.

"Arthur White? Sure I know him. I know he's a vicious maniac and the police are after him."

The man stiffened. "P-police?"

"Yeah. They were around here yesterday. Looks like he's given them the slip."

"And where do you think he could have s-slipped to?" he asked softly.

"Rumor has it he's joined a cult."

The man looked down at Blaine's lap and the open notebook. His eyes lingered on the sketch of the card. "How interesting." He gave a half smile. "You've been most h-helpful. Thank you." Then he got into the car and drove away.

At the end of the week, there was still no sign of Arthur. Blaine went to see his mother, with Liz there to supervise. Helen's face was mottled with tears and tiredness, and her nails were gnawed down to the quick. When Blaine came in, she flinched away and sat crouched in the corner of the sofa, thin arms wrapped around her body, as she rocked and wept.

"No, no, I mustn't see you. He wouldn't like it. He told me, he *warned* me, he'd leave if we weren't good enough. You pushed him to the edge and now you've driven him away. All he ever wanted to do was take care of us, and what will happen to us now? I can't *bear* it, oh—"

Liz walked Blaine to the door. "She'll come round," she said wearily. "But I'm getting the doctor to visit later. It may be that your mother needs to be looked after . . . professionally, for a while."

Blaine nodded dumbly. He wished he had never gone into the study, never found the card.

And yet he carried his torn corner with him at all times, as if for luck. The top of the dancer's head was visible above the tear, and there was part of the first line of writing on the back:

The Arcan

Following his visit to Helen, however, Blaine wanted to forget about Arthur and everything else. He went to walk on the seafront.

Like most of the town, the promenade's row of seedy bed-and-breakfasts and discount shops had seen better days. The amusement arcade that lined the rusting Victorian pier was closed at this time on a Sunday. Nonetheless, a group of people were sitting around one of the plastic picnic tables outside the entrance. They looked exotically out of place.

There was a blonde in a sharp white suit and sunglasses, even though it was a dour winter's afternoon. She was seated opposite an older, darkly glamorous woman in an evening gown. A young man lounged beside her, fashionably disheveled. He had a sleepy smile and tousled hair. The fourth was a black man, dressed as if for a business meeting, grizzled and stern.

As Blaine drew closer, he noticed two things. One, that the group appeared to be playing a card game of some sort, and two, that although they were talking among themselves, the sound was small and blurred, as if he was listening to something far away. The chill wind that had begun to whip off the sea didn't ruffle their clothes or hair, let alone set them shivering.

Out of some instinct, Blaine felt in his back pocket. As he did so, the black man rose to his feet and put out his hand.

"I believe you have something belonging to our Game."

His voice was heavy as granite. The other three didn't even look up. Without quite knowing why, Blaine proffered his bloodstained piece of card.

"I want to find the man who's got the rest of this card," he said.

"He has joined the Game as a Knight of Wands, and become lost in the Arcanum."

"Arc-what?"

"The place where our Game is played."

"Will he come back?"

"He could. He has everything to play for."

"Then I've got to go find him."

Below them, the gray sea sucked and mumbled on the gray stones. A seagull cawed. But for Blaine, everything except the man in front of him had faded into the distance.

The man looked at him carefully. "You have brought only a scrap of card. You cannot become a knight of our courts or compete for our prizes.

"However, your actions have altered the State of Play. You are responsible for this Knight of Wands joining the Game, and because your intervention was by accident, we have no choice but to let you into the Arcanum. Your role in the Game will be that of a chancer. Some call it the Fool."

He picked up a new card from the table and gave it to Blaine. This one showed a figure dressed in motley-colored rags, poised at the brink of a precipice. The lettering on the back was the same as on Arthur's.

"Temple House? Where's that?"

"There are many cities with a quiet square, an ancient house, a door that is just ajar. All players in the Game of Triumphs will find their way to it."

Blaine tightened his grip around the gilt edge of the card. His hand was shaking slightly. "And . . . and who are you?"

"I am Ahab, king of the Court of Wands. And these are the Game's other masters: Alastor, King of Swords; Odile, Queen of Cups; and Lucrezia, Queen of Pentacles."

At this, the other three looked up at him and smiled. The wound on his arm flared. Blaine was suddenly afraid, and turned to go. When he looked back from the end of the street, the four cardplayers had gone.

Arthur White became the subject of an official missing-person inquiry. The police traced his credit card to a petrol station in central London, but that was three days after his disappearance, and there had been nothing since.

Blaine took the train to London at the end of the week. Someone from school had a brother living in Hammersmith, and Blaine arranged to stay on his sofa for the first few nights. After that, who knew? Ever since meeting the King of Wands, nothing felt real to him except his pursuit of Arthur. He did not really question what the game was, or what would become of him when he entered it.

He had slipped away without saying goodbye to Liz, to spare her having to try and persuade him not to leave. Instead, he left her a thank-you note, with a vague story about trying to track down his father. He left a letter for Helen, too, for when she got out of the clinic where she was "resting."

And so Blaine went to London and found his way to Temple House, Mercury Square, and all the strangeness of the Arcanum. But nearly a year later, he had found no trace of Arthur White.

> *In altum tollor,*
> *Nimis exaltatus;*
> *Descendo minoratus,*
> *Funditus mortificatus!*

> *I am raised on high,*
> *Exalted too much;*
> *I descend diminished,*
> *Utterly destroyed!*

In the warm peace of the Seatons' basement, the drum of the dryer spun slowly round. Blaine was staring at a sketch of Fortune's Wheel. The lines of poetry written at its side thrummed through his head, as if in time to the machine's cycle. He had soon realized that Arthur's research contained only red herrings and dead ends. Yet he kept the notebook with him anyway, as a kind of talisman.

Occasionally, Blaine would call Liz and tell her lies about what he was doing and where he was staying, but his mother rarely came to the phone. In Arthur's absence she had set herself the task of proving to him that she was everything he wanted her to be. Part of her penance was exiling her son.

And this was Blaine's fear: that Arthur would find a way to come back, triumphantly and unbeatably, having escaped the Arcanum and won some great prize in the Game. Blaine must find him first. Not to destroy him—not at first. No, Blaine wanted to drag Arthur back to expose him, and make him face what he'd done. Arthur must be forced to let Helen see who the true monster was.

Blaine understood that by confronting Arthur with the notebook and card, and then involving the police, he had forced his stepfather to flee into the Arcanum. Such a cautious, canny man would never otherwise have taken the risk. Blaine was responsible, as Ahab had said, for making Arthur a knight and himself a chancer.

Now the reign of Ahab, King of Wands, was over. The nature of the Game had changed. But whatever it took to defeat Misrule, Blaine would do it, so he could pursue Arthur White across every square on the Arcanum's board.

ETERNITY

CHAPTER EIGHT

THE NEXT MORNING WAS FINE and bright. A great day to save the world, as Toby remarked when he met Cat by the steps of Temple House.

Cat did not respond. She did not want to be in this dismal, ruined place. She did not want to hear more of the High Priest's threats of doom. Her fears were evenly split between what was waiting for them in the Arcanum and whether Bel could be trusted to keep away from the scratchcards.

"Do you reckon Flora and Blaine will be at each other's throats by now?" Toby speculated. "It'd be funny if they both turn up with matching black eyes."

"No it wouldn't. And anyway, those two get on OK."

"They're still a bit prickly, though. You know what I think it is? Unresolved sexual tension. After all, opposites are supposed to attract. First they bicker, then they kiss. . . ."

Cat gave his ankle a swift kick.

"*Ow!* What was that for?"

"To shut you up. Look, they're coming."

Flora was back to her usual immaculate self. Blaine looked better, too, less tired, and with some color in his face. What's more, his layers of shabby sweatshirts had been replaced by a fleece jacket and blue polo shirt. Cat found herself disliking the change of clothes intensely.

There was no more opportunity for talk, for as soon as the other two reached the steps, the door to Temple House opened and the High Priest was glowering down at them from the entrance. He offered neither greeting nor comment, and turned to march across the hall and up the stairs without checking that he was followed.

The battered shutters in the ballroom had been flung open, letting a flood of morning light into the room. It gave a diamond brightness to the heaps of glass on the floor, as well as starkly exposing the pockmarked plaster on the walls. Of the mirrors that had once lined them, only one panel of glass still hung, though damaged, in the middle of the wall at the end of the room. As the High Priest advanced toward it, the chancers realized the panel must belong to the door that led to the crypt. Beforehand, the entrance had been concealed almost seamlessly within the mirrors.

Their guide took out a bunch of keys. One of them was small and silver, with an oval—or rather, a zero—forming the gripping end. "Oh," Flora exclaimed. "That's the same as the key we found."

"I am the guardian of doors," he replied stiffly. "It follows that I am the master of keys also."

"That's good for you, but I'm not going through any strange doors till I know what they lead to," said Blaine. As the glass panel sprang open, he looked down the narrow flight of steps with suspicion. He had not been with the other three when they had discovered the hidden staircase to the crypt and found the Hanged Man suspended in his prison of tree and stone.

The High Priest shrugged dismissively. "You do not know what you seek, either. I am here to show you the paths you might take, but the choice is yours." And he turned his back on them and began the descent.

Toby promptly followed him. After a brief hesitation, Flora went, too, then Blaine. Cat was last.

The stairs were steep and went on for a long time, down the height of the house, past its foundations and deep into the earth below. The five of them proceeded through what felt like miles of cramped darkness, until finally the blackness began to fade and gave way to a lamplit room.

Toby and Flora were some way ahead of Cat and Blaine, and reached the bottom of the stairs while the other two were half a flight or so behind. The stairs turned in at a right angle for the final descent, and so Cat was still in darkness when she heard Toby exclaim in anger and alarm. Flora's voice was also raised in protest.

When Cat stumbled into the room, she, too, cried out. She was face to face with the King of Swords, playing cards with the three other Game Masters.

"It's all right," Flora told her. "They're not—awake. They can't . . ."

In fact, it was apparent that they couldn't do anything. The kings and queens were as pale and motionless as wax-works, seated around a circular table of green baize, each with their right hand resting on a card. The left hand was upturned, with what looked like a spherical die lying on the palm. The cards were blank and their eyes were open in wide, unblinking stares.

The rest of the room had suffered none of the damage wreaked on the house above. The black-and-white floor and paneled walls were polished smooth; the golden curtain that hung in the arch was neither torn nor stained. The only flaw in the place was a picture whose gilt frame enclosed a canvas so grimy with age it was impossible to discern the image. But that had been the case the first time they saw it.

Cat's eyes kept darting back to the macabre tableau in the center. "What's *happened* to them? I thought Misrule had banished them from the Game."

"So he did," the High Priest replied sternly from across the room. "The four men and women you see before you are only the shadows of the rulers you deposed, and their livings selves endure in torment."

He drew closer to the table. "Tell me . . . do you know how a knight may become a king?"

"I do," said Toby promptly. "The knight has to win every triumph in the deck, but not use them. Move after move, round after round, risking everything again and again. The

Game Master he wins the most cards from is the king or queen he kicks out."

The High Priest nodded. "In such an event, the defeated ruler is forever expelled from the Game, though they will spend the rest of their life trying to return to it. But that is not the punishment Misrule imposed.

"The Game Masters you overthrew have been returned to their past rounds within the Arcanum. Under Misrule's sentence of exile, they are doomed to eternally repeat every card they were ever dealt in the Game. This time, however, no matter how cleverly or courageously they play, each move will end in defeat. They must suffer the pains of that failure—imprisonment, transformation, torment—before moving to the next card, and the next failure, endlessly."

He rapped the screen of a little portable TV that they had not noticed before, set in the corner of the room. Shapes and movement began to swim out of the static. Blurred forms fleeing some unseen terror, or else fighting some unknown enemy . . . mouths opening . . . eyes widening . . . arms flailing . . .

As the chancers watched, they realized that the figures on the screen were the same as those around the table. The Game Masters had used a range of modern technology to monitor play in the Arcanum, peering into computer monitors and TV screens as if they were crystal balls. Now it was their turn to be spied upon.

Flora looked back to the immobile cardplayers. They were not as frozen as they first appeared, for the hands resting on the cards would occasionally twitch, jaws clench and shoulders quake. She knew all too well how a player in the Game could be trapped both in and outside the Arcanum. At this very moment her sister's body lay immobile in a hospital bed while her living spirit waited for rescue in the Eight of Swords. But Flora didn't want to equate her sister's fate with that of the kings and queens.

She moved as far away from the table as she possibly could. "Very well," she said to the High Priest. "Why have you brought us down here?"

The old man raised his brows. "So that you can restore the rule of the courts, of course. Just as only a fool could release Misrule, it will take a king—or queen—to bind him."

Everyone began to talk at once, in a babble of protest and confusion. Blaine spoke the loudest. "No way. There's no way in hell we're letting those bastards back in. No."

"Absolutely not," Flora agreed. "It's only been three days since they were thrown out of power. My sis— Well, there are people who get trapped in the Arcanum for years, sometimes *forever*."

"Time passes differently in the Arcanum," the High Priest answered. "Be assured that their present suffering feels as boundless as their reign over the courts once did. These four cannot win again."

"I don't understand. If the kings and queens can't be brought back—"

"Then we must find new ones." The old man's cloudy eyes regarded them steadily. "If each of you were to take a card from under their hands, play its move and win, then the outcast kings and queens would return to their past lives . . . and *you* would become the new Game Masters."

There was an incredulous pause.

"You mean," breathed Toby, looking at the rigid gathering around the table, "I could be the next King of Pentacles? Or Swords, or—?"

"A king of sorts. You would have no players to command, prizes to award or forfeits to impose. Misrule saw to that when he overturned the rule of the courts. Meanwhile, he has his own pack of tricks to play with.

"But you would inherit the cards of the Game Masters' decks. Though you may neither give nor claim them as prizes, the cards can be used in your search of the Arcanum, to deal your own round and plot your moves."

"And what would we be searching for?" Blaine asked.

"The greatest triumph of them all. It is the prize above all other prizes, and so only a king or queen, a player above all players, may win it.

"Behold—"

The High Priest slowly raised his arms. As he did so, the blackened canvas on the wall began to lighten, revealing new shapes and colors.

The chancers recognized it at once. A dancer encircled by a serpent hovered over the earth, in the Triumph of Eternity. Its image glowed with eerie beauty, more detailed than the picture on the knights' cards of invitation they'd seen. The four faces within the wheels at each corner were clear and bright: a lion, an eagle, a bull and a man.

"Why isn't this painting upstairs, with the other pictures in the gallery?" Flora asked.

"Because Eternity has never been won. There are as many ways to win it as there are moves in the Game, yet the conditions change with each turn of the Wheel."

Even as they watched, the artwork began to fade, dissolving into murk and grime.

"The nature of its supremacy is this," the High Priest continued. "Whoever holds Eternity has dominion over all other triumphs—yes, even Fortune, and most certainly the Hanged Man. Eternity is the Great Triumph, and what the Game Masters have been searching for throughout the long history of our Game.

"Each of you must play the part of the outcast kings and queens, to win where they fail, and become Game Masters in their place. Only then will the Great Triumph be within your grasp, and only then will you be able to defeat Misrule."

"But if none of the other kings and queens ever got close to finding Eternity, what hope do *we* have?" said Cat, trying not to sound too obviously dismayed. "You said yourself we'd be Game Masters without any of the real powers or perks."

"The odds are doubtless against you," the old man replied calmly. "Nevertheless, if a fool can become a king, who knows what else is possible? Perhaps chaos creates chances that order does not. If there is any hope, it is that the Master of Misrule's victory has sown the seeds of his own defeat. Although," he added, "that is a faint hope indeed."

The High Priest turned away to gaze at the blackened

canvas of Eternity. The TV screen again showed static. It was up to the chancers now to make a decision.

They looked at each other uncertainly. In unspoken agreement, they left the man to his painting and held a whispered conference by the stairwell.

"The old chap makes some fine speeches," Cat said in an undertone, "but so did the Hanged Man. It could be another trap. What happens if we go on as substitutes for that gang round the table but don't win? We could end up banished as well—or worse."

"We all witnessed Misrule expelling the old kings and queens," Flora said, "so if the High Priest says they can't come back, I believe him."

"It sounds like a good deal to me," Toby put in. "We only have to play one card each to become Game Masters. And once we find Eternity, we won't just have our own prizes, but *every other* triumph as well. We'll rule the Game and save the world!"

"For the moment, I'm more worried about saving ourselves," Cat retorted.

"Same difference," said Blaine starkly. He was thinking of Helen and Liz. The woman who had given him his last job, washing dishes at a hotel. The boy who'd taken his place at the Soho squat. London's millions. The world's billions. Thanks to what he and the others had done, nobody was safe from the Game. "You know what the visions in the mirrors showed. Humanity enslaved to some mad lottery, and all because the four of us mucked about with something we didn't understand. This isn't just about us and our prizes anymore."

Before the others could respond, he turned back to the High Priest. "So what do we do next?"

The old man looked across the table, his expression inscrutable. "You see that each of the former kings and queens rests their hand upon a card. To play it for them, you have only to take the card and enter the Game. But since the exiles play without beginning or end, at what point in their round you will enter, and what card will be revealed by the Arcanum when you get there, I cannot tell."

"I see." Blaine lightly touched the scar on his arm. Through a spasm of coughing, he said, "Then I'm going in."

"Me too," said Toby. "It's meant to be."

"And me," said Flora, looping her hair neatly behind her ears and straightening her clothes.

Cat glanced back at the stairs. She was trying to recall the image of morning light at the window, the moment where choice still seemed possible. But in spite of her distrustful queries and cautions, she knew Blaine was right. None of them could walk away from this.

"OK," she said. "I guess that makes four of us."

The High Priest looked at their apprehensive faces and smiled a little. "A bold move. You will not, however, be without help. I believe you are already in possession of dice?"

They laid them on the table.

"Though I cannot tell where your next moves will take you, I can load at least one roll of the dice." He ran his finger along the tip of each triangle. "There. Wherever you throw them in the Arcanum, the next threshold they raise will return you directly to my temple. And I have something else to give you."

The old man reached for the small metal ball that lay in Alastor's upturned palm. It was solid silver, the material symbol for the Court of Swords.

He used the ball to sketch a rough rectangle on the paneled wall, as one might scribble with a piece of chalk. The lines glowed faintly. With a plucking motion, he peeled the rectangle out of and away from the wall, except that it was neither part of the wooden surface nor thin air, but a playing card. He placed it facedown on the table before taking up Lucrezia's golden ball and sketching another rectangle. Another card peeled away. Ahab's ebony sphere was followed by Odile's crystal one and two more cards.

One by one, he turned them over.

The first card depicted a sword, around which a tempest raged.

The second was a gold disc that sprouted green buds.

The third was a wooden staff, from which embers flew.

The fourth was a jeweled chalice overflowing with water.

They were the four aces of the Lesser Arcana, and each card was capable of unleashing all the strength and fury of the element it represented. The High Priest shuffled the cards, and held them out facedown for the chancers to pick. Flora drew the Ace of Swords, and Blaine the Ace of Pentacles; Toby held Wands; Cat, Cups.

Flora looked up from her card. "We used these to free the Hanged Man, so why can't we use them to recapture him?"

"It is too late for that; only Eternity can bind Misrule now. But the aces shall protect you against other perils."

"And what about the magic-ball things?" Toby asked. "Aren't they what the Game Masters gave knights who won a triumph?"

"They are the amulets of the courts," the man said reprovingly, "and tokens of their power. As such, they can only be forged from the blood and bone of kingship, and you are not Game Masters yet. If you succeed in your task, and return to my temple as kings and queens, I will show you the ways of their decks and amulets, and make divinations for your quest." He indicated the table. "But now is the time to make your first moves. Choose your cards and claim your courts."

Instinctively, each chancer moved to take the card from the king or queen who had been foremost in bringing them to the Game. Cat was playing for the King of Swords; Blaine, the King of Wands; Toby, the Queen of Pentacles; and Flora, the Queen of Cups. Once they had slid the cards from under the limp hands of the former Game Masters, the kings' and queens' eyes had slowly closed. Drained of all previous signs of life, their bodies became even more rigid than before.

When they had made their choice, the High Priest bowed his head toward them in grave salute. He gestured to the golden curtain and the words engraved over the stone arch from which it hung: *regnabo, regno, regnavi, sum sine regno.* "It is time to follow me," he said, "and enter the Arcanum. There is no need of thresholds when I am with you."

His eyes were hooded, the lines and hollows of his face cast into stark relief by the light he was standing near. Even in his quaint uniform, it was difficult to believe they had ever thought of him as a mere doorkeeper.

Beyond the curtain, a labyrinth of shadowy chambers lay before them, like the cells in a honeycomb, though not as regular. Oil lamps set in alcoves flickered on arches and pillars, and there was the smell of incense and old stone. A carpeting of dead leaves skittered on the floor.

Once, the oil lamps had lit the way to Yggdrasil, and the man who hung from its branches in a living sacrifice. Now when the chancers reached the chamber of the Hanged Man, there was nothing there but a blackened tree stump and dead leaves. Lamps illuminated the curved frame of four archways set in the room's circular wall. The silence and solemnity of the place had already worked on them: their minds felt emptied yet at peace. In a kind of trance, they stepped forward to take their places between the columns. Each carried an ace in their pockets and a card in their hands.

Meanwhile, the High Priest stood by the remains of Yggdrasil. He took out a deck of blank cards from within his coat and began to shuffle them in his hands, intoning ancient words in a sibilant murmur.

As he did so, the leaves on the floor of the crypt began

to swirl about more agitatedly. There was a papery snap and rustle. And the higher the leaves blew, and the faster they twirled, the more difficult it was to tell if they were shriveled foliage or burned playing cards. They rose up in a swarm, twisting giddily around each of the chancers, higher and faster again—

—until the dark flurry thinned . . . subsided . . . settled . . . leaving four empty archways behind.

The High Priest slumped, exhausted, and let the cards fall from his hands.

THE HIGH PRIESTESS

CHAPTER NINE

CAT'S EARS BUZZED WITH the sound of shuffling cards. When their cascade fell away and the fluttering shadows cleared, the playing card she was holding was no longer blank. There gradually emerged a picture of a woman sitting between two pillars, with a horned diadem on her head and a lunar crescent at her feet. This must be the move she had to win to become Queen of Swords. The Triumph of the High Priestess.

Her first thought was, OK, it could be worse. And her second: What the hell is a Priestess doing in a parking garage?

She was in another underground vault, but this crypt was made of concrete pillars, ramps and parking bays, all very dirty-looking under the pallid glare of fluorescent tubes.

Although the cars were empty, the place was not deserted. Something whisked around a pillar, and there was a tinkling sound, followed by a giggle.

"Who's there?" Cat asked sharply.

There was more giggling, then a young girl—not more than twelve or thirteen—sidled out from the shadows. She was a skinny, sallow little thing, who looked as if she'd been playing in a dress-up box. Her torso was draped in an assortment of silk scarves, and she was wearing a flounced skirt that was much too long for her, its tiers sewn all over with little gold discs. It was these, and the bangles loading her arms, that made the tinkling noise. Her eyes were outlined in smudged black kohl, and she wore a crookedly perched headdress of two crystal horns.

"If you're looking for that man, he's already had his turn," the girl announced.

"What man?"

"The young one who was just here."

Cat looked around nervously, but could see no sign of the king whose move she had entered. Was Alastor hiding and watching somewhere?

"He was very handsome, I thought. . . . Ooh, I like your necklace." The girl reached out to stroke the plastic four-leaf clover around Cat's neck. It was a cheap trinket, but she seemed fascinated by the glitter coating. "Can I have it?"

"Um . . ."

"You can use it to pay me, if you want." She had suddenly become curt and businesslike. "I can't do the prophecy without an offering. And that's what you're here for, right?"

"Right." This person might not look like the woman on the card, but Cat knew that appearance didn't count for much in the Arcanum. As a prize, the High Priestess's triumph represented mysticism, the powers of prophecy. Perhaps she really would learn something useful from the girl—something important about the Game . . . or her parents.

"Come on, then, slowpoke!" The High Priestess hitched up her skirt, revealing bare feet with chipped red nail polish, and set off in a zigzagging dance through the parking bays.

She brought Cat to a ramp leading to a lower level. Instead of fluorescent tubes, this story was lit by tea lights set in flickering circles around the bases of the concrete pillars. It felt warmer, almost stuffy, and there was a nauseating smell of scented candles and exhaust fumes.

The Priestess let her skirt fall, trailing its ragged hem carelessly behind her, and walked to a pillar wrapped in black-and-yellow hazard tape. A tripod-like iron chair was set in front. She climbed on, adjusted her headdress and sat up very straight. Her hands were folded neatly on her lap.

"You are now in the presence of Sosostris herself," she intoned. "The holiest of holies, Belladonna, Lady of the Rocks. I am Madam Equitone, Queen of the Borrowed Light. I am Persephone and the pomegranate; I am Ariadne and her labyrinth. You have come to my sanctum, but will you dare hear my prophecy?"

Cat nodded.

"I must have the card and my offering."

Cat gave her the triumph card and undid the lucky charm necklace, not without a superstitious twinge. Still, she had got off lightly: a Rolex watch and several wedding rings were among the Priestess's other fripperies.

"The offering is deemed worthy. Let the divination commence."

The girl hung her head and made a low droning sound from deep within her chest. "Ommmmmmm." She began to shake, rocking from side to side, so that the diadem flashed in the candlelight. "I see . . . yes . . . I see . . . ommm . . . a tall . . . dark stranger. . . ."

"Oh," said Cat, nonplussed.

"He's ever so good-looking. Lovely brown eyes."

"You, er, can see the color of his eyes?"

The High Priestess collapsed into squeals of laughter, so that her flounces tinkled and bangles chimed. "Of *course* not!" Afterward, she leaned forward confidentially. "But wouldn't it be nice if I could?"

Cat gritted her teeth and counted to ten. She wondered how Alastor would have handled this.

"Maybe I could ask you some questions," she suggested. Her thoughts were already churning with possibilities. How were my parents involved in the Game? If I defeat Misrule, will the Triumph of Justice punish their killer? And will I *ever* be free of the Arcanum and its crazy cards?

The girl shook her head. She put a strand of hair in her mouth and chewed it broodingly. "It doesn't work like that. The Spirit speaks through me however it likes. Booor-*ring*."

She sighed and covered her face with her hands, muttering something indistinguishable. Then she leaned down from the tripod and ran her fingers through a slick of spilled petrol. On the ground, it had a rainbow sheen, but the stain it left on her hands was black and sticky. Deliberately, she smeared the oil over her mouth. She then struck a match on the arm of the tripod and tossed it into the puddle.

The gasoline shot into flames. Behind billows of toxic smoke, the High Priestess gripped the arms of her tripod and convulsed all over with a harsh choking sound. Her mouth was black and clotted, and her rolling eyes were a blinded white. As soon as the fire started, Cat backed away in alarm, her hands tensed around the Ace of Cups. But almost as quickly as they had begun, the flames died down to a smolder, and the High Priestess became calm and still.

When she spoke, her voice was high and cold and very clear.

> *Then the glory of the Lord went up from the cherub, and stood over the threshold of the house; and the house was filled with the cloud, and the court was full of the brightness of the Lord's glory.*
>
> *As for the wheels, it was cried unto them in my hearing, O wheel.*
>
> *And every one had four faces: the first face was the face of a bull, and the second face was the face of a man, and the third the face of a lion, and the fourth the face of an eagle.*
>
> *And when the cherubim went, the wheels went by them:*
> *O wheel—*
> *O—*

She sagged limply in her seat, and Cat thought the prophecy was finished. Silence rang in her ears. But then the girl raised her head and began to speak again. This time, her manner was brisk, almost abrupt.

"Hear my prophecy: Eternity awaits you, but only the cherubim can summon it. You must make them offerings so that they rise again. Otherwise, Misrule's wheel shall burn at the turning of the year. For now, the Empress holds the answer to what you seek."

Her head rolled on her neck, her eyelids drooped and her face slackened. Then she opened her eyes and yawned. "Did I say anything interesting?"

"Um . . . kind of."

Cat thought the first part of the prophecy might be describing the wheels portrayed in the Triumph of Eternity. She remembered the painting the High Priest had shown them, and how the wheels in its corners had animal faces inside. Then "the glory of the Lord" probably referred to the Master of Misrule. But who were the cherubs, and what kind of offering did they need? And as for the Empress . . . Could *she* have the answer to Cat's more personal quest— the identity of her parents' killer?

Sudden hope flared. Cat thought of what Toby had said about Eternity allowing them to control the Game and all of its triumphs. It would give her Justice along with Misrule. But if she became Queen of Swords at the end of this move, she could go where she liked in the Arcanum. . . . She might even have the Empress among her own cards. . . . She could go and ask—

The High Priestess spat on one of her silk scarves and set about scrubbing the oil off her mouth. "Goody. Don't forget there's a falsehood, though."

"Falsehood?" A car alarm was beeping close by, but Cat was distracted by something else she'd heard—a kind of rasping groan—echoing around the floor below.

"Mmm. There's always one untruth in my prophecies. Trouble is, I never know which one." She peeped at Cat slyly from behind her scarf. "You'll have to ask my brother."

"The High Priest?"

"Don't be daft. No, my brother's Asterion. He's kept down there."

She flapped her hand at the floor. As if in response, there was another groan, this one ending with a bellow.

Cat's heart seemed to jolt.

"It's funny, isn't it? Here I am, telling you lots of important things, things you need to win the Game, and you don't know which of them you can trust!" The High Priestess's giggle sounded particularly strange coming out of her blackened mouth. "Asterion can tell you, though. He's the only one who knows when I'm not speaking the truth. But if you want to ask him, you'll have to be quick—he'll be starting the change soon."

"The change?" Cat asked.

"Yes. From man to . . ." The High Priestess patted her horned headdress. "Well, you'll find out soon enough!"

Cat felt another jolt. "How do I find him?"

The girl poked her tongue out at her. "Follow the arrows, silly."

There were, indeed, large yellow arrows painted on the floor to direct the traffic. The one closest to them was indicating a ramp down to the next level—down to where the groaning was coming from. There was nothing Cat wanted less than to go deeper into this place, to where sounds of pain and fury echoed underground. But it was pretty clear that winning this move meant getting a workable prophecy. So she left the High Priestess to play with her lucky charm, and followed the arrow trail.

It was on the next story that she found the King of Swords. Alastor was slumped against a concrete pillar, a gaping wound gored in his side. He was breathing, but only just.

Now Cat truly understood the nature of Misrule's punishment. If Cat didn't find a way to win this card, and break the cycle of failure that Alastor was trapped in, he would survive the move only to suffer something equally terrible in the next one. And the next. And so on, for all eternity . . .

She looked at her onetime nemesis, bleeding on the floor. His eyes were closed. She remembered his former power, the steely chill beneath his charm. Alastor had had countless years, centuries even, to rule the Game and manipulate his players. Many of his knights had suffered just as he did now. But Cat could feel no sense of triumph. For both their sakes, she had to get on and finish this move, and defeat whatever monster had defeated him.

The level below was empty, but the groaning was louder, interspersed with bellows and the shrilling of more car alarms. Cat followed the yellow arrows through the pillars and down another ramp, then another. The ceilings were getting lower, with only a few stuttering fluorescent tubes here and there. By now it was very hot and the over-powering smell of oil and exhaust was making her feel sick.

Four levels down from the High Priestess, Cat found her brother. In the center of the floor, a man was strapped down on a concrete slab. He was huge and muscular, wrapped around with metal chains. His naked torso glistened with sweat as he twisted and heaved against his bonds.

The man had a broad, strong face and thick, curly black hair. His nostrils flared and his eyes rolled as Cat approached. She came to a halt by a pillar a little distance from the slab.

"I—please—um—I've had the oracle. Can you tell me, please, which—"

He roared at her. It didn't sound human at all.

"Stay back," he said thickly. "Back." Getting the words out made him grunt with effort, his mouth flecked with foam. Tufts of black hair sprouted on his chin and out of his nostrils and eyebrows, and ran up from his chest to grow over his face, which bulged and broadened. The change the High Priestess spoke of had begun. But the eyes that turned to Cat were wide and hazel, and filled with human anguish.

"P-please tell me. Which is the false prophecy?"

He roared again, and the chains clanked. His body was swelling into even greater strength and bulk. Two dark brown lumps had begun to protrude from the curling hair on his forehead.

Cat prepared to ask for the third time. She could tell his power of speech was fading; his face was nearly all animal.

Although she was light-headed with fear, she tried to keep her voice as cool and clear as the High Priestess's voice of prophecy. "Asterion," she commanded. "Tell me the falsehood."

And out of the beast's mouth, a human voice spoke.

"The false . . . the falsehood . . . is the last. *The—the Empress holds the answer to what you seek.*"

Of course.

Of course that would be the lie. Just another Arcanum cheat, Cat thought savagely. Another false hope, another dead end.

But she didn't have time to dwell on her defeat.

As Asterion gave a last terrible groan, the horns of a bull sprang from his head—long, curving and cruel. A Minotaur was born.

Cat fled. Those chains wouldn't hold him for much longer. She couldn't see the way back through the pillars to an upward ramp and so took the nearest one, which led down again. This next level was even hotter, darker and more cramped, and its yellow arrows pointed in every direction. It's a labyrinth, she thought despairingly. The floor here was stained with something dark and sticky; she didn't think it was oil.

What had been the trick to Flora's maze? *Every turn is left. . . .* There were no corners here, though—only a forest of crookedly parked vehicles and concrete posts, and arrows that pointed everywhere and nowhere. She had no clue, let alone a thread, to guide her. But unlike an ordinary player in this move, Cat didn't have to search for the threshold out of here. She could raise her own, and get straight back to Temple House. She must throw her die and—

But a clanking, crashing sound followed by a bellow announced that the Minotaur had broken his chains. His rage seemed to shake the ceiling. He was coming for her. In her panic, she decided that even the few moments she would need to roll the die, raise the wheel and toss the coin would take too long. She had to find some kind of refuge first. Or get into one of the cars, try her hand at joyriding . . . But the few doors she checked were all locked.

Cat ran through the pillars in a frenzied imitation of the High Priestess's zigzagging dance from before. The roars of the beast had a disorientating echo: the noise bounced off the walls and ceiling and posts so that she had no real idea of how close the creature was. She was moving so haphazardly, and so fast, that she nearly slammed into a wall before skidding to a stop. But her whimper of terror changed to weak laughter when she realized the dead end was actually a car lift.

Slowly, creakily, the door began to raise itself from the floor. It was separate to the lift itself, which was a hydraulic platform on chained gears. She flung herself onto the platform, repeatedly jabbing the buttons to close the door and send the lift up. Slowly, creakily, the door began to close . . . and came to a screeching halt a quarter of the way down. The door had jammed. The lift, however, began to rise. "Oh God," Cat moaned aloud. "Please, please hurry." It was moving up inch by torturous inch.

She could see the Minotaur now. He was perhaps fifteen feet away, and standing beneath one of the few working lights. Under the fizz and flicker of its fluorescent tube, the curve of his horns jutted upward in silhouette, almost high enough to touch the ceiling. From the neck down, his body was still a man's, but the bulk of straining muscle was too grotesquely exaggerated to look human. He pawed his foot on the ground and lowered his head, ready for the final charge.

Cat took out the Ace of Cups and tore it in two.

A jet of water erupted from the floor just outside the lift and surged across the room. The lift continued to inch upward. Cat crouched on its floor, only a couple of feet off the ground, and watched as the water gushed forth in ever greater quantities—her own personal geyser bursting through the concrete. It was a brown, oily torrent that foamed angrily against the pillars and thrashed all round the beast, who was bawling with shock as well as rage. The water rose with astonishing speed. Her last view before the lift climbed to the next story was of the Minotaur's horns tilting to one side as he floundered in the flood.

CHAPTER TEN

FLORA RECOILED AS THE FIRST snowflake fell on her cheek. Snow had ceased to be picturesque ever since the midwinter's night she had found Grace lying in the park, and after her experiences in the Eight of Swords, even the thought of it made her skin crawl. But if she was going to be the next Queen of Cups, she couldn't allow herself to be put off by a little bad weather.

The card she had taken from Odile was the Five of Pentacles. Its move began outside a church, below a stained-glass window that glowed with rainbow warmth. A choir was singing inside, very high and sweet. Flora's first impression was that she was in front of an Arcanum version of St. Bernadine's, but the more she gazed at the walls, the higher they seemed to tower, so that their scale increased to that of a great cathedral.

The illustration on the card was almost exactly like the scene in front of her, right down to the two ragged figures who had just appeared from behind a funeral monument. As the beggars approached, Flora backed away, holding the Ace of Wands for reassurance. The die in her pocket was a comfort, too. She reminded herself that she could create a threshold and escape to Temple House whenever she wanted. But the beggars ignored her, limping painfully toward the entrance at the west end of the building.

Flora walked after them. The doors opened onto a cavernous hall—the cathedral's nave—lined on either side with an arcade of clustered columns, built of the same sooty stone as the exterior. They soared up to the roof and branched out into a dizzying tracery of ribbed vaults. The spaces in between the columns were full of leaping shadows cast by ranks of candles wavering in the draft.

Despite the fact that the architecture was unmistakably that of a cathedral, she couldn't see any religious apparatus or imagery. The circular window over the west doors was in the design of Fortune's Wheel, while the high arched windows along the aisles were filled with stained-glass illustrations of triumph cards. Both the woodwork and the stone bore intricate carvings of pentacles, swords, cups and wands.

Although Flora had slipped through the open doors quietly enough, the moment she was inside, they slammed shut with a crash. The choir abruptly ceased singing and the entire congregation turned to look at her. All the pews were filled with people as ragged and starved-looking as the pair she had followed in. It was unnerving to be the focus of their silent stares, alone and exposed in that great space.

Soldiers guarded the ends of the pews. They wore black combat uniforms and balaclavas and carried guns. As Flora began her first faltering steps down the nave, four of the soldiers broke away from their positions to form an escort. Hemmed in from behind and at the sides, she had no choice but to keep going.

They came to a halt when they reached the transept— the aisle that cut across the nave to give the building the shape of a cross. Its mosaic floor was in the design of a pentacle, a five-pointed star within a circle, and hooded figures in scarlet robes were seated on each of the star's points. A bronze reading stand had been set in the middle. Across the transept, the eastern end of the building—where one would expect the choir stalls and altar to be—was cut off by a wooden screen, guarded by more gunmen.

One of the soldiers behind Flora gave her a shove, so that she stumbled forward to stand inside the star. The robed figure opposite raised his head to examine her. His own face remained overshadowed by the hood.

"We are the Five of Pentacles, the Game's High Order of Inquisitors," he announced in a dry, papery voice. "You have been brought before us to prove yourself a True Player, and a champion worthy of the Arcanum."

"And how do I do that?"

"Each of the Five of Pentacles has a question for you," the man replied. "Answer all five correctly, and the Inquisition will be satisfied. One wrong answer, and the Trial by Inquiry will be followed by the Trial by Ordeal. If you prevail there, you may still prove yourself a True Player and win the move. If not . . ."

"Yes?"

"Your Game will be over, and with it all your hopes of reward."

Flora decided against asking what the ordeal entailed, and what kind of state she might be in at the end of it. She knew that nothing could be worse than the Eight of Swords and its maze of briars. If she could survive that, she told herself grimly, she could survive anything.

"Very well," she said. She produced the Five of Pentacles playing card, and handed it to the robed figure on her right. "Then I'm ready to take your trial."

As if on cue, the choir began to sing again. They must have been hidden in one of the chapels off the transept, for she never saw them. But their voices rang out angelically, in a cascade of golden notes. "*Cursus Fortune*," they sang, "*variatur in more lune: crescit, decrescit et eodem sistere nescit. . . .*"

Flora went to take her place behind the reading stand, so that she was facing the congregation. The lectern was a larger version of the one at St. Bernadine's. She gripped its cool, polished sides and felt a little calmer.

In spite of everything, it seemed she could almost be taking part in some kind of mad game show. The scarlet robes of the Inquisitors were theatrical as well as threatening, and the people in the pews looked as raptly attentive as any studio audience. Flora decided to imagine that the church was filled with people she knew. Tilly, Georgia, Charlie and the rest of her crowd were lined up in the front rows, cheering her on. Her parents were watching proudly from the back. Cat and Blaine and Toby were close by, too, crossing their fingers for her. The thought of them warmed her, a little.

Proceedings began with one of the soldiers striking a gong. Once its shivering ring had died away, the hooded figure immediately to Flora's left began the cross-examination. He spoke in exactly the same parched voice as the first Inquisitor.

"Hear and consider your first question. Who is your ruler in the Game?"

She took a deep, steadying breath. The question wasn't as straightforward as it might appear. She was playing this move on behalf of Odile, the Queen of Cups, but since Misrule had overthrown the reign of the courts, he was the only Game Master with any power. There was also the fact that she was technically still a chancer, and chancers weren't supposed to come under the rule of anybody at all. But then she thought of the choir's song, and felt a new certainty. "Lady Fortune," she replied.

The ragged audience gave a sigh of relief. All five Inquisitors slowly nodded. "Your answer is accepted," pronounced the one who had asked the question.

Boiiing! went the gong. Flora supplied imaginary cheers from her imaginary support team.

Now it was the turn of the second man along. "In

a Game ruled by Fortune, how do Fate and Luck work upon a player?"

This was something Flora had thought about before, and struggled with. She took her time to prepare her answer.

"Out of all the cards I might have played, Fate dealt me this one. Luck, however, will help determine how difficult or easy I find it to win. And . . . um . . . there's also the matter of Free Will."

At this, the congregation rustled and murmured, so that the soldiers had to strike their rifle butts on the floor to command silence. The Inquisitors, meanwhile, exchanged looks. "Free Will?" repeated the second of the five.

"Yes," Flora said firmly, although she was quaking inside. "I play the Game out of my own Free Will, just as I choose to answer your questions as I see fit. So Fate imposes necessity on a player, Luck provides her with the opportunity for victory or defeat and Free Will decides if and how that opportunity is taken."

As soon as she'd finished, she began to think that she had made a stupid—and dangerous—mistake. Far better to let her original answer stand by itself than to complicate it with unnecessary philosophizing. . . . The hooded heads turned to each other, their dry lips moving in silent conferral.

Eventually, the second Inquisitor spoke again. "Your answer is accepted."

The gong was struck, and the third question asked.

"What was the Hanged Man's first name?"

Ooh, I don't know . . . Harry? said Flora to herself,

barely managing to stifle a snort of hysterical laughter. It took a minute or so to compose herself. "The Mas—" she began, and stopped herself just in time. The Hanged Man might be the Master of Misrule now, but that was not what his card used to be called. She had suddenly remembered what Cat had said outside Temple House after they'd seen Misrule in the mirrors, and the nearness of her miss set her trembling. "The Traitor," she answered.

The five heads nodded. "Your answer is accepted." Again, the gong rang. Again, the audience sighed in murmuring relief. Three down, two to go.

"In a game of dice with the Magician," said the fourth Inquisitor, "what would be the odds of you throwing a winning six?"

Flora remembered her meeting with the Magician, with his crooked grin and showman's patter, and smiled. "Zero," she said. "Because he'd have loaded the die."

Boiiing! Her fourth answer had been accepted. Her body tightened in readiness for the final challenge.

"Hear and consider your last question. Which card is the cross sum of Death?"

Flora frowned. *Sum* implied a mathematical calculation of some sort, and numbers were not Flora's strong point. Her mind was a roaring blank. Come on, come on, she implored herself. *Think.* Death was the thirteenth triumph. . . . All right . . . so thirteen was an unlucky number. . . . What other numbers were like that? In the Bible, 666 was the number of the Beast—that is, Satan. And wasn't the Devil the sixteenth triumph? She couldn't remember. But there surely wasn't another card with such close associations with Death. "Um . . . that would be . . . the Devil?" she guessed.

The congregation appeared to be holding its breath. The candles sputtered and the shadows danced.

Then:

"Your answer is rejected," all five Inquisitors announced in the same dry voice.

The gong was struck again, but much louder this time, so that the noise clashed and boomed through Flora's head. She had to put her hands up to her ears. They were still ringing when the Inquisitor behind her spoke.

"The Trial by Inquiry has ended in failure. Yet you have one final chance to redeem yourself. It is time for the Trial by Ordeal to commence."

The people in the pews quivered and moaned; a few began to weep. Flora's hand curled fearfully around her ace and die.

The five Inquisitors rose from their seats. At their signal, the soldiers who had been guarding the wooden screen moved it away to reveal that a pyre had been erected in place of the altar. A gagged woman was bound to the stake. Her pale hair was dark with sweat, her white skin greenish with fear. It was Odile, the onetime Queen of Cups.

"Behold the heretic," said one of the robed figures as he lit a taper from one of the candles. "You, though, still have victory in your grasp. All you have to do is take this taper and set the pyre alight."

Flora looked around wildly. "I thought—but isn't—this is *my* trial—"

"The ordeal by fire is hers. Yours is an ordeal of choice. Or Free Will, if you prefer."

"You want me to choose to *burn a woman alive*?"

"We want you to prove your dedication to the Game. This is your last chance to win in it."

Odile moaned from under her gag. Flora had to look away. She was here to win on Odile's behalf, and so release her from her punishment. But what if Flora's only way of winning this move was to kill the person she had come to save?

The Five of Pentacles were watching her from under their hoods. The beggarly audience rustled in the pews.

"In our Game," the Inquisitor with the taper said softly, "a true winner knows that it is every player for himself."

"Herself, in this case," said Flora tartly. She had come to a decision. She took the taper, and stooped to put it to the pyre.

The wood was dry, and caught alight quickly. As the first tongues of flame licked delicately at the tinder, the choir began to sing, in darker yet more triumphant tones than before:

> *In altum tollor,*
> *Nimis exaltatus;*
> *Descendo minoratus,*
> *Funditus mortificatus!*

Very slowly, the five hooded figures of the Inquisition brought their hands together in stately applause. The soldiers joined in by hammering the butts of their rifles on the floor, while the congregation cowered and wept. Smoke plumed, and as the flames began to crackle and hiss around the Queen of Cups' feet, she writhed hopelessly against her bonds. The gag had slipped, and soon her screams could be heard even over the choir.

Flora tore her ace in half. At once, the Ace of Swords, Root of Air, unleashed a mighty wind that howled down the cavernous length of the building. The Inquisitors' robes whipped around in a flurry of scarlet as the gale sent them and their soldiers in a slithering tumble across the floor. The congregation clutched their pews like half-drowned sailors clinging to a wreck. With a clang, the bronze lectern fell to the ground. Only Flora was still able to stand. Wind roared around the pyre, and for a horrible moment she thought it would fan the flames so that they only flared more strongly. But the tempest was too great for any fire. In a matter of seconds, its flames were blown out, the woman's cries stopped and the building was plunged into darkness.

CHAPTER ELEVEN

BLAINE'S NINE OF SWORDS depicted a person hunched on a bed with their hands held fearfully over their eyes, as if waking up from a nightmare. It wasn't nighttime here, though. The window on his left looked over an assortment of ugly modern offices on a dull afternoon. Below there was a small yard and a Dumpster daubed with a lopsided black wheel on one side. Although Blaine didn't like the look of his card at all, he was slightly reassured by the sight of a threshold. He felt for his die and was reassured some more. There would always be a way out.

He walked down the corridor into a lobby. Something about the place reminded him of school. The walls were painted the same sludgy institutional beige and the floor was lined with the same scuffed linoleum. But the smell was different: sour and antiseptic, medical.

A hard-faced nurse was sitting at a table in front of a pair of double doors. "Visiting hours are over," she informed him without looking up from her charts.

Blaine set the card down in front of her. Eventually, she condescended to look at it before turning her inspection on him.

"All right. I suppose you'd better come through." She got to her feet, grudgingly, and entered a numeric code in the keypad beside the door. "They're restless this afternoon. Don't say I didn't warn you."

Past the doors, Blaine found himself in a hospital ward. It was more dilapidated than the corridor, with the linoleum stained and curling at the edges, damp patches on the ceiling and rust on the bed frames. All the beds were filled with people sleeping, although, as the nurse had said, there wasn't much rest involved. Most were drooling and muttering, twisting jerkily beneath the bedclothes. One old man near to Blaine began to thrash and shout, and another nurse, with the air of someone repeating a familiar chore, came and emptied a syringe into his neck. The man froze into silence.

Instead of a single person waking from a nightmare, it was a roomful of people in the midst of one. Blaine felt tension hum through his body. But the nurse on duty didn't pay him any attention. Her uniform was soiled, and her yawns were noisy.

The next ward was smaller, and more like a common room, with sagging armchairs grouped to face a television fixed high in a corner of the wall. The patients here were awake but barely conscious, all strapped to their seats and staring listlessly at a TV game show. One of them was the black man, Ahab, who had been King of Wands. His towering stature and grizzled hair were the same, but his expression was vacant as he drooled and mumbled in his chair.

With a shudder, Blaine increased his pace. Whatever test was coming, he wanted to find it and face it as soon as possible. He went down some stairs and into a gallery lined with cells. Through viewing panels of reinforced glass, he could see the inmates—dressed in the same thin beige pajamas as the other patients—howl and beg, and hurl themselves against the padded walls.

At the other end of the gallery, a creaking lift opened and the nurse who'd been on duty in the lobby stepped out. She looked at Blaine. "Are you ready for your visit now?" she asked.

This must be it. . . .

He shrugged. "Sure."

"Come along, please." She rapidly led the way around corners and along corridors until they reached a plain white room. There were three women inside. One was sedated on a bed, twitching and drooling like the people in the first ward. Another was strapped to a chair, staring blindly into space. The third was crouched in a corner, rocking from side to side as she chattered and cackled to herself. All three looked exactly like Helen.

Bile rose in Blaine's throat and he backed clumsily toward the door. "What's the matter?" asked the nurse disapprovingly. "Aren't you even going to say hello? She's been looking forward to your visit all day."

152

"No she hasn't," he muttered. His mother wasn't here. She couldn't, *mustn't,* be.

The woman on the bed moaned. The one strapped to the chair turned her head and looked at him emptily with bloodshot eyes. But the one in the corner leaped up and screamed, "Go away! You're a monster! Monster! Monster!"

"Let me out of here," Blaine said harshly. The nurse was standing in front of the door and he had to push her out of the way.

He staggered into the corridor, breathing hard. The scar from the knife throbbed and he could feel cold sweat on his back. It was like being in Arthur's study again, but worse. His very own living nightmare. The nurse took him by the arm as if to lead him back into the room, and he shook her off, swearing.

"There's no call for that," she said primly. "I think you need to calm down, young man."

"And I think you should f—"

"Now, now," said a genial voice. "What's all the fuss about?"

A rosy-faced, gray-haired gentleman in a white coat had come out of the room next door.

The nurse looked smug. "There," she said to Blaine. "Doctor will sort you out."

"I don't—" He lapsed into a fit of coughing and it took him a while to catch his breath. "I don't need to see a doctor."

"Oh, it won't take a minute." The man smiled and beckoned Blaine into his office. In contrast to the ramshackle state of the rest of the hospital—or asylum, or whatever it was—the room was inviting. It had a plush carpet and comfortable chairs, and flowers on the windowsill. The medicine cabinet on the wall looked out of place. Blaine remained, tense and mistrustful, in the doorway.

The doctor settled down behind his mahogany desk. "How are you feeling?" he asked in a fatherly way.

"OK."

"That's a nasty cough."

"It's getting better."

"You were very agitated back there. Something's obviously upset you."

"It was nothing. I'm over it now. She— It wasn't real anyway."

The doctor wrote something on his pad. "Hmm . . . interesting."

"Like I said, I'm fine."

"Of course you are," the man replied with a humoring smile. "Still, perhaps we should both take a little look at what set you off. Just to straighten things out, you understand."

He got to his feet and opened a hatch in the wall near the medicine cabinet. It revealed a glass panel, like the ones in the cells, for looking into the room next door. "Can you tell me what you see in there?" the doctor asked.

Blaine hesitated. Knowing that this was a test didn't make it any easier to work out the right answer. Steeling himself, he went to take another look at the three Helens. It still made his guts cramp. He described the scene as briefly and impassively as possible.

When he'd finished, the doctor sighed and summoned

the nurse, who had been waiting by the door. "You mustn't worry," he told Blaine. "There's nothing to be afraid of."

"I know. It was just the shock."

"The shock of an empty room?"

"But it isn't empty. I've just told you what—" Blaine stopped. Too late, he realized the trap he'd fallen into.

"Ah." The doctor looked at him regretfully. "The fact is, that room's unoccupied. There's nobody there."

"Yeah, there is," Blaine said uselessly. "And the nurse saw them, too. She brought me to the room as a visitor. She told me Hel—that woman, those women—had been looking forward to seeing me." Though he already knew it wouldn't be any good, he turned to the nurse in appeal. "That's right, isn't it?"

"It's right that you should see Doctor for your consultation," she replied blandly.

"You lying b—"

"Come, come!" said the doctor, still in the same genial manner. "First you told me that you were getting yourself into a state over nothing, and that you knew it 'wasn't real.' *Now* you're getting upset that no one else believes in this fantasy of yours! Next you'll be saying that all of us are illusions, too, and none of this hospital actually exists."

Blaine laughed shortly. "Stranger things have happened."

"Paranoid hallucinations," the doctor told the nurse in an undertone. "Very sad. We'll start him off on the lethecocytus chloride."

All Blaine's instincts shrilled a warning. Before the doctor could reach into his medicine cabinet, he swiveled round and began to sprint down the corridor. He needed a head start of only a minute or two to throw his die and raise a threshold. However, he didn't get even that. Two male orderlies had just emerged at the other end of the corridor, and at the nurse's shout they grabbed at Blaine as he skidded past. He lashed out but they were too strong for him, and a few moments later he was frog-marched back to the doctor's office. One of them wrested the die out of his hand. With both arms seized, he had no way of reaching his ace.

The doctor's plump pink face creased in concern. "It's for your own good, you know," he told Blaine as he filled a syringe with muddy green liquid. "And we'll get you something for that cough of yours, too."

Blaine pulled to the side, trying to wrench out of the orderlies' grip as the nurse began to roll up his sleeve. She tutted over the scar. "Dear me, you *have* been in the wars." The doctor moved forward, still calm and cheerful, so that Blaine was trapped between the point of the needle and the wall behind him.

Sagging limply between his captors, he hung his head. "I'm sorry," he murmured weakly. "I'm just really scared of needles."

The doctor smiled. "You won't feel a thing."

Blaine sagged some more and half closed his eyes. As soon as he felt the first prick of metal on his skin, he jerked his leg up to knee the doctor in the groin. The man went *"Ouff!"* and doubled over, dropping the syringe on the floor. Blaine lunged out with his leg again. His arm stung, for the doctor had still managed to empty about half of the solution into it. The nurse darted away to press an alarm button while one of the orderlies bent to retrieve the syringe. Blaine kicked it away and, in the resulting scuffle, managed to break free from his captors.

For the second time, he was sprinting down the corridor. An alarm wailed and the lights over the doors began to pulse a warning red. A couple of nurses attempted to get in his way, but he thrust a trolley of medical instruments at them. Once he was through the doors at the end of the ward, he pulled the trolley after him, and jammed it at an angle under the doors' handles. As a makeshift block it wouldn't hold for long, but it was the best he could do.

He had reached a small, dingy foyer. There were stairs to his left, a lift immediately in front of him and a window on his right. When he heaved it open, he found he was looking down at the other side of the yard he'd seen from the lobby. Relief rushed through him. If he was going to use the ace, he needed to maximize his chance of escape by playing the card as near to the exit as possible. And now he saw that the Dumpster with the threshold was only a few flights of stairs or a short lift ride away.

But it might already be too late. He could feel the drug beginning to work. There was a fuzzy green haze on the edge of his vision, swirling around the floor and creeping by the walls. . . .

The next moment, there was a shattering clatter from the trolley as the doors burst open.

The doctor and nurse were standing in the entrance to the ward. Simultaneously, another nurse and two orderlies arrived at the head of the stairs.

"It's all right, son," the doctor told him, raising his hands in a soothing gesture. "You've done your best, but you're confused and you're tired. It's time for you to take a rest."

Blaine was about to retort that he was fine, thanks. But when he glanced at his arm, he cried out in revulsion. It was covered with blood, as warm and slippery as when Arthur had first slashed him with the knife. This couldn't be right: he'd had only a little injection, and there wasn't any pain. But blood was pumping out of his old wound nonetheless, a great crimson spurt pouring slickly onto the floor, where it dissolved into the sinuous green. He felt faint just looking at it.

The doctor's plump, rosy face merged into Arthur White's prim, narrow one. "You need me to look after you," murmured Arthur's tight mouth. "Only I can help you in the way you need."

"I can look—after—my . . . myself," Blaine said with difficulty. "I'm not . . . not my . . . mother—"

The doctor regarded him sorrowfully. "It seems to me that you're in quite a muddle, young man."

True enough. The blood had stopped gushing from his arm and his flesh was clean and healed again, but this only made things worse. Nothing could be trusted as real or unreal. With a ping, the doors to the lift finally opened, but there was no rescue there. The interior of the lift was lined in a thicket of long, dirty needles. Their rusting spikes were like the spines of some monstrous animal.

Get a grip, Blaine said to himself. Don't let them fool you. Get in the lift and escape. But it didn't make any difference. A treacherous little voice was whispering that it wasn't the drug at all, that he'd been going mad even before he'd been given it, when he thought he saw three Helens in the ward. He looked back at the window, and the threshold so far below, and heard himself saying, like a little boy, "I want—I want to go home."

"If you're capable of discharging yourself," the doctor answered, in tones of infinite reasonableness, "then it's possible we got our diagnosis wrong. Prove to us you're sane. Leave our hospital." He smiled knowingly. "Win your move."

His staff moved away from the stairs. The exit was clear. But the stairs weren't any better than the lift. They were gushing with blood, as Blaine's arm had been doing just a moment before. Instead of concrete and linoleum, each step was a slab of flayed flesh. He reeled backward, gagging.

The doctor regarded him pityingly. "Poor boy," he said. "You've had a hard time of it, haven't you? A nice, long sleep will sort you out in no time." And he removed another syringe from the pocket of his nice white coat.

But the pocket reminded Blaine of something he'd almost forgotten in his confusion. His die had been confiscated, yet he still had a card to play. Panting with effort, he brandished the ace at the green haze in front of him, then tore it in two.

"Get away from me!"

It was the Ace of Pentacles, Root of Earth. It should have shaken the hospital to its foundations, pulled the building down in a quake and buckle of angry earth. Yet after the torn pieces of card fluttered to the floor, the bricks and mortar stayed exactly as they were.

More visions began to squirm out of the green mist. A gaunt and disheveled Helen who begged him, weeping, to be a good boy. The silver-haired man with the stammer. Arthur, smiling as he brandished the knife. In his desperation to escape them, Blaine lurched back to the window. Here, too, the view was changing. The patch of concrete far below was rippling into greenness. It was a different green, though: brighter, and fresher. Grass grew there. A hill was rising out of the city, a rolling wave of soil and grass and daisies, reaching up to his window. The ace's path of earth to the threshold . . .

With a groan of relief, Blaine heaved himself onto the window ledge.

But the doctor shook his head sorrowfully. "The hallucinations will only get more vivid, I'm afraid. It's clear you've lost all sense of reality."

And suddenly the hill glimmered before Blaine's eyes, and turned transparent, so that he saw his own body lying broken at the foot of the building. A bloodied smash of flesh on concrete.

"It's just another trick," the doctor said gently. "You're trapped in your own mind, and now your own mind wants you dead."

Blaine looked back into the building, at the dour nurse and the ward of lunatics behind her, at the shining point of the doctor's syringe. He hesitated, swaying, on the brink.

"I don't care if it does. This is still better."

With that, he dropped out of the window, onto the green slope that flickered between solid ground and gaping void. Except that the moment his body fell onto the ghost-hill, it solidified, and he was tumbling on warm earth. With each rich scent of summer grass, Blaine could feel the poison in his blood grow weaker. The suffocating green haze had cleared. And he half rolled, half ran, down the daisy-sprinkled slope toward the wheel.

CHAPTER TWELVE

TOBY RECOGNIZED THE SETTING, or rather, he recognized the part of London that the Arcanum had adapted it from. It was St. James's, the imposing Westminster street lined with nineteenth-century gentlemen's clubs. Their well-heeled patrons would hardly have known what to make of it now. The stately buildings were blackened by explosions and pockmarked by bullets; some had gaping holes torn out of them, while the road was strewn with glass and rubble.

As Toby watched from the shelter of a doorway, a soldier in camouflage brought a rocket launcher forward. Three more gunmen ran into the street, firing continuously to give him cover. An explosion followed, and the rocket seared across the road, sending a military jeep up in flames. In response, sniper bullets hit the street in front of the soldiers, whipping the air with ricochets.

Toby felt as if he could have been in the middle of

a news report on one of those distant, dusty battles in distant, dusty countries. This bit of the Arcanum was a lot better than the one with the shopping mall. In fact, he thought approvingly as he looked at his card, it was the kind of setting he would have expected for the Chariot.

The Seven of Swords depicted a man sneaking away from a military camp with a bundle of swords in his arms. In the distance a small group of soldiers emerged from a dust cloud. Colorful pavilions gave the battleground scene the glamour of chivalry, in stark contrast to the wreckage around him.

"Ow!"

Someone had grabbed his leg. Toby twisted around to see a man in civilian clothes slumped against the wall a little farther in. His face was contorted in pain and there was blood on his shirt and in his hair.

"You need to—to get back," the man rasped. "Take proper cover. This is no—place—for sightseeing."

As if to prove his point, there was an eerie whizzing sound and the ground immediately outside the doorway shook with smoke and dust.

With a groan, the man managed to drag himself upright. "Mustn't let army find us. We have to go—farther—farther in," he said. "Help me."

The man slung an arm across Toby's shoulders, and by supporting some of his weight, Toby helped him to hobble deeper into the building. The place had been so completely gutted that only the bare structure remained, littered with burst sandbags and chunks of masonry. At last, they came to a room at the back of the house overlooking a narrow street, and the man collapsed onto the floor.

"Our insurgency is gathering pace," he mumbled. "Occupiers can't hold city for long. Here"—his hand fumbled toward Toby's playing card—"you've got to make the drop. Take the card. I tried . . . got caught in cross fire . . . too late . . ."

"What do I do with it?"

"Deliver to our agent—our agent—on—on the inside. Ministry of Operations." He licked his cracked lips. "Seven of Swords gives the sign—proceed with mission."

There was a thunderous bang from the front of the building. It was followed by shouts. Toby tensed, and glanced out the broken window into the street.

"Soldiers'll be here soon." The man roused himself a little, though the effort made him gasp and screw up his face. "Listen. The drop's in occupied territory: Church of St. Savior. Leave the card—in the confessional."

"St. Savior's? Where's that?"

"Behind the ministry. You'll need to . . ."

"Yes?"

Toby was afraid he was losing him. He put his hand on the man's shoulder and shook him.

"There's a supply tunnel," he murmured, closing his eyes with a grimace. "Turn right—end of street, two blocks up, alley left of department store. It'll get you—under—under the checkpoints. Don't . . . delay. . . ."

Toby shook the man's shoulder again, but his body

sagged and he didn't respond. A little blood trickled out of his mouth. He was gone.

There was a thump of approaching boots and the crackle of a transistor radio. With one last look at the body on the floor, Toby scrambled out of the window.

In his haste, he landed awkwardly and scraped his leg, but it wasn't bad and he kept going, bent double, expecting to feel the whiz of bullets around his head at any second. Turning right down the street, he reached a row of dilapidated apartment buildings, which, he was relieved to see, didn't resemble any part of London he recognized. The anonymity of the city made it easier to think of himself as moving through a film set or computer game.

The Seven of Swords had taken him into a shattered urban landscape strewn with mangled vehicles and rubble. Bombs had gouged huge fissures in the ground, and columns of smoke and dust clouds filled the sky. Although he appeared to be moving away from the line of battle, the sound of gunfire and explosions echoed everywhere. It was a glaringly bright afternoon, hot and colorless. There seemed to be a lot of flies. Bodies, too.

From fear of snipers, Toby kept to the shadows as much as he was able, hugging the sides of buildings and darting between the precarious shelter offered by burned-out cars and the remnants of makeshift barricades. In spite of everything, he found he was enjoying himself. This was what the Game was about—the snap of adrenaline, the running of risks that made one feel so dangerously alive. . . .

Eventually he reached the department store the man had told him about, a hulking shell of a building with a couple of mannequins still propped in its blasted windows. There was a drain cover in the alley to its left. After checking that he was unobserved, he tugged the grating open, revealing an unpleasantly dark hole with thin rungs set down its side.

With a sigh, Toby got out the pocket flashlight attached to his key ring. This wasn't the first time it had come in useful in the Arcanum. Once he had lowered himself through the hatch, he found himself in a narrow tunnel, so low that he had to crawl on his hands and knees.

After about fifteen minutes, he came to a slightly wider section, which had been used for storage. There was a small pile of ammunition, bundles of tools and tarpaulin, and canisters of paraffin. About ten yards farther on, he found a ladder and a trapdoor. He waited a few anxious moments before cautiously pushing up the hatch. It opened into a cellar, completely empty except for a piece of matting that had been laid over the tunnel's entrance.

The rest of the house was stripped out and deserted, but otherwise intact. Its surrounding streets were much less ravaged than the neighborhood Toby had first found himself in; there were even some bedraggled civilians about. He saw patrols of soldiers, too, whose uniforms bore the insignia of a silver sword on a black background. Although he knew he should be downcast at the enormity of the task ahead, he felt a warm thrill as he looked around, knowing that all this

activity—every face, every stone, every sight and sound—
had been conjured into being on his behalf.

He found the Ministry of Operations around the next
corner: a fortified block of ugly brown brick, with a tattered
sword flag hanging from the top story. A dusty stretch of
grass occupied the center of the square outside, but there
was no church behind it or in any of the streets nearby. All
that remained of the drop's location was a smoking crater
and a few shards of stained glass.

OK, Toby reasoned, time for plan B. He could see
people working in the windows of the ministry; one of
them must be his target. Perhaps if he got past the sentries
and into the building, the Arcanum would provide its own
clues? After all, he had his Ace of Wands, the Root of Fire,
to fall back on if things went wrong. . . . But thinking of the
ace gave him an idea. He didn't necessarily have to deliver
the Seven of Swords to anyone. The card wasn't valuable in
itself. It was just a signal to the agent to proceed with the
mission, whatever that might be. To win the move, Toby
simply had to find a different means of communication. He
had to give another sign.

Grinning to himself, Toby slipped back to the house
with the tunnel, and the underground storage area. Here he
collected one of the canisters of paraffin and put it in a plastic bag. He already carried matches in his pocket. It was
comforting to have the die there, too, as his own personal
escape route, but it occurred to him that if he fell into enemy hands, the Seven of Swords might be incriminating, so

he decided to leave it behind. As he concealed the Ace of Wands inside a tear in the lining of his jacket, he briefly wondered what the other three chancers were facing. Whatever it was, he thought smugly, he'd bet it couldn't compete with espionage in occupied territory.

Once he had returned to the square, Toby made for the far north end from the ministry. He spent a while scuffing the grass with his feet and loitering about in what he hoped was an innocuous manner. Then he used his keys to puncture a hole in the bag and the bottom of the plastic container inside. When he had made sure the paraffin was seeping out in a clear and steady trickle, he walked—trying to look as aimless as possible—in a straight line to the other corner. From there, he turned and trudged in a diagonal direction across the lawn, squeezing the container to ensure that the liquid was leaving a substantial trail along the grass.

Out of the corner of his eye, he was aware that the sentries outside the ministry were looking at him and conferring among themselves. One of them stepped forward to the edge of the grass.

"You! Boy! Come over here."

Increasing his saunter to a jog, Toby covered the last few feet of his course. There was only just enough paraffin to finish it. Already, two of the guards were moving to intercept him. His hands trembling in fear and excitement, Toby lit a match and dropped it on the ground.

For a horrible moment the match just smoldered, weakly. Then, with an excitable whoosh, the grass lit up and fire raced along the trail of paraffin that Toby had laid: a long diagonal line leading up to a short horizontal one. Within seconds, a giant 7 blazed across the square. Well, he thought, if that doesn't get the message across, nothing will. Already, the windows of the ministry and the other surrounding buildings were crowded with people watching the display.

There was no time to savor his success. Toby had managed to sprint only a few yards before a kick from one of the guards swept his feet from under him, sending him crashing down onto the pavement. Almost before he knew it, his hands had been wrenched behind his back and his captors were searching his pockets. One of them held up the die. "A gambler, eh?" he jeered before stamping it under his boot.

The next moment, Toby was bundled through a side entrance to the ministry and marched into the basement. Cells lined the corridor. Most were empty, but as he passed one on the left, a woman's face pressed against the bars. Underneath the mash of blood and bruises, he thought he could make out the features of Lucrezia, Queen of Pentacles. But before Toby could react, he was hustled on and shoved into a windowless cell. The door slammed shut behind him.

He didn't know how long he was left to sweat it out. It could have been three hours, or one. He sat on the floor, his back against the wall, and tried to hold his nerve. Without his die, and with no sign of a threshold, he was trapped. At least they hadn't found his ace, he told himself. He still had a powerful defense. The weapon of last resort ... But the longer he waited, the harder it was not to fill his head with gruesome imaginings of what that last resort might be. Lucrezia's pulpy face was warning enough.

It was almost a relief when the two guards returned. Without speaking, and barely looking at Toby, they unlocked the door and hustled him down hallways and up long flights of stairs. From what he could see of it, the place was run-down and chaotic: a warren of badly lit rooms filled with people huddled over screens and switchboards. At the top of the building, he was shown into a small office lined with maps, where a man in military uniform was working at his desk. Toby had to wait a further five long minutes before he looked up from his paperwork.

"Ah yes. The arsonist. Perhaps," he said with chilling quiet, "you would care to explain what your demonstration in the square was in aid of?"

Toby attempted a careless shrug. "It wasn't in aid of anything. I like setting fire to things, that's all."

"So you would have us believe you are just a common hooligan."

"Yeah."

"And the significance of the seven?"

"It's a lucky number."

"Hmm. I do not think, however, it will prove to be lucky for you." The interviewer leaned across the desk. "I am a reasonable person," he said. "And a patient one. Other members of this administration are not so patient. You will find explaining things to me is much more ... bearable ... than having to talk to my colleagues. Do you understand?"

Toby paled in spite of himself. "There's nothing to explain," he said defiantly.

"Very well." The man smiled coldly. He called to the guard outside the room. "Take our young friend down to the interrogation suite. I'm sure a few hours there will make him more conversational."

He went back to his paperwork.

Toby's guard escorted him along the corridor. The other guard was just ahead, at the top of the stairs. Toby's stomach twisted. Was this the right point to play his ace? He wished he had a better idea of what starting a fire up here would do—what chance of escape it would give him. But perhaps the Arcanum would provide its own way out, after all. . . .

Before they reached the stairs, they had to pass a door on the right. Toby hadn't really taken it in on the way up, but he noticed it this time because it was open. It revealed a small storeroom. As they approached it, Toby darted inside, closed the door and twisted the key in the lock.

It was done on impulse, with the vague hope of buying time. It was only when he stood with his back against the door, breathing hard, that he realized there was a window.

He pushed the handle. The window opened onto a courtyard at the back of the building, five floors below. From this height, it felt like miles. Meanwhile, the door thumped and rattled. He would have a minute at most before the guards forced their way in.

Toby grasped either side of the window frame and pulled himself up. On the brink of the drop, giddiness churned through his head. He saw that the roof sloped down to either side of the window, with a lead gutter running along its edge, almost in line with the window's ledge. He was slim and slight. Could it take his weight?

Quaking all over, Toby forced himself to stand on the narrow ledge, hands grasping either side, looking into the room with his back to the courtyard. Then he began to shuffle toward the gutter.

Inside, the storeroom door burst open with a shout from the guards. Hugging the slope of the roof, Toby left the last few inches of the window ledge—so perilous before, now a haven of stability and refuge—and put his weight on the gutter. It sagged, but stayed firm.

A soldier's head came through the window. He tried to grab Toby by the leg but Toby managed to lean out of reach, clutching at the roof's stone tiles. The gutter creaked and protested at the strain, and his heart stuttered with terror. The man's fingertips brushed his ankle. Toby's hands scrabbled over the tiles, searching for some kind of grip. Ivy wound across the tiles, its roots thick and fibrous, and he dug his fingers into it. Come on, he told himself. *Work*. He screwed up his eyes, sweating and grunting, and sought new handholds, thrusting his cramped fingers through cracks in the stone tiles, scrambling around the gnarled ivy roots. The muscles in his arms burned all over. Slowly, torturously, he hauled himself up the slope.

There was a valley in between the two peaks of the roof, and after he'd slithered down, he lay there for a few moments, panting, but also giggling weakly to himself. Spider-

Man, eat your heart out. A siren was already wailing, though, and the sound of voices sent Toby scrambling to his feet again. More soldiers had accessed the roof from a skylight at the other end of the building: pursuit was not far behind. And to escape onto the roof of the next building, he would have to leap over the alley between them. It would mean a running jump of about six feet.

There was no time for hesitation. Toby sprinted along the tiles, and hurled himself into the air.

At first, he felt that he was moving in slow motion, speeding up only as he fell. Before he knew it, his feet hit the ledge of the roof, and for a few hideous seconds he hung there upright on the edge, his arms flailing for balance. Gravity tipped him forward, the smack of his hands on the lead sheeting sending shocks trembling through his body.

But as Toby resumed his flight, ducking and diving through the parapets and peaks and chimney stacks, he felt no fear. Now it was like his last time in the Arcanum, at the end of the Chariot, when Mia had given him his quest. Confidence and luck sparkled through his veins. The bomb-blasted, smoking city spread around him was like the biggest film set in the world. He wasn't even surprised when he felt pins and needles on his palm. Of course a threshold must be in reach. He found its wheel built into the brick patterning of a chimney, and when he raised the coin, he actually laughed aloud.

After all that, he thought, I didn't even have to use my ace!

Chapter Thirteen

CAT WAS DROWNING. The flood that had engulfed the Minotaur had caught up with her before she could manage to toss the threshold coin, and now she was sinking helplessly into its depths. She thrashed around in the muffling dark until her confused senses realized the air wasn't being strangled out of her by water, but by cloth. She was swaddled in thick, heavy folds of the stuff. At last, she fought her way free, to find herself standing in a swath of gold brocade just inside the entrance to Temple House.

Something strange, though, had happened to the hall. The marble floor, checkered in black and white, had grown impossibly wide, or else Cat had grown impossibly small. It was as if she was a pawn standing on a giant's chessboard. And yet she was also bestriding a toy landscape of miniature mountains, forests and rivers, towns and plains, whose scurrying figures were as small and inconsequential as ants.

Black and white. Large and small. The empty board, the teeming landscape, the marble hall. One and the same.

Cat closed her eyes on the confusion and groped for the way out.

Except that Temple House was no longer in the city she knew. The square outside and the buildings surrounding it were utterly strange. Yet she knew that she was not in the Arcanum. This was indisputably her own world.

Standing at the bottom of the steps to the house was Alastor, King of Swords.

There was no trace of the wounds inflicted by the Minotaur, yet he did not look like the man Cat knew. Alastor appeared thin and worn, and older than she remembered.

He looked up to where Cat stood in the entranceway, lapped by her swirl of golden drapes. She expected to see hate and bitterness, but his gaze was empty as a dead man's. The wheel on Cat's palm burned as, one by one, cards began to slip out of Alastor's pockets and dance through the air. They spun toward her hand like iron filings to a magnet, and in the twists and turns of their flight, she glimpsed a scattering of triumphs among the cards of the Swords suit. But the moment they reached her grasp, the cards melted away.

For the last time, the queen of the Court of Swords faced its fallen king. As Alastor stared past Cat into the hall and the great checkerboard, the despair that suffused his face was more frightening than anger. He stretched out a hand, hungrily. The door slammed shut between them.

The crashing noise reverberated in her head. With every echo, Cat seemed to see the door swing shut again and again, each time closing on a different view. She glimpsed Lucrezia, Odile and Ahab, each looking up at her with grief and loss and terrible longing.

The door slammed shut for a fifth time, leaving Cat alone in blackness. There was nothing except the sound of her quick, shallow breathing, and an unseen weight of stone. Then one lamp, then another, winked into life, and she was back in the crypt, looking into the strained, pale faces of the three other new kings and queens.

They left the Hanged Man's chamber in silence. Speech of any kind would have felt irrelevant. But when they reached the room with the golden curtain, a new shock awaited them. The High Priest was lying sprawled on the ground in front of the arch. There was a single crumpled playing card clutched to his chest.

Flora knelt beside him to check for signs of life; Toby, to prize the card free. He was not breathing, although they could find no sign of injury. His eyes were open in the same trapped, unblinking gaze as the past Game Masters had when they last sat around the table.

There was no one around it now. Instead, they pulled back the curtain to find the Master of Misrule sitting cross-legged on the table, tearing greasily into a chicken leg. The hair that flowed to his shoulders was as soft and white as thistledown, and he was dressed in a rich and glittering version of the Fool's patchwork rags.

"Your Royal Highnesses," he said, bowing low from the waist.

"What've you done to the Priest?" Blaine demanded.

The Master of Misrule widened his already wide blue eyes. "His card has joined my discard pile. And there he will wait, until such a time as I see fit to reintroduce him into play." He tilted his head at them in mock concern. "What's the matter? Don't you like what I've done to the place?"

The wave of his arm indicated everything from Temple House to the boundless reaches of the Arcanum.

"Of course, I couldn't have managed it without you!" He laughed merrily, and gnawed some more on the chicken leg.

"Without cheating us, you mean," Flora muttered.

"Cheated? But I bestowed the prizes you asked for! It is no fault of mine if they were not quite what you expected . . . for didn't I warn you that every card has two sides?" The curve of his cheek and the gentleness of his smile were like a child's, yet something cold and ancient seemed to peer out from behind his face. "Have no fear, my friends. You will soon see how glorious our Game has become."

"The High Priest already showed us," said Cat, lifting her chin, "and I don't think much of it. There's more than enough bad luck and random nastiness in the world as it is."

"Wisely spoken, Your Majesty." Misrule clasped his hands together and nodded eagerly. "Why indeed should some men live in comfort and ease while others starve in gutters? What absurdity dictates the tyranny of birth! How capricious opportunity is, how narrow the span of one man's destiny!

"Chance has always been at the root of men's fortunes, good or bad, but its influence is flimsy and fleeting. I seek to redress this imbalance. And so my Lottery shall render every man, woman and child equal in vulnerability and opportunity alike. Each player will live an infinite variety of lives, suffer and celebrate a thousand destinies. The prince shall become the pauper. The sinner, the savior. The detestable may be beloved; the dying can rise again. . . . Until, that is, the next spin of my wheel, when the cards will once more set all at liberty from their fate."

Flora's face was pinched with loathing. "How can you talk of liberty? You're far more of a tyrant than any of the old kings and queens. You're out to play *God*."

The man laughed, showing even white teeth. His lips shone greasily from the meat. "A god at play is a generous one. I have no need of thunderbolts; I will impose no laws on tablets of stone. I have only to ensure that the wheel spins and the cards turn, for what lies on their reverse, and who receives them, is still Fortune's lot. I am her consort, not her conqueror.

"I once told you how the Game began, as a Lottery of the people. When I tried to advance its powers, I was cast down and condemned. And so my beautiful Game became a secret, hidden thing, crippled by boundaries and corrupted by false laws. But just as you released me, so will I release the Game. Beyond the thresholds of the Arcanum, its destiny will be fulfilled."

"Not if we can help it," Toby retorted.

"Ah yes . . . your brave new round!" When he had talked of the Game's origins, Misrule had become grave and still, but now his lighthearted tone returned. "All manner of play delights me. I did not set the Game free only to frustrate its sport. You may wander the Arcanum for *all* Eternity if you wish. And besides," he continued, licking his chicken bone clean, "although Fortune loves a fool, she likes to toy with kings even better."

With that, the Master of Misrule took the drumstick between his hands and broke it. In a snap of bone, the room in the crypt disappeared, and the former chancers found themselves standing in Mercury Square.

"Well," said Flora shakily, "that was interesting."

Dazed, Cat turned round to face the steps of Temple House. A toss of a coin . . . the slam of a door . . . a snap of bone . . . In real time, she had barely had the chance to catch her breath after her last move, and yet its ordeal already seemed misty and muddled, like something from long ago. She looked back at the others. "Did you see the giant chessboard, too? And the other kings and queens, with their cards?" she asked.

They nodded.

"It was strange," Flora murmured. "It's not as if I'd expect them to be overwhelmingly grateful for being set free. After all, we're the ones who wrecked their Game in the first place. But they . . . they looked so . . . *ruined.*"

"They've lost everything," Toby replied solemnly. "After centuries of ruling the Game, what could life in this world

179

possibly offer? Perhaps for an ousted Game Master, even suffering in the Arcanum is better than being banned from it."

."More fool them," said Blaine.

"And more power to us!" Toby's face brightened. "C'mon, guys, we *did* it. We're the new generation of Game royalty! All hail the King of Pentacles! Wooo-HOOO!" He let out a victory yelp that echoed around the square.

Flora smiled a little but shook her head. "What's the use of grand titles if we don't have our Game Masters' decks?" She spread out her empty hands. "One minute the Queen of Cups' cards were there—floating toward me—and the next they had gone. Nothing."

Toby inspected his own palm. "Hmm. There must be a way of getting them back. Maybe we need to find those magic-ball-amulet thingies first."

"Or maybe Misrule has stolen them," said Flora. "Who knows? Without the High Priest to guide us, we haven't a clue. About *anything*."

Cat opened her mouth to tell them about the oracle, then thought better of it. The words of the prophecy were hopelessly entangled; she needed to straighten them out in her own mind first. In the meantime, Toby's confidence was irrepressible.

"Well, we've got at least one card up our sleeves. Look!" With a flourish, he pulled out the card he had taken from the old man. "It's blank at the moment. But the High Priest must have meant us to have it, as our next move. Perhaps it will take us to the rest of the deck."

"We don't know that for certain," Cat cautioned. "It could lead to anything."

"Doesn't matter," he replied. "Once we're in the Arcanum, the Game will show us what to do. We'll just keep going until we get some answers. I lost my die but I've still got my ace, by the way. What about you guys?"

It transpired that they had two dice but only the one ace between them.

"Better than nothing," Toby said. "And you never know, our last moves might hold some clue as to what's in store for the next one. Here, Blaine, what card did you get?"

Blaine glanced up from trampling leaves in the gutter. "Nine of Swords. And I don't want to talk about it."

"What d'you mean?"

He lowered his brows heavily. "Exactly what I said."

But Toby didn't back down. "I'm sorry, but what affects one person affects us all."

"He's right," Flora told Blaine. "The High Priest was the only person who could have told us what to do next. But we're on our own now. When it comes to the Game, all we have is each other."

Cat noticed that Flora had turned a little pink.

They went to a greasy spoon in Soho that they'd met up in before and whose chief recommendation was that the spacing of its tables and noisiness of its customers helped even the most outlandish conversation go unnoticed.

It wasn't even noon, yet the idea of food was comforting.

Plates of fries revived unsettled appetites; everyone began to relax as they eased into the bustle of the café.

In the end, Blaine was the first to relate his experience in the Arcanum. It was a curt and cut-down summary that set the tone for the others' narratives. Even Toby's account was relatively restrained. Flora spoke third.

"... and I still don't know what a cross sum is, let alone who or what Death's is supposed to be," she said in conclusion.

"The Emperor, obviously," said Toby.

Flora rolled her eyes. "Well, it's obviously not obvious to me."

"The cross sum of a number is what you get when you add its digits together. Death is the thirteenth triumph, right, and one plus three equals four. The fourth triumph is the Emperor. So if you think about it, that last question was actually the most straightforward of the lot. . . . Pity you wasted that ace, though."

"*Excuse* me—I didn't 'waste' anything, thank you very much," Flora retorted. "I used the card to save Odile's life."

"She would have survived anyway. That's the point of Misrule's punishment: whatever horrible things happened to them in one move, they'd always regenerate safe and sound in the next one. Think of their doppelgängers in the crypt—there wasn't so much as a scratch on them."

"I'm still not convinced. And there's no need to look so pleased with yourself, Toby," she added. "It was only sheer dumb luck you didn't have to use your ace as well."

"Not necessarily. The fact is, whatever card you get

dealt, there's always going to be *some* way of winning it, even if you haven't got an ace to help you. For example—"

"You haven't heard about my card yet," Cat interrupted, hastily launching into a description of the High Priestess. As she'd expected, although everyone was interested in the Minotaur, it was the oracle that got their attention. After explaining the falsehood about the Empress, she did her best to relate the main prophecy.

"OK, here goes. The prophecy began with a lord standing over a threshold, and filling a house with cloud and a court with glory. Then the Priestess described four wheels: one with a bull in the middle, and a man and a lion and an eagle in the others. Like in the picture of the Triumph of Eternity. But there were cherubs mixed up in it, too—riding the wheels or something. Anyhow, we have to make some kind of offering to the cherubs because they're the only ones who can bring us Eternity."

"Cherubs?" Toby pulled a face. "Like on Valentine cards?"

"Those are cupids, technically," said Flora. "*Cherub* is the singular of *cherubim*, who were originally powerful angels, and part of the heavenly host. But the only angel-type cards I can think of are the Triumphs of Love and Fame."

"Hmm." Cat helped herself to the last of the fries. "Well, we have to find some way of working out who they are and what kind of offering they need—or else Misrule and his wheel are going to kick into action. At the turning of the year, the girl said."

"So the big showdown will be on New Year's Eve!" Toby failed to keep the relish from his voice.

"I might have got things garbled," Cat warned them. "It didn't help that the Priestess was speaking in this fancy ye-olde-worlde style. *Thee* and *thou* and whatever."

"I'm beginning to think it could be biblical," said Flora. "Both Tarot and triumph cards use religious imagery, you know."

"Or religion uses Game of Triumphs imagery," said Cat. "After all, the Game and the Bible are both old and creepy and don't make much sense. Maybe the Bible pinched some of its ideas from the Arcanum."

Flora rolled her eyes. "Amateur theology aside, the business with the wheels and cherubim sounds familiar. It's the kind of apocalyptic vision the book of Revelation goes in for."

"Or the prophet Ezekiel," said Blaine quietly. "'Then the glory of the Lord went up from the cherub, and stood over the threshold of the house; and the house was filled with the cloud, and the court was full of the brightness of the Lord's glory. . . .' Does that sound right, Cat?"

"Hell, yeah. That's it *exactly*."

Flora laughed. "You'd be top of any Bible study class. Maybe Charlie wasn't so wrong about you and the priesthood, after all."

Cat and Toby looked confused; Blaine, uncomfortable. He coughed. "The last time we were in this café," he said, "I asked how you people first got mixed up in the Game, remember?"

"Yes," said Cat. "And you said that you'd got involved because of something you read in a book."

"A notebook. It was written by the man I'm looking for." Blaine moved to touch his scar before self-consciously pulling back from the gesture. "He filled it with research on the Game. Or rather, some of it's about the Game. Mostly it's the usual hocus-pocus Tarot crap. Anyway, there was a reference to Ezekiel chapter 10 in his notes on the Triumph of Eternity. When I looked up the passage, it didn't mean much. But now . . ."

"Do you still have the notebook?" Toby asked eagerly. "Have you checked out all the references yet? Can we see it?"

"It's back at Flora's place."

Toby got to his feet. "Then what are we waiting for?"

"Don't get too excited," Blaine warned them as they approached the Seatons' house. "There're no earth-shattering secrets waiting to be discovered in this thing. Most of it's any old occult rubbish."

"You never know. As Toby said, everything and anything could be important," said Flora, getting out her keys.

The door opened before she could reach for the lock. Mina stood in the hall, hands on hips.

"Miss Flora! I try to call! Why you no answer your phone?"

"Oh . . . I'm sorry—I, er, my battery's dead." Flora came to a flustered halt in the doorway, with Cat, Toby and Blaine hovering behind.

Mina eyed them doubtfully. Apart from her scratches, Flora was as neat as ever, but then her most recent visit to the Arcanum had not involved any physical exertion. The others were distinctly bedraggled: Toby still had bits of ivy in his hair.

"Yes, fine, Miss Flora, but why you no tell me you have friend staying over? Your parents, they phone, they ask about you, and I do not know what I am to say."

Flora flushed. "It's all right, Mina. I'm going to talk to them myself. Honestly, there's nothing for you to worry about."

Suspicion struggled with the concern and affection in Mina's face. "But my job is for worrying about you, yes?" Then she sighed. "OK. So you do that. I know you are good girl, always. And Mr. Charlie is waiting for you now."

"What?"

"In the study. He try to call you, too. Miss Tilly has also come visit, but she went to the shop." Mina turned round and headed in the direction of the kitchen. "Let me know if I to get snacks for your guests."

"Thank you!" Once Mina was gone, Flora said hurriedly, "Look ... I'm awfully sorry, but I think we'd better postpone. Can we meet back at the square at, say, four o'clock? It's only because—"

"I hope no one's leaving on my account." Charlie had emerged from a room to the right. He was holding a battered leather notebook.

Blaine shouldered past the others. He stood only a few inches away from Charlie, quite controlled, but with pent-up force visible in every line of his body. "What the hell are you doing with that?"

"I found it."

"*No.* It was in my bag. Under my bed, in my room."

"Yes—the bedroom Mina was tidying. She must've decided to give the bag a good scrubbing along with everything else. I found the book lying on the kitchen table while your bag was being disinfected or deloused or whatever."

"Opportunist theft is still theft." Blaine hadn't taken his eyes off Charlie's face.

"Stop it, Charlie. Just give him his book," said Flora tightly. Toby and Cat exchanged glances.

With insolent casualness, Charlie held up the book and walked slowly backward into the room. Blaine advanced toward him, matching him pace for pace, until they were squaring up to each other in the center of the study. Helplessly, the others followed. In this moment of confrontation, Flora found the contrast between the two boys disconcertingly blurred. The blue polo shirt she'd lent Blaine was an ironic match for Charlie's green one. The hardness in Charlie's face was new, too; he looked older, more sharply focused, than she would have thought possible. He opened the book and brandished the pages so that everyone could see them.

"Devils and death's-heads and burning towers. Not exactly the sort of material a protégé of St. Bernadine's should be interested in, is it?"

"This has nothing to do with you," said Blaine, his voice dangerously quiet. "You don't know what you're getting into."

"I'm not the issue here. It's Flora I care about." All of

a sudden, the arrogance left Charlie's voice. "I mean, for God's sake—this thing is covered in *bloodstains.*"

Blaine paused. For the first time, he really took in his surroundings: the book-laden shelves, the desk, the filing cabinet. This room was a world of luxury away from Arthur's study, yet the fittings were essentially the same. Charlie's reaction to finding the notebook wasn't all that different to his own, either. Although he was still angry, he managed to take a step back, keeping his voice level.

"The blood's mine," he said. "But the stuff in the book isn't." He pushed up his sleeve. "It was written by the man who gave me this scar. He got married to my mother. He bullied her and made her ill, and hit me. I didn't know what any of the book meant, just that it was important to him, and so I stole it. When he pulled a knife on me, that's when I left. I'm staying with Flora only because I have nowhere else to go."

There was the sound of bustle in the hall. Gripped as they were by the unfolding drama, nobody had noticed the bell ring, or heard Mina go to answer it. But suddenly a pretty brunette was in the doorway, swinging a bottle of Diet Coke in a shopping bag.

"The *Lord of the Rings* Role-Playing Society!" she exclaimed, smiling at Cat. "That's right, isn't it? You came to see Flora in that coffee shop off the King's Road before Christmas."

Oblivious to the atmosphere in the room, Tilly looked from the pale, scruffy girl to the boy in the blue polo shirt to the one with bits of ivy in his hair. "It was about a game of Orcs versus Elves, or something. . . ." Her eyes slid back to Blaine and she gave a self-conscious laugh. "Come on, Flo, aren't you going to introduce us?"

Everyone else was still frozen in place.

Blaine abruptly turned to Flora. "We'll meet later, like you said. Excuse me." He took the book from Charlie's unresisting hands and pushed past Tilly into the hall. The front door slammed.

"Satisfied?" Flora asked Charlie through gritted teeth.

"I'm sorry. But I had to know that you were safe."

They stood staring at each other as Tilly looked on, bewildered, from the side.

"Right now," Cat told her, "it seems the Orcs have the upper hand."

Chapter Fourteen

Cat and Toby made their own exit shortly after Blaine's. As soon as they got outside, Cat could see that Toby was fit to burst with exclamations, and before he could launch into anything, she got in, "OK, then, so I guess we'll meet up later. Bye."

"What, you're just going to go home?"

"I could do with putting my feet up. There's something about being hunted down by bloodthirsty mutants that really takes it out of a girl."

"There's still lots of preparation to be done, though. Wouldn't it be better if all four of us camped out at Flora's? For one thing, if I tell my parents I'm staying with a friend, they won't worry if I'm out late or gone for ages. Then we could make her place a proper team HQ. It'd be fun."

"*Fun?* Since when is any of this remotely fun?"

"I'm just saying we should make the most—"

"For God's sake! Give it a rest. We're already doing as much as we can."

"I'm not sure we—"

"It's all right for *you*." Cat was close to her snapping point. *"You've* always wanted to save the world. But Blaine and his stepdad … Flora's sister … my parents … the Game's mixed us up in all sorts of other bad stuff, as well as Misrule, and we're still dealing with it. You don't understand what it's like for me, for any of us, because you treat everything like one big happy-go-lucky adventure."

"But—"

"I need to go now, Toby. I'll see you at four."

He looked hurt, but she walked rapidly away all the same, in the opposite direction to where he'd go to catch his bus. When she turned the next corner, she found Blaine leaning against a wall, almost as if he'd been waiting for her.

Cat went and stood beside him. She didn't say anything at first. Her reflection floated in the window of a car parked opposite. Face to face with her own wintry sharpness, Cat wished she could be someone else, just for a little while. Someone accessible and comforting, who could give a hug as easily as a smile.

Instead, she cleared her throat. "Mind if I have a look at the book?"

Blaine passed it over silently. She flicked through a few pages.

"Are you sure your stepdad's in the Arcanum?"

"The King of Wands told me he'd got lost there, but could still get out. He said he had 'everything to play for.'

And when you come to think of it, the Game Masters haven't lied before."

Cat considered this. The old kings and queens were coldhearted and calculating. However, it was true that she'd never caught them in an outright lie.

"There's been no sign of him inside or out, so I reckon he's still stuck in some move. I'm sure of it, in fact."

"And—and your mum? Where is she?"

"Back home. A neighbor checks on her. After everything that happened, she finds it easier if I'm not there." He stared down at his feet. "My stepfather had—has—quite a hold on her."

Cat swallowed. "There're monsters in the Arcanum," she said finally, "monsters and darkness, and things strange enough to send you mad. But at the end of the day, none of it's any worse than the stuff you get in the real world, or the things that real people do."

Then she reached over and pushed up Blaine's sleeve and, gently and deliberately, placed her hand on his arm, so that it rested on the line of puckered skin left by the knife. He tensed, and she thought he would move away. Instead, he brushed her hand with his own, light as a whisper. Their eyes met.

The ringing of her cell phone made them both start. Cat jerked away, flooded with an inexplicable guilt, as if she'd been found out at something.

"Sorry," she said with effort. "My aunt. Won't be anything." She pressed the Ignore button.

Blaine had begun to cough again. "She raised you after your parents died?"

"Mmm. Bel was only nineteen when it happened."

"And she treats you right?"

"More than right." Cat wanted to explain how it was between them, but she had never before tried to find the words for a love that was lived in but not looked at. She and Bel came first for each other, that was all. "It makes me wonder what her life would've been like if she hadn't had me to worry about. Bel's always been restless—moving around, chopping and changing—but she's smart enough to do anything. People start off wanting her, and end up needing her. It's just the way she is."

"Must be hard, having to keep the Game a secret from her."

"Yeah. That's what the Game does, doesn't it? It puts up barriers, creates obsessions. Sometimes I . . . sometimes I think that's the worst thing about my parents' deaths."

"How do you mean?"

She took a deep breath. It seemed today was going to be a day for revelations. "One or the other of them might've got an invitation to the Game. That's why they were killed: someone was looking for it."

Blaine didn't say anything, but shifted closer to her again, so that his arm was next to hers. This time its warmth steadied her.

And so Cat told him about going into the Six of Cups, the Reign of Past Pleasure. About wandering through layers of long-lost memory brought to new life. About being three years old again, and playing under her parents' bed, where she found a richly colored card tucked in the slats. And how after that the memories had shifted and grown shadows, until there was no pleasure, only a gathering foreboding. . . .

At this point, Cat had to halt the narrative. This part was still too raw, too real, to be shared with anyone. Instead, she related the barest of facts: an unseen stranger with a stutter demanded her parents give up a card belonging to the Game; her mother told him there'd been a mistake, but he shot them nonetheless.

"I'm sorry," Blaine said at the end. She felt his gaze on her, the weight of its seriousness. His voice was almost formal. "I'm sorry it happened, and I'm sorry you had to see it."

She shook her head, not to deny his words but to distance herself from the truth of them.

"As you see, everything's a mystery," she continued, trying to sound practical rather than plaintive. "I don't know if and how the invitation was hidden under the bed without my parents knowing, or what happened to it afterward. But if my parents knew about the card, why didn't they hand it over? Was it just that the killer didn't give them the chance? Or was it so important to them that they thought it worth risking their lives for?"

Not for the first time, Cat wondered what the Game could have offered her parents that they didn't already have. They were young and in love; they had a home, a child. . . . Such a fulfilled family *shouldn't* have needed anything else.

"Getting invited to the Game doesn't mean they did anything about it. Or ever intended to," Blaine pointed out.

"I'd like to think so." She sighed. "Still . . . the Game gets a hold on people, and quickly. That's why Misrule is so dangerous, right? People can't resist his scratchcards, just like I couldn't resist trying out the Arcanum."

"D'you regret it?"

"I don't know. Maybe I'd be better off—happier—still believing that my parents were killed in a car accident, but that'd be living a lie. As for the Arcanum, it's hellish most of the time, and I should hate it, and yet . . ."

"It can be beautiful, too."

"Yeah."

"I remember one of the first times I went in," Blaine said slowly. "It was a really cold, wet night, early in the year, and I was trying to find a shelter. Then this man started following me around, offering to help, said he knew how to take care of me. I didn't like the look of him, so when I came across a threshold, it seemed like a good way out."

"And was it?"

"It took me to the Triumph of the Sun. I found myself in a meadow, with all these white horses. Yellow flowers and white manes blowing in the breeze. I've never seen skies so blue. Even weeks later, when I was out in the cold and the rain again, just thinking about that meadow made me feel warm."

Cat watched the London street in front of them, picturing it unraveling into fields of green and gold. She thought of the bygone luster of Temple House, remembered the glow of oil lamps on ancient stone. "It's my life before the Game that feels otherworldly now. Strange to think that without it I'd never have met Flora or Toby. Or you."

Blaine pushed himself away from the wall and stretched, getting ready to move on. "Don't be so sure of that. Fate works in mysterious ways." But his voice was light, and she couldn't tell if its mocking note was meant for himself or her.

Instead of catching a bus home, Toby decided to walk for a while. The altercation with Cat had shaken him more than he cared to admit. Although his arms and shoulders ached from his rooftop exertions, his body was still charged with adrenaline. His tiredness was evident mostly in the jittering of his thoughts. The images that accompanied them were colorful but remote, already the stuff of legend.

He wandered along a couple of streets like the one on which Flora lived, the houses rising on either side like the iced tiers of a wedding cake. The next corner led to a row of boutiques. A window display of silver-and-scarlet baubles put him in mind of the shopping mall in the Chariot, and he wondered what Mia was doing now. It occurred to him that she, too, could have been a phantom of the Arcanum when he last saw her, but he immediately dismissed the idea. Perhaps she had not been quite the dreamy schoolgirl he remembered, but if anything, she had seemed more real as a person, not less.

Toby came to an incredulous halt. It was as if thinking

of Mia had summoned up other ghosts from his past, for he had just seen Seth, lounging at a table outside a bar.

As usual, there was a girl draped over him. Toby tried not to stare too obviously at her thin caramel limbs and mane of glossy hair.

"Er, hi, Seth."

Seth looked at him blankly. "Do I *know* you?"

"Well, sort of. Back at school . . ." His voice trailed off.

"One of the squirts, right?" Seth was smirking and the girl didn't bother to hide her yawn. "The one who liked dares." Lazily, he flicked a bottle top in Toby's direction, just like he had in the clock tower, all those months before. "Run away and play, squirt."

Toby thought of Cat's taunt that he didn't take their quest seriously, and felt anger boil helplessly inside him. He knew he wasn't stupid or ugly or uninteresting. Why, then, did these people make him feel so? If he was a true king of the Arcanum, how come he couldn't stand up to a jerk like Seth?

I could bring the Game of Triumphs to its knees, Toby thought. I could save the world with all the powers of Eternity, and yet once I return from the Arcanum, I will still be nothing but background noise.

After she said goodbye to Blaine, Cat took the rest of the afternoon easy. She had a long shower and spent a while getting dressed, taking the time to paint her nails in smooth, careful strokes. It felt good to concentrate on this one thing. Afterward she lounged on her bed, listening to music and flicking through Bel's gossip magazines. Like the nail polish, the mags weren't something she usually bothered with, but they provided a different kind of otherworldliness to lose herself in. She found it amusing to skim pages of rock royalty, pop princesses and beauty queens while testing the sound of her new title: Cat Harper, Queen of Swords.

Although the idea of this should have been fateful and threatening, just now it felt mildly comic. As Cat slipped into a doze, she was conscious only of a dim happiness. I wish I could have seen those white horses, she thought.

The slam of a door startled her into wakefulness. She found Bel stomping around the kitchen with more than her usual vigor.

"Hello," said Cat through a yawn. "I thought you were still in staff training today."

"Got let out for good behavior, didn't I? Which is more than I can say for you." Bel's tone was snappish. "Why didn't you answer your phone when I called?"

"Sorry. I was in the middle of something. You didn't leave a message. . . ." Cat took another look at Bel's face. "Is there a problem?"

In answer, Bel pulled a battered hardback book out of her bag and smacked it down on the table. Its cover, a rainbow of psychedelic swirls, proclaimed *The Wondrous World of Tarot*. Until recently, it had lain under Cat's bed. "What are you doing with that?"

Cat couldn't help feeling they were acting out a bizarre parody of Charlie and Blaine, in confrontation over the leather notebook.

"I found it when I was cleaning your room."

"Since when do you clean?"

"Since you stopped bothering."

Cat winced. What with one thing and another, her usual chores hadn't been much of a priority recently. And it was true that her room had looked tidier than she'd remembered.

"Well?" Bel demanded.

"Well, what? It's nothing. Just a tacky book someone lent me."

"Which someone? One of that gang you were with in the caff at lunchtime?"

Cat stared. She and Bel didn't have these sorts of conversations. It was like being in some lame soap opera, something out of one of those magazines. "Have you been *spying* on me?"

"I saw you in the window, on my way to the post office. You were with that boy, the moody, thuggish one who's been hanging around. Plus another kid covered in leaves and muck, and some cheerleader type in the corner. An odd-looking bunch, aren't they? Not your usual type of friends."

But I don't have a type, Cat thought with an unfamiliar spurt of resentment. We never stay in one place long enough.

"Are they the ones who got you mixed up in this?"

Cat was afraid that guilt showed on her face, in spite of herself. "Mixed up in what?" she asked as lightly as possible.

"This Tarot card junk. It's morbid and nasty and I don't want you getting involved. All that mumbo jumbo is for people who're wrong in the head."

"Bel, it's just silly fortune-telling. Like horoscopes."

"Or those scratchcards you got so worked up about?"

"That's different. They—"

"I don't care. I'm having none of it. Not in my house."

It could almost have been funny, Bel laying down the law like this. But although her eyes flashed, and her hair seemed to flare redder, the way it always did when she was riled, Cat could see that her aunt's hands were trembling as she lit a cigarette.

"Why are you being weird? I don't get why you're so freaked out." Then a horrible thought struck her. The force of its impact was physical, and she had to sit down, as if winded. "Wait—unless . . . Bel, has this got something to do with my parents?"

Bel's lighter dropped onto the floor with a clatter. "I don't know what you're talking about."

"*No.* Don't mess with me, Bel. Not after everything. I need to know."

The power balance had changed. Now it was Bel who was looking shifty, Cat accusing.

"All right," said her aunt, heaving a shaky sigh. "Fine. It was your mum. She set a lot of store by those Tarot cards, till it got to the point she'd hardly make a decision without them. That's what these things do, see. They start off as a bit of fun, and before you know it, you're hooked."

"My mum was . . . hooked?" Cat whispered.

Bel looked even more uncomfortable. "Not really. I think she was just looking for some . . . distraction."

"I didn't know this. I didn't see this."

"See it? You were barely more than a baby. How could you?"

In the Arcanum. But of course the Six of Cups had given back only rose-tinted memories—the past's pleasures. The memory of tangling her arms in her mother's hair and being swung up onto her father's shoulders. Candles on the birthday cake, stars on the Christmas tree. Her father's smile and her mother's kisses, their every glance abundant with love ... There had been no shadows in that paradise. At least, not until her three-year-old self found an invitation to the Game.

"Did Mum ... did she ... did she ever talk about trying to win—trying to—using the cards to—" But Cat couldn't go on. The shadows had lengthened, solidified, and the perfection of her memories was spoiled.

Bel leaned across the table. "Listen here, puss-cat. Nobody's one hundred percent sunshine one hundred percent of the time. That doesn't mean your mum and dad didn't have a good life, or that they didn't love each other and you. Don't ever think different."

Cat gulped, blinking furiously to keep back the tears. "OK."

"And I'm sorry I had to bring any of this up. It's just ... well, you haven't been yourself lately. Stands to reason, what with finding out about the murders and everything. But coming across that Tarot book gave me a shock. I started fretting you'd been sucked in by all kinds of crazy ...

Anyway, I should've known better. Should've reacted better, too."

"Don't worry about it. Because you're right—Tarot's a load of rubbish and I don't want anything to do with it."

Bel smiled, relieved. "That's my girl."

THE TOWER

CHAPTER FIFTEEN

FLORA ARRIVED AT MERCURY SQUARE with the relevant passage from Ezekiel typed out, but even with the full text in front of them, nobody was any more enlightened as to the High Priestess's prophecy. Wheels, cherubs, cloud and creatures were as much a mystery as they'd always been. And there was more bad news on the Lottery front.

"I checked for updates online," Toby explained. "The websites are full of Lottery of Luck stuff. They say the cards have started popping up in other cities and countries, too. Just this morning there was a stabbing in Earl's Court—two blokes fighting over who got to play a scratchcard they'd found. One's dead; the other's in intensive care. Of course it turned out to be tails."

Blaine grimaced. "There're definitely loads more posters and flyers about. A grand prizegiving is set for New Year's

Eve, apparently. I saw it advertised on those massive video displays at Piccadilly Circus."

"That's not good," said Cat. "Remember my prophecy? 'Misrule's wheel shall burn at the turning of the year. . . .'"

The sun was setting, and the sky over the rooftops was a medley of crimson-washed clouds on a lilac sky, shot through with low amber light. At Cat's words, the red-stained horizon seemed to take on a particular menace.

"Time for us to get going, then." Toby held up the playing card he had taken from the High Priest. Like the other cards the old man had given them, it was blank on one side, with a pattern of interlocking wheels on the other. "Our first move in the Quest for Eternity. Who wants to do the honors with the die?"

He looked around at the others' tense faces.

"C'mon, team, this isn't the moment for hanging back. We're kings and queens of the Game now—"

"If you're going to say, 'With great power comes great responsibility,' I *will* kill you," Cat told him.

Toby grinned. "Not quite. Except—well—it's just . . . OK, none of us ever thought we'd end up fighting the Forces of Darkness. But here we are, with not much more than a blank card and a murky prophecy to go on. So . . ." He took a deep breath. "I suppose what I'm trying to say is, never mind about being in the grip of Fate and Luck and the rest of it. We're our own people doing our own thing. And that's what'll count, in the end."

"The end of what?" Flora asked. But nobody cared to answer.

The sunset filling the windows was exactly the same as the one over Mercury Square, but was even more spectacular seen at this height. Across the river, the jumble of office blocks and apartment buildings was silhouetted against the horizon, windows as small and bright as sequins.

"So what's the story?" Blaine asked Toby as, slowly, the illustration on the playing card swam into view.

"Er . . . Hold on. . . . Oh." Toby's face fell. "It's the Tower."

The Tower was one of the more infamous triumphs. As a prize, it gave the winner the ability to inflict destruction on a grand scale. As a move . . . well, the omens weren't good. The image was of a crumbling edifice struck by lightning as falling bodies, their faces contorted in screams, plunged from its heights. At the top of the illustration was a broken crown.

And the four kings and queens were in a tower, all right. A skyscraper, by London's standards: a mirrored pillar of glass and steel that reared up among its fellow monoliths in a Game of Triumphs version of Canary Wharf. The state-of-the-art office fittings were sleek and minimalist, and looked solid enough. But that didn't count for anything in the Arcanum.

"Why would the High Priest send us here?" Flora asked.

"He must have left us some instructions. Or our Game Masters' decks." Toby began pulling out drawers and flipping through folders.

Cat snorted. "I don't reckon kings and queens of the

Game keep their magic cards in a filing cabinet. In fact, I think we should cut our losses and—"

The door to the neighboring office opened.

"Not *you* again!" said a querulous little voice.

It was the High Priestess. She looked even more bedraggled than the last time Cat saw her, for the horns on her headdress were festooned with weeds, her damp hair hung in rats' tails and her gaudy scarves were sadly waterlogged.

"What—what are you doing here?" Cat asked blankly.

"I'm looking for my brother. We never used to be able to wander the Arcanum, but things are changing. Now he's lost among the cards and I can't find him." The girl sniffed plaintively and bent down to wring out her wet skirts. "It's all *your* fault. Whyever did you start that horrid flood?"

"I'm, er, sorry," Cat said. "It was my only way of winning the move."

Flora, Toby and Blaine exchanged looks. "So you're the High Priestess?" Blaine asked the girl. "The one who gives oracles?"

"The original and the best." She cocked her head at him, suddenly cheerful again. "Mmm, what nice eyes you've got. . . . Brown, aren't they?"

This was followed by a smirk in Cat's direction. Cat ignored it. "We're looking for the Triumph of Eternity," she said determinedly. "In the prophecy you gave me, you said that only the cherubim could summon Eternity. And that we had to make offerings to them first."

"Did I? How peculiar. A cherub is a type of angel, you know."

"Well, yeah. . . ."

"I'm only telling you because people often get them confused with Cupid. Who is *entirely* different and a *lot* more fun." The girl gave another sidelong glance at Blaine and gurgled with laughter. "But if you want me to prophesy what Cupid's got in store for you—or about anything else, for that matter—I'll need payment up front."

Cat had forgotten about the oracle's fee. "Anything shiny will do," she explained to the others. "Jewelry or whatever."

Blaine raised his brows. "Whoops. I must've left my diamond cuff links back at the squat."

Flora touched the little gold crucifix at her throat. It had been her sister's. She bit her lip.

"We can use this."

As quickly as possible, so as to get it over with, she undid the clasp and handed the necklace to the High Priestess, who nodded approvingly.

"Let the divination commence."

There was no burning oil or rolling eyes this time. Instead, the High Priestess wandered over to one of the floor-to-ceiling windows and breathed on the glass. She used her finger to draw a wheel in the condensation. As she did so, the smoky vapor spread. Strange symbols appeared within it, runes or hieroglyphics of some sort, which the girl examined gravely. She bowed her crystal-crowned head and the bangles on her wrists chimed.

"Yes," she said. "The cherubim. They are the fallen gods of the Game's city. To find them, you must start with the

Eight of Cups, and the guide who awaits you there. To summon them, you must renew their first offerings on the Game's board.

"The first offering is a knight, who sleeps entombed.

"The second is the fledgling of empire.

"The third is the Queen of Cats' King of Beasts.

"The fourth is led in triumph by its horns.

"These four will summon the cherubim. Yet only you can release them: outside the Arcanum, where the Game's play meets the play of your other world."

Then she breathed on the glass for a second time, and the mist faded away, taking the runes with it.

"All clear?" the High Priestess asked her audience.

"As mud," Cat muttered.

"Thank you very much," said Flora hastily. "You've been extremely helpful."

"Whatever." The girl yawned.

"That's funny." Toby frowned. "Can anyone else hear something? A kind of squawking noise?"

Everyone tensed. Their ears strained to pick up the sound. It quickly grew into a harshly croaking chorus as a flock of huge black-winged birds, the size of small planes, swooped into view. More and more joined them. Together, they formed a seething thundercloud of tattered wings and flashing eyes and claws. The sunset turned black under their shadow.

One moment the birds were high and distant; the next they were diving toward them, screeching loud enough to rip the sky in two. Their gaping beaks spat jets of forked lightning onto the city below. Before the five people in the tower could react, almost before they had time to be afraid, an explosion in the stories above set the whole building shuddering.

Through the window in front of them—its glass a mesh of cracks—they saw the monstrous flock streak away as swiftly as it had come, leaving a pulsing web of fireballs in its wake. They were perhaps four or five floors below the top of the skyscraper, but they could feel the heat of the conflagration overhead, and spumes of oily black smoke were already uncoiling from the ceiling.

The High Priestess clapped her hands, eyes sparkling. "Oooh! Isn't this *exciting?*"

Ominous crashes and crackings sounded as tongues of flame began to lick into the room, their flickers tinged with blue. The office block immediately next to theirs was already a column of fire, boiling and writhing upward, and spitting out a shower of metal shards. Its flames had a curious blue tint, like those on a Bunsen burner.

"That'll—be—us soon." Blaine was racked by coughing. "Let's get out—out of here—"

Cat turned toward the threshold wheel, which appeared as a screen saver on one of the nearby computers. But before she could reach out to it, another blast ripped through the windows on the other side of the room. This time, the force of the impact slammed them onto the floor. Before their appalled eyes, a wave of fire rolled toward them.

There was barely enough time to scream, even if they'd

had the breath to do so. Feeling as if he was moving in slow motion—though his actions were almost too instinctive for thought—Toby reached into his pocket.

A second later, the four of them, and the High Priestess, were enclosed in a sphere of flame.

This fire was bright yellow rather than livid blue, and its heat did not scorch their hair or skin. Instead, it seemed to beat back the conflagration's advance. Toby shakily held up the two pieces of his Ace of Wands.

"Fight fire with fire, right?"

Cat's eyes were watering so badly she could hardly focus on the computer screen and its wheel. Blinking hard, she ran her fingers over its lines to conjure the coin while the others crowded awkwardly around her. In order for several players to leave the same move at once, they all had to be touching the wheel when the coin was thrown. The High Priestess, meanwhile, was regarding the inferno admiringly. "This is *much* more dramatic than my move," she remarked to nobody in particular.

Cat stared down at her palm. "Something's wrong."

"What d'you mean?" Blaine rasped.

"The coin. It's . . . different." It was tinsel-bright silver rather than gleaming black, with a laughing head on one side and a serpent's tail on the other. Just like on Misrule's scratchcards. The High Priestess giggled.

Outside their protective bubble, wicked blue flames rippled and roared.

With deep misgivings, Cat tossed the coin into the air. Instead of sinking back into the flesh of her palm and flipping the four of them into a new move, the coin transformed mid-descent into a chocolate button. She rubbed disgustedly at the brown smear it left on her hand, then started to cough. Her breath tasted bitter in her throat.

"Let me try," Flora said hoarsely. She traced the wheel and got the same sparkly silver coin. When she threw it, a little white mouse tumbled through the air. Toby's attempt produced a plastic whistle.

"Try to make a new threshold, Cat, with your die," he said.

The same thing happened.

"It's Misrule," said Cat despairingly. "He must have fiddled with the thresholds so we can't get out."

"Bastard," said Blaine. "This ace won't hold forever."

It was true: their sheltering yellow fire had begun to falter against the onslaught of the blue.

Toby's predominant feeling was one of outrage. "This—this is all wrong. There *has* to be another way. We're *kings and queens!*"

"Really?" the High Priestess remarked brightly. "Well, in that case, why don't you use the amulets of your courts? I'm sure they'd work the thresholds just as well as those boring old coins."

More blue flames pooled on the ceiling, down the walls and along the floor, which began to buckle and creak. Smoke was roiling everywhere; the rest of the room was barely visible, except for a fleeting glimpse through the windows of red-stained sky.

"But—but we can't find—we don't have—"

"Silly! They're in the palms of your hands."

Cat stared at the faint line of the wheel's scar. She tried to remember how the High Priest had described the amulets. Something to do with the "blood and bone of kingship." Blood and bone . . .

She circled the scar with one finger, round and round.

And round again . . . until there was a hardness at her fingertip, a chill heaviness growing out of her flesh. From the root of her bone, from the beat of her blood, she summoned the essence at the heart of Swords. Metal rising, coldness rolling. Silver. A plain silver ball the size of a marble. An amulet.

Cat held her trophy up as the others gaped at her through a blur of choking smoke.

"*Told* you," said the High Priestess. "Well, I suppose it's time I was off, too." She smoothed her muddy draperies and straightened her headdress before leaning down to spin one of her bangles on the floor. "Bye-bye, everyone. Have fun."

In the fleeting time it took for the hoop of gold's revolutions to slow, falter and stop, the girl had vanished. Meanwhile, the protection given by the Ace of Wands had almost burned out. A few seconds more and the place would be a fireball.

"Keep hold of me," Cat managed to wheeze. She did not know what exactly the amulet could do or how she should use it but there was no time to lose. So she hurled it at the computer screen, smack into the middle of the threshold.

This was not like the toss of a coin, which flipped

a player, in a blink of eye and flash of metal, from one move to the next. As the die crashed into the wheel, everyone jerked forward. Their surroundings seemed to be whirling in one direction while they were irresistibly propelled in another. It was like being pulled in two directions at once while spinning at high speed.

Cat's last thought before the world changed was, OK, so now I know how a roulette ball feels.

The crimson clouds were the same. So was the wash of lilac sky and amber light, the square's railings and the stump of apple tree. Apart from their bloodshot eyes, and the reek of smoke clinging to their clothes, it was as if they had never left.

"Nice one, Cat," said Blaine creakily. His lungs felt swollen and raw as he took in deep, grateful breaths of air.

Toby was already circling a finger around his palm. "Do you realize what this means?" he said, repressing the last of his splutters. "We can conjure up cards just like the High Priest did! *This* must be how Game Masters control their deck."

Clutching his golden amulet, Toby bent to trace a rectangle on the trampled earth around the apple tree. A moment later he was holding up a card. He seemed to have plucked it out of nowhere, but there was a small stack of others beneath it.

"Two of Pentacles!" he exclaimed gleefully. "And look—here's the rest of my Pentacles suit."

Soon the others were following his example. Each found

they had a number of triumphs in addition to their court cards—presumably the winnings their predecessors had collected before being deposed. All the same, there were some notable gaps. Nobody expected to find the Triumph of the Hanged Man, but the High Priest, the Tower and all four aces were missing, too. None of the cards that Misrule had bestowed as prizes, or that they had played on behalf of the old kings and queens, appeared.

"It looks like once a card gets played, it's gone," said Blaine. "One strike and you're out. Well, we were warned our Game Master powers would be limited."

"But everything in the Arcanum happens for a reason," said Toby. "Like the High Priest leaving us the Tower to play. He must have known we'd get a new prophecy."

"I'm not so sure," said Cat. "Misrule could've planted the card on the old man as a trap. I reckon the Priestess turning up was a fluke."

"Either way, we've lucked out with our cards." Toby stroked the gilt edge of his deck admiringly. "Aren't they gorgeous?"

They discovered that if they moved the palms of their hands along the surface of a card toward their bodies, its illustration turned blank. Repeat the movement, and the picture returned. However, if they swept their hands over a card in the opposite direction—away from themselves—the card itself vanished. In this way, they could get rid of the whole stack in an instant. With their amulets literally at their fingertips, it didn't take much longer for a deck to be drawn up again.

The process was mesmerizing. Played about with like this, even the cards with dark associations lost their dread. Cat gazed at the Ten of Swords—the scene of murder that had first ensnared her in the Game—as if entranced.

Flora's voice snapped her out of it. "All right, everyone. We've got the cards, the amulets and a brand-new prophecy. Any thoughts?"

Cat shuddered. "Well, whatever the offerings involve, they're only going to summon the angels. It's still up to us to release them, so they can use their powers on our behalf."

"Release them how? And from what?" Toby asked.

"From the Arcanum, maybe," Cat said. "Mystic Meg seems to think that means playing the Game here, in our 'other world.'"

"We can worry about that part when we come to it. At least we already know our next move." Flora held up a card. It showed a hooded figure in a desolate, moonlit landscape. "The prophecy said a guide was waiting for us in the Eight of Cups. The guide might be able to tell us more about the angels, and what kind of ritual is required to summon them. Let's hope we don't actually have to slaughter anything."

"There's only one way to find out," said Toby cheerily.

Cat prepared to raise a threshold with her die. She had her amulet ready as well, to use instead of Misrule's treacherous silver coins. But to her surprise, she didn't need it. This threshold coin was plain and dark, just as it should be. It looked as if Misrule's powers over the Arcanum were not as widespread as they'd feared. Perhaps the disruption to the Tower's threshold was a one-off.

Everyone's spirits rose. As Cat tossed the coin, her thoughts, like the others', were preoccupied with winning Eternity. How defeating Misrule might mean the recovery of their own rewards . . .

She was certainly not thinking of the Minotaur, or his role in the High Priestess's first prophecy, and its hidden falsehood.

CHAPTER SIXTEEN

THE SETTING FOR THE TOWER had shared a close resemblance to the city they knew, but the Eight of Cups' location was unfamiliar. They were in a marshland of boggy pools, with rocky outcrops ahead and an overcast night sky above them. The other side of the threshold was apparent only in the remains of a garbage dump, for the wheel sign was in the spokes of a rusting bicycle propped against a waterlogged mattress and an old fridge. The reeds alongside sprouted lager bottles and syringes.

There was a stench of dirty water and rotting weeds. Ghostly lights flickered over the pools and within the chill mist that crept around them.

"Ugh," said Flora. "What a wretched place."

"It looked nicer on your card," said Toby. "And where's the moon got to?"

As if on cue, the ragged clouds melted away, and a mother-of-pearl moon sailed into view.

It was extraordinary the difference it made to the landscape. What had seemed murky and desolate was now flooded with eerie beauty. Opalescent light danced on the water and reeds, giving the mist that rose up from them a rainbow tint. Even the air smelled sweeter.

"We should stick close," said Cat, "and wait for the guide the High Priestess told us about. All too easy to get lost in this mist."

Everything had become too dreamlike for her to be truly anxious, but as the haze condensed into a billowing, creamy fog, and the others sank away into its depths, she felt a stirring of unease. Then she saw Flora emerge, her figure dim and gauzy, and farther away than Cat had thought.

Except it wasn't Flora. The woman's hair was darker and longer than Flora's. Her face was Cat's face, and Bel's, too, but different from both: shockingly familiar, impossibly real.

"M–Mum?"

Her mother smiled, and reached out her arms.

From the cloudiness behind, someone called out, "Wait—" but Cat didn't hear them. She was lurching into the mist and moonshine, their rainbow glisten flooding her with almost unbearable happiness. So her mum hadn't really been shot by the stranger. She'd managed to escape into the Arcanum. All this time, she'd been waiting for Cat to find her and bring her home—

Cat flung herself forward, blindly. She was pulled into an

embrace of soft, yielding flesh, and felt warm breath and tickling hair against her cheek. Both their faces were wet with tears. Cat closed her eyes. Without knowing it, she had been waiting her whole life for this moment.

"Cat, thank God. I—I was so frightened—I—"

It was Bel. Bel, dressed in her croupier's uniform of tight black skirt and low-necked satin blouse. Her eyes were wide and startled, darting round at the fog. Mascara had smudged down one side of her face. She held on to Cat by both arms.

"I don't understand. Where are we? What's happened?"

"You!" Cat choked out. She twisted herself free and backed away. "Why is it *you*?"

"Cat, don't look at me like that. I—"

"What have you done to my mother?"

"Nothing! It wasn't me. It wasn't my fault, I swear it. . . . Please, wait—don't leave me here!" begged Bel.

Cat would have thought that if she was going to be terrorized by a phantom, it would have been the man with the stammer and the gun, yet somehow this was worse. She could feel wetness ooze around her ankles and mud suck at her feet. She didn't care. She just wanted to get away. But the Arcanum-Bel still held out her arms imploringly.

"I'm so sorry, Cat. I didn't mean for it to happen. I didn't know what I was getting into. You have to believe me. Please—you have to forgive me. Please . . ."

The fog swallowed her up, and Cat was alone in the stinking, sinking bog.

"Toby? What are you doing here?" Mia asked, peering at him through a veil of mist.

"I'm searching for Eternity. So we can stop the Master of Misrule." Toby looked round for the others, but they must have wandered off somewhere. It was odd how little this troubled him.

"Oh. Right. Of course you are."

"So . . . what are *you* doing?"

She lowered her voice. "I'm looking for Mr. Marlow. Our fight isn't finished, you see. Two knights playing for the same triumph at the same time; only one can win. Those are the rules."

"But I thought you had to start a new round—"

"Shhh!" Mia held up a hand. "What was that?"

"What was what?"

She looked around nervously. "He's hiding in the fog. I saw him just a minute ago."

Toby drew nearer to where Mia was standing.

"Look! There—oh God—I saw something move." Mia's voice was taut with fear. She beckoned him farther into the gloom. "Follow me, this way. . . . We have to hide."

Toby's breaths came shallow and fast. The moonlight was playing tricks on his vision, so that everywhere he looked, he saw shape-shifting shadows loom out of the fog before falling back and dissolving into nothing. More worryingly, he could feel the ground beginning to soften.

"Mia, stop," he hissed. "We're in a swamp. It isn't safe."

"That's why we have to get away. Then we can circle back and catch Marlow before he catches us. Come *on*."

He stayed where he was.

"I'm not going any farther."

Mud sucked and tugged at his feet.

"It's our only chance."

"No."

"*Your* only chance."

Grace looked different than she had in the Eight of Swords. Her hair was wet and straggling, and the red evening dress was stained with mud. "Come on!" Grace called out from the nothingness. "Quick, Flo-Flo. We have to hurry!"

"Wait," Flora entreated. *"Wait."*

She hastened after her sister again, although this time there was no snow or briars, no drunken revelers, only pearly cloud, and cold waters seeping underfoot. Even as she strained for a glimpse of scarlet skirts and golden hair, she knew it was pointless. The apparition was as insubstantial as water vapor. Yet Flora stumbled on.

The fog rolled and rose around. Flora could barely see her own hand in front of her face. But it cleared a little, and she saw a tall, blond figure, standing—waiting—a few feet ahead.

"Grace!"

"Flo?" said Charlie's voice.

Tall, blond Charlie. He looked just as he had when they had parted in the study, a shock of hair falling over his clear blue eyes, a disconcerted frown on his face. Flora cursed the Arcanum, her sister and most of all her gullible, useless self. You fool, she thought. Did you really think it would be as easy as that?

221

"Flo—what is this place? I'm dreaming, right?"

She laughed bitterly. "Ghosts don't dream."

"How do you mean?"

"I mean," she said wearily, "that's all you are. An illusion. Another phantom of the Game."

"Funny," mused Charlie. "It doesn't feel like being asleep. So perhaps you're right. Perhaps I *have* died without realizing it. This is pretty much how I imagine limbo to be." He smiled at her. "Though I'm glad you're here to keep me company."

Flora turned away and looked for signs of the others, of real life, but there was nothing. It was just the two of them, alone in the fog blindness.

"Why did you think I was Grace?" Charlie asked.

"Because she was here."

"Her ghost?"

"Sort of." Then, forcefully, "But my sister's not dead."

"No. No, of course not."

"That's why I have to win Eternity: to bring her back. And to save the real you, along with everyone else." She regarded him ruefully. "Though you don't know it yet, I've put you in terrible danger. Misrule is my fault."

"I'm not sure I understand. . . ."

"It doesn't matter."

"It does if you're upset about it. I was thinking about Grace earlier. Today was one of Will's visits to the clinic, you see."

"Nice that someone still bothers."

"I suppose, even now, he feels a little guilty."

"Guilty?" Flora repeated sharply. "Why?"

Charlie tilted his head back to look at the sky, where a sliver of moon had briefly appeared. "Is this where you go, Flora?" he murmured. "The secret place where none of your friends can follow . . . Is this your other world?"

She shivered. The air felt colder, and the smell of slime and weeds had returned. "Listen, whatever-you-are, you have to tell me. Tell me why Will would feel guilty."

"Oh. It's just one of those stupid things. You see, Grace had a bit of a crush on him. During his playboy phase, unfortunately."

"That's—that's ridiculous."

"A couple of their friends knew about it. It's no big deal."

"Shut up. You're lying. Shut up. You're just another Arcanum lie, another trick—"

But her protestations were hollow. Flora had always wondered what had driven Grace into the Game, and what prize it could offer that her sister didn't already have. What, then, if this thing with Will had been more than an unrequited crush? Had Grace gambled on the Triumph of Love to make her dream come true? "Liar," Flora spat, though it wasn't any good. The phantom Charlie had spoken truths that the real person never would. Her sister had risked everything, lost herself, broken their family . . . and all because of a *boy*.

"Flo, don't cry. Everything's fine, you know: this is just a dream. And if it's not real, nothing matters because there's nothing to lose. I can say what I like. I can do what I want. . . ."

He leaned in, tenderly.

"It's *your* fault," she screamed. "You and your stupid brother. Your fault!" And she hit him across the face.

It made a satisfyingly loud smack. Her own hand tingled from the impact. Then Flora blundered away into the fog.

Blaine had been waiting for this moment for a long, long time. He'd dreamed of it, too—of being in a wasteland of cloud and shadows. Of knowing that Helen was lost and alone, crying for help, while Arthur stood over him and wouldn't let him pass. Arthur's eyes would gleam and he would moisten his prissy mouth in anticipation, the way he used to just before he'd hit him. *Boys will be boys,* he'd say as he pulled out the knife.

This was different. This was Arthur's nightmare. Blaine was king, a master of the Game, and the Arcanum was his hunting ground. As he crept through the coiling haze, he couldn't always see his stepfather, but he could sense his haphazard, halting movements, only a little way ahead. He could taste Arthur's fear. He could hear his whimpering, panicked breath and smell his sweat.

Blaine wouldn't need a knife. There were pools underfoot, shallow, but still deep enough to choke the life out of a man. . . . Stealthily, he pursued his prey farther into the marshes, along an increasingly tortuous trail. Each time he thought he had finally caught up with Arthur, his quarry would twist away, or the spectral fog-shapes would shift again, and Blaine would be left grasping a fistful of air. As time went on, he grew more and more confused by what he was following, and why. It seemed endless, these loops through the mud, these spirals through the mist.

A woman was crying somewhere. The sound was muffled and rhythmic, an almost mechanical keening, and was as familiar to him as—

Blaine paused. The sobs were disorientating and made it even harder to concentrate. He moved on. But although the noise grew fainter, it seemed to him there was something he had forgotten, something he needed to do.

He found her lying beside a boggy pool. Her disheveled hair hung down over her face, and she was tearstained and exhausted. She looked at him blindly.

"I thought it was *her*. I followed her. I thought it was over, that everything was going to be all right. But it wasn't her at all. It was just a trick."

Blaine crouched beside her. Above them, the tattered clouds cleared to reveal the moon. It wasn't the mother-of-pearl disc from before: its face was pockmarked and yellow. The pale billows and iridescent sheen had evaporated, leaving marsh slime and reeds, and a damp sky. Blaine took her hands in his.

"I know," he said tiredly. "It's OK, Cat. Nothing's what we thought it was, but I'm here, and I'm real. We'll be OK."

CHAPTER SEVENTEEN

BLAINE AND CAT SEARCHED for the others for a long time, but in the end they had to admit defeat. Although the fog had lifted, trails of vapor made it hard to see far ahead. Several times they slipped into pools where the mud sucked oozily, until at last they managed to reach higher, stonier ground. But though they called for Flora and Toby until their voices were hoarse, nobody answered.

"Do you think they're ... safe?" Cat faltered.

"Toby's smarter than he looks, and Flora's tougher," Blaine said brusquely. "They'll be all right, wherever they are." He rubbed his eyes. "But I don't understand. The Priestess *told* us to start with the Eight of Cups. The guide—"

"There was never any guide," said Cat. She was angry, but mostly with herself. "It was a lie—I see that now. The Priestess always tells one lie in every prophecy."

Blaine swore. "God. Of course. You told us about it in the café."

"That's why I had to face the Minotaur the first time around—to find out which bit of the prophecy was dodgy. It's my fault. I forgot."

"We all did. And even if we hadn't, it wouldn't have done us much good. The Minotaur might've known when his sister was lying, but he wasn't around to ask, was he?"

"I guess." Cat looked down at her hands. "Blaine . . . who did you think you saw? In the mists?"

"My stepdad."

"I saw my aunt. I—I thought it was my mum at first. That bit was like something from a dream. But Bel felt—acted—so real. *Solid.*"

"Yeah. It's just the usual Arcanum mind-messing crap."

Messy, but effective. The encounter with the phantom had stirred up fears Cat wasn't ready to admit to. *I'm so sorry, Cat. I didn't mean for it to happen. I didn't know what I was getting into. . . .* What had Bel got into, though? Cat was beginning to realize that there was a lot about her aunt that was still a mystery. Like the fact that Bel hadn't told her she'd lived in London before. It was the latest in a line of revelations, some big, some small, that nagged at the back of her mind. The way Bel had freaked out over the Tarot book was odd, too, almost as if . . .

But, no, she was being ridiculous. Of course Bel didn't know anything about the Game that had caused the death of her sister and brother-in-law. If she had, there was no way she'd have joked about Misrule's scratchcards. "This triumph card gimmick," she'd called it, and laughed.

Blaine was right, Cat decided. The Arcanum was making her paranoid, and she had to resist it.

"All right. So what do we do next?" she asked.

They looked at each other somberly.

"We go on," he said, "and hunt down these four creatures from the prophecy. Just like Flora and Toby will be doing, wherever they are. And whether it takes four of us, or two, or one, somehow we'll find a way of making things right."

Cat nodded. No matter what dangers lay ahead, she was ready for them. Although the state she was in when Blaine found her—collapsed and weeping, helpless as a child—should have been the ultimate humiliation, somehow she wasn't embarrassed. They were beyond that now.

"OK. Somewhere in the Arcanum, there's a bull, a lion, an eagle and a man. And the prophecy gave us clues to where we might find them."

"Right," said Blaine. "The man would be the knight in a tomb, presumably. Then the lion's the king of the beasts, and the bull must be the creature 'led in triumph by its horns.' What was the eagle again?"

"Something to do with empires."

Blaine frowned. "I've got an idea the Triumph of the Emperor has an eagle on it but I don't have the card. How about you?"

"Nope. Nor the one with a woman taming a lion. The Triumph of Strength, I think it is. Toby or Flora must have those two. But my Four of Swords has got a knight's statue on a gravestone. He could be our man."

"It's a start."

"And you know what?" Cat added. "There mightn't be a bull on any of the cards but there *is* one loose in the Arcanum. Or half of one, at any rate. The Minotaur."

"I thought you drowned him."

"The High Priestess didn't think so; she seemed pretty sure he's wandering around the Arcanum, just like her. It must be because of Misrule messing with the Game—the boundaries between moves are breaking down."

Blaine flipped through the stack of cards he'd drawn up with his amulet. "Um ... OK ... How about trying the Six of Wands, then? There're no animals on it but the illustration *is* of a triumphal procession. And our bull is meant to be led in triumph, right?"

They exchanged tentative smiles. It felt good to be working out the prophecy together, as if it was merely a puzzle or a crossword clue. Something abstract and manageable.

"So d'you want to start with trying to find the man or the bull?" Cat asked. "My Four of Swords or your Six of Wands?"

"If the High Priestess is looking for the Minotaur, too, it might be a good idea to get him out of the way first."

"Fair enough." Cat dropped a mock curtsy. "Lead on, Your Majesty."

Blaine grinned, and rolled the die. A new threshold, another move.

The Six of Wands took them into the middle of a carnival. The pavements were packed with people cheering a street parade as the sun blazed and a succession of floats trundled past to the oompah-pah of a marching band.

After the traumas of fire and mud, the party atmosphere should have been a relief, but Blaine and Cat found it over-whelming. All the noises were blaring and all the colors were gaudy, from the holiday clothes of the crowd to the garish floats and the town houses painted in vibrant pinks and yellows and blues. Every building was decked with bunting bearing the image of wands, and there was a hot, sharp smell of frying meat, exhaust fumes and burned sugar. Someone presented Cat with a stick of cotton candy and Blaine with a bottle of soda; somebody else placed card-board crowns on their heads.

The carnival displays were on the backs of trucks or on platforms towed by cars, with a few on horse-drawn wag-ons. The floats were adorned with figures from the Greater Arcana, though the triumphs had never looked so cheerful. Death was a prop from a Halloween party, his plastic skele-ton face grinning atop a rocking horse. The Lovers were two naked shop mannequins decorated with felt fig leaves; the Fool was a red-nosed clown; the Tower, a pink papier-mâché version of a Disney castle.

"Look!" Cat grabbed Blaine's arm.

This time, the oracle hadn't failed them. There was the Minotaur, following the High Priestess's float. The mutant was in a narrow cage on a trolley, pulled along by chains attached to his horns and held by three soldiers in ceremonial uniform. Behind them marched a troop of baton-twirling cheerleaders.

His body was the same exaggerated hulk that Cat remembered. Yet the Minotaur's huge, shaggy head was bowed, his eyes were glazed and he made no attempt to break out of his prison. The spectators certainly showed no fear at his presence. As the cage trundled past, people threw confetti and flowers, women blew kisses and men cheered.

Blaine attempted to force his way through the throng, moving parallel to the parade. "Keep up—we mustn't lose him."

Working their way along the tightly packed pavement proved impossible; the best they could do was to push their way to the barricades at the front. Blaine helped Cat scramble over the makeshift railings, and together they ran to join the procession. The floats were moving at such a slow pace that it was easy enough to swing up onto the nearest vehicle.

It was the Chariot: a red Christmas sleigh drawn by white fiberglass reindeer, with just enough room for two on the seat. They had forgotten they were still wearing the cardboard crowns, but as the spectators applauded and whistled and showered them with chocolate coins, it seemed the least they could do was give a regal wave or two. They ate some of the chocolate, passed the soda bottle between them and grinned.

As the sun shone, the cheerleaders pranced and the music played, the Eight of Cups seemed as insubstantial as its mists. A stream of rainbow bubbles bounced in the air. But the horned bulk of the Minotaur loomed ahead, a dark stain on the brightness.

The procession wound its way to an oval arena whose tiers of benches were buzzing with more spectators. The arena itself was just a plain, sandy space, about the size of two tennis courts, its railings decked with balloons and flags. A man in a white suit and chains of office was standing on a platform to the right of the entrance gates. His grin was even shinier than his suit, and he was flanked by two beauty queens in prom dresses and tiaras. A large plasma screen had been erected above.

The carnival procession forked at the entrance and proceeded to encircle the arena. When they saw that the Minotaur and his entourage had come to a halt in front of the gates, Cat and Blaine took the opportunity to get down from the float and draw near to the entrance themselves.

A drum rolled, and the mayor's voice echoed confidently around the gathering.

"Welcome, one and all, to our city's carnival day. What a parade, and what a spectacle it's been!"

The crowd whooped its assent.

"And now is the moment we've been waiting for. Friends and citizens, honored guests, we must solemnize as well as celebrate our festivities. It is time to make the final offering at our Triumph Games. Let us hail the sacrifice!"

The Minotaur's image was beamed on the plasma screen overhead, almost as large as life, as a little girl in a pink fairy costume skipped up to the stage. She was carrying a double-headed ax, which she presented to the mayor with a curtsy. He brandished it on high, and the blade winked in the sun.

Meanwhile, the Minotaur's escorts had unlocked the cage and opened the gates, prodding their prisoner through with long poles, so that he shambled into the center of the arena. Released from their chains, his curved horns were as brutally sharp as ever. But Cat remembered his face before he had made the change from man to monster—how his eyes had been human, and anguished.

"Blaine, I get that we're supposed to be making a sacrifice of some sort, but...the ax...this arena...It feels wrong. Messed up. What if we've made a mistake? The Minotaur isn't a proper bull, after all."

"I know. Still, we're not committed to anything, not yet. We'll just have to play along and see what happens."

There was no chance to talk further, for the mayor himself had turned to them, beaming and beckoning.

"Welcome, my friends. Come on, come on, don't be shy!"

Before they knew it, they had been ushered onto the platform and found themselves standing on either side of the mayor. "A big hand, please," he cried, "for the latest players in our Triumph Games!"

The crowd yelled its approval. The little girl in the fairy costume skipped and smirked. Under cover of the noise, Cat leaned toward the mayor's ear, trying to be discreet. "Um ... We're here for the Minotaur."

"Well, of course you are! He's waiting for you now."

The mayor's grin flashed brilliantly around the screen. "All *you* have to do is fetch him."

He signaled to one of the beauty queens, who stepped forward to present Cat with a battered leather collar set with six iron studs in the shape of wands.

"Just slip it over the beast's head, and he'll be good as gold," the man told them. "A lamb to the slaughter, one might say! No need to look so anxious," he added, patting Cat on the arm. "We'll ensure you're well equipped."

"With the, er, ax?"

"Good Lord no! It's only used for ceremonial purposes."

At this, another girl handed Blaine a metal rod, about three feet long, with a rubber handle at one end and two metal prongs at the tip.

Blaine looked at it disbelievingly. "That's it? A cattle prod?"

"Ah, but it's two against one." The mayor clapped him on the back jovially. "It wouldn't do to skew the odds too far in your favor. Now then, best of luck, and put on a good show, won't you? We're all counting on it!"

He grabbed them by the hand and swung their arms up in salute as the audience roared with approval. This time, it was their own image filling the plasma screen.

Since there was nothing else for it, the two of them went to stand by the gates to the arena, accompanied by a fanfare from the band and a frenzy of flag waving from the spectators.

"The Minotaur's not acting the same as he was with the

High Priestess," Cat muttered. "It's almost like he's been doped or something."

"Let's hope so."

Now that he was freed from the cage, they could see that the creature's body was bruised and battered, and that his movements lacked the savage force, and indeed grace, that Cat remembered from before. His bloodshot eyes were dull. But he was still formidable—over eight feet tall, his musculature as craggy as a rock.

Cat tested the weight of the collar. Her throat felt very dry. "How do you want to do this?"

"Our best chance is to sneak up on him from behind, I reckon. I'll distract him with the prod and try to draw him off." Blaine rolled his shoulders and shook out his arms, as if preparing for an ordinary fight. "Then you can try to work your way around and throw the collar over him from the back. After that . . . Well, let's hope it's somebody else's turn to deal with him."

"OK."

"We'll be fine. I promise."

Cat nodded as coolly as she was able. "I know."

Together, they walked through the gates. The band had ceased playing and the crowd was utterly silent, except for the crying of a child somewhere. On the screens at either end of the arena, their own faces loomed into the sky.

Blaine went forward to meet the monster.

The Minotaur lowered his head at Blaine's approach, snorting and blowing. As his bare right foot raked the ground, he raised a cloud of dust. A moment later, the Minotaur swung round to stare at Cat, and the leather collar. Before he could lumber in her direction, Blaine made as if to run at the creature, then swerved away and back at the last moment.

And so the dance began. The beast's wits were certainly befuddled, for he seemed unable to make up his mind as to which of his adversaries he should take on first. The Minotaur's reactions were so sluggish that Blaine felt as if he was locked in a crazed version of blindman's buff as he swooped first near, then far, pausing to draw the creature in, only to sway out of his path at the last minute. If Blaine showed signs of being backed into a corner, Cat would make a sudden movement or give a shout to draw the Minotaur off, to rapturous applause from the crowd. Similarly, whenever the Minotaur seemed ready to lunge at Cat, Blaine's feints with the cattle prod would goad him into another change of direction. Yet the creature was never distracted long enough for Cat to creep up behind him, or get close enough to risk flinging the collar around his bulging neck.

And as the flies droned in the heat, dust rose from the sand and the crowd whooped, it became apparent that while the two humans were beginning to flag, the beast was regaining his speed and strength. They couldn't keep this up for much longer. A couple of times, Blaine got in a jab with the cattle prod, so that the creature flinched from the electricity's fizz and backed off, tossing his head and bellowing. Yet as the Minotaur grew angrier, he also became more alert, as if the shocks had sharpened his blunt wits.

The creature grew bolder, until the moment came when Blaine slashed at him with the prod and the Minotaur didn't bawl or back away. Instead, he used his brawny arms to block any further assaults, and began to close in on his tormentor.

This time his advance was steady, purposeful and impervious to all Cat's attempts at distraction, all the screeches from the stands. In the Minotaur's shadow, Blaine looked like a small child waving a stick.

Cat realized that it was now or never.

She raced across the arena, and leaped up against the beast's broad, muscled back.

THE EMPEROR

CHAPTER EIGHTEEN

TOBY WAS IN TROUBLE. After Mia had gone, he tried to make his way back to where he had last seen the others, at the Eight of Cups' threshold by the dump. It didn't take him long to realize that he was hopelessly lost. The path, which had begun muddy, rapidly grew wetter and boggier. Soon he was floundering knee-high in a swamp. The more vigorous his efforts to free himself, the deeper he sank.

"Help!" he called out, and giggled weakly in spite of himself. It was all so *pathetic*. Stuck in a bog, bawling for rescue . . . Of course, there was no one to answer his cries. Everyone had gone, swallowed up by the marsh, led astray by its phantoms. The sludge was nearly up to his waist, and although he knew it would only make things worse, the spurts of panic rising in his chest made it impossible not to obey his body's instinct to thrash its way out of danger.

"Help," he cried again, at one of the mist-wraiths. Perhaps the ghost of Mr. Marlow was about to emerge and finish him off. Or Misrule himself. Although it was hard to be dignified when he was waist-deep in mud, he pulled himself as upright as he was able, ready to face what he had to.

"Toby," said Flora flatly.

She was standing on a clump of reeds and was almost as white as the fog.

"Are you really you?" he asked suspiciously.

Flora sighed in exasperation. "Don't be idiotic." The mist lifted a little, revealing a scoop of yellow moon. "All right. I'll be back in a minute."

He resisted the urge to beg her not to leave him.

Splashing and squelches sounded from behind. And exclamations of disgust. "Ugh. This swamp ... Vile ... Everything *stinks*. . . ."

Flora came back lugging the mattress from the dump. She spread it across the reeds, making sure it would support her weight, and gingerly lay down on her stomach. Then she reached out to Toby. "Here, take my hand. Please try not to get more sludge over me than you can help."

After several minutes of clumsy struggle, she managed to pull him free. The bog released him with a comical belch. Toby flopped out on the mattress, under the clear night sky, and laughed with relief. Then he looked around him.

"But, Flora ... where are the others?"

After much discussion, Flora and Toby came to the same conclusions as Cat and Blaine. There was nothing to do but press on in search of the creatures from the prophecy, in the hope that wherever the others were, they, too, were able to continue the quest. They would just have to trust to luck, and the Game, that they would find each other again.

Toby held the Triumph of the Emperor, whose illustration included the image of an eagle on a scepter. Flora's Triumph of Strength depicted a woman taming a lion. They decided to start with trying to find the eagle. The Emperor was an authority figure of sorts, so even if it turned out that they had misinterpreted the oracle, it was possible he could set them right again. "Plus, an imperial palace will be a big improvement on this swamp," said Toby.

Flora was distastefully brushing mud off her trousers. "I wouldn't get your hopes up. This is the Arcanum, remember."

Flora's pessimism proved justified. Once they had raised a threshold with their die, the card took them to the shell of a building that might have been impressive once but now lay in ruins, open to the skies. A sallow dawn was just breaking. As wind moaned sadly through cracked columns and tumbledown arches, the monumental nature of their task struck them with new force. Both thought again of Cat and Blaine, and the treacherous marsh pools they had left behind.

After wandering through a series of empty chambers and courtyards, they reached the main hall, the entrance to which was partly blocked by a mound of rubbish, marked off by red rope. Close to, they saw it was more like loot: statues, paintings, tapestries, glassware and goblets piled in a dust-furred heap. The other side of the hall ended in a broken colonnade, with a broad flight of steps leading down to a terrace. A man was sitting on a throne beneath the portico.

His skin was as fragile and lined as a cobweb, and his beard was cobwebbier still. He was wearing a tarnished breastplate, and had a dried laurel wreath on his head. Propped against the throne was a golden orb and scepter with a heraldic eagle at the end, just like on the playing card.

"Good, er, morning," Toby began. "I'm the King of Pentacles, and this is the Queen of Cups."

"Then I bid you welcome," the old man replied in a voice as withered as his laurel leaves. "For I am a king also, lord of all I survey." He tilted his head to indicate the paved terrace and the cliff edge beyond. Below it was a windswept plain of dead trees and rocky ground.

"It looks very extensive," said Flora politely.

The Emperor fidgeted with his beard, coughing, and leaned forward to peer at them with filmy eyes. "Hmm. You strike me as a strangely *muddy* species of Game Master. Kings and queens of the courts don't go grubbing about in the Arcanum. They deal the cards and roll the dice, and scheme and gamble from afar. Which seems a poor sort of rule—but then, who am I to talk?" His tone grew melancholy. "An aged man is a paltry, tattered thing. I, who commanded the boundless reaches of empire! The soldiers and sages, the lords and ladies, golden smithies and starlit domes . . . They've all gone. Everyone, everything." A tear slid down his wrinkled cheek. "Everything but my faithful Juno."

"Juno?"

"My queen of the heavens. See! She has been feeding, and now she comes back, replete." His ancient face became almost childish with pride. "Come here, my darling!"

There was a sound of great wings beating the air as a gleaming shadow swooped through the columns to perch on the armrest of the throne. As the eagle folded its wings, its feathers ruffled with a curious creaking sound.

The bird was made of gold. From powerful talons to feathered breast to cruel curved beak—every piece was metal, except for its ruby eyes. It bent its head to allow the Emperor to pet its chill neck, and uttered a hoarse cry. Something like rust stained its beak.

"Did you feast well, little one?" the Emperor crooned.

A gust blew across the terrace, carrying with it the stench of rottenness. Flora moved from under the shadow of the portico onto the steps. In the wan light, she could see a pale heap lying on the terrace with a glistening dark hole in its side.

"My last visitor," the old man told her. "A knight from your Court of Cups, I believe."

"You—you fed him to the eagle?"

"The player failed. His task was to steal a flame from the mountain, but the torch blew out. And so his liver is meat for my Juno here. . . . I don't see why this should disturb you," he added fretfully. "You are Game Masters, not common knights. *Your* days of risk are over. *You* may come and go as you please."

The eagle flapped its wings with a muffled metallic clash. Each golden feather looked razor sharp.

"You're right," said Toby abruptly. This wasn't an occasion for deference, he had decided. It was time to show the Arcanum who was boss. "The two of us are Game Masters. And while you might be Emperor in these parts, we're in charge of all the triumphs—including you."

"Toby," Flora hissed. "For goodness' sake! We can't just march in expecting—"

However, the Emperor did not seem affronted. "You wish for tribute?"

"Yes. We wish for the eagle, in fact. It's part of our bid for the Great Triumph."

The old man stared at the barren plain. "Ah, Eternity. I have vast deserts of the stuff; it is what all empires come to, in the end. As for their beginnings . . . Well, you must know the story of how the Game arose."

"Of course," said Toby impatiently. "The city lottery. But your eagle—"

"The city was a republic," the Emperor continued, as if Toby hadn't spoken. "A great republic, with winged and glorious gods. Yet when the city fell, the gods' fame fell with it. Even their names are forgotten."

Toby and Flora exchanged looks. Both remembered the High Priestess's description of the cherubim: fallen gods of the Game's city.

"There were no courts then," the Emperor continued, "but four guilds, which ruled the city between them. And when the Game grew to greatness, and a temple was built in its name, each of the guilds dedicated an offering to the gods. The guild of farmers presented a bull; the guild of soldiers, a lion; the guild of priests, an eagle; while the merchants' guild brought forth a man. And each was slaughtered on the temple's foundations."

Flora's eyes darted back to the torn body lying by the rocks. Her own flesh crawled. With such origins, no wonder the Game was so bloodstained.

"Like the gods they were given to, those first sacrifices are embedded deep within the Game. Here they endure— bull, eagle, lion, man—though in each round their form is a little different, their purpose new."

The Emperor combed his beard with shaking fingers.

"Now, most worlds are round, like an egg, but the Arcanum is the great checkerboard. It is said the temple's foundation stones still rest at its corners. And you are set to renew the first offerings, and summon the gods of old.... Who knows what cataclysms will be unleashed upon our board?"

"That's a risk we have to take," said Toby. "Starting with Juno."

He reached out a hand toward the bird, which spread its clanking wings, a span of at least eight feet, and snapped at him savagely. Toby flinched away just in time, as its husky cry rose to join the Emperor's wheezing laughter.

Flora pulled Toby aside. "Slow down," she said. "There's no point making demands until we're sure of what we want. Remember the words of the prophecy: 'the *fledgling* of empire.' That means a chick. A baby bird." She turned back to the Emperor. "Excuse me, Your Majesty, but . . . does Juno have a nest?"

The old man feebly pointed upward. "She roosts on the mountain's peak and guards its flame."

"There," Flora said to Toby with only a trace of smugness. "You see? We don't need Juno, but Juno's fledgling. So we have to find her nest."

"Mmm-hmm. Onward and upward," the Emperor mumbled. "Onward, upward . . ."

Toby followed Flora to the left side of the terrace, where a rough path wound farther up the mountain. Of course she was right about the wording of the prophecy; he was annoyed he hadn't thought of it himself. And yet . . . He cast a final glance back at the throne: the doddering old man, the eagle preening its feathers, the scepter and orb lying in the dust like discarded toys. Something was niggling at him. But whatever the thought was, it remained tantalizingly out of reach.

The palace had been built on a wide spur of rock that jutted over the plain. Behind its ruined walls, the mountainside towered implacably upward, its summit shrouded in cloud. A dim glow smoldered within the vapor.

"Mount Doom, I presume."

Flora pursed her lips. "If your next remark involves hobbits, you're on your own."

"OK. Last one to the top's an Orc!" Toby retorted cheerfully as he started on the path.

It didn't last long, meandering into a rough track that

petered out among a scrubby patch of bushes. Soon the steepness of the slope forced them to climb at a sideways tilt, one hand clutching at the ground for balance, their skidding feet sending a scurry of loose stones rattling in their wake. Flora, who had wrenched her ankle before Christmas, found it particularly hard going. And it got worse. The rocks became more jagged and the bushes more spiny, and the thin soil was replaced with grit and ash. In spite of the cold wind and clouded sky, it was hot work. The higher they climbed, the warmer the ground felt beneath their feet, and a smell of sulfur began to taint the air.

When they finally clambered, breathless, to the summit, they found a scorched wasteland from which twists of vapor writhed and hissed upward. The air was thick with sulfurous heat; the cindery ground within was cracked with rivulets of molten red. Outcrops of rocks pierced the surface.

In the center of this wilderness was a tall tree, as jagged and black as the rock it grew from. One bough, however, right at the top, gleamed with gold. There was a thorny tangle perched on its tip; high above that, a shadow wheeled through the sky. Juno was circling.

To get to the tree would mean a deadly game of stepping-stones across the smoldering embers; to reach the nest would mean a dizzying climb through spiky branches, up to where Juno's beak and talons would be waiting.

"This is hopeless," said Flora.

"But not *impossible*."

Crouching down on the farthermost edge of solid ground, Toby stretched out a leg to the nearest rocky foothold, testing the distance. "It's not actual lava, you know. There's a sort of ash crust keeping most of the heat in. And, look, I'm sure we could reach this bit of rock all right."

"And where would we go from there? We'll either get boiled alive or torn up for bird food."

Toby was ready to dispute this but somehow couldn't find the words, let alone the energy. His feebleness was more than just physical tiredness: the tainted air and stifling heat were making it hard to think. Instead, he got up to join Flora at the lip of the summit, looking out over the Emperor's dominion.

Seen from this height, it was vaster than either of them could have imagined. Apart from the mountain on which they were standing, the entire view was flat and featureless: barren rock curving away to the horizon, as far as the eye could see. Toby raised his hand to the sky, spreading his fingers and then clenching them, as if to grasp the world—a globe of gray in the palm of his hand.

And at this thought another one came to him: beautiful, shining, perfectly formed. He laughed out loud.

"Flora! We're looking in the wrong place."

"What do you mean?"

"Our baby bird isn't nesting on Mount Doom. It's been in the palace the whole time."

"But the Emperor said—"

"He said where Juno's nest was. He didn't say anything about what we'd find in it."

"What's your point?"

"You'll see," he said maddeningly.

Before Flora could interrogate him further, he launched

into a helter-skelter descent from the summit. She called after him angrily, but he ignored her and she had no option but to scramble behind him, and save her breath for the long climb down. It was quicker than their hike up, but not easier. Down they went, sliding and slithering among the dust and rocks and thorns, with grazed hands and bruised knees, grit in their eyes and stones in their shoes.

By now the sun was up, though it cast a poor, weak sort of light. When they finally reached the terrace, the ruined building looked less imposing than it had in the glimmers of dawn: its classical portico was municipal rather than palatial in style. Flora remembered the red rope around the treasure heap. On the other side of the threshold, she thought, there must be a museum where the relics of empire were more respectfully housed.

"Back so soon?" said the Emperor.

He was sitting up straighter, so that his chin was no longer slumped into his beard. For the first time, the remnants of strength could be traced in his profile, his proud hooked nose and fierce brows.

"We've come for that trib—tribute—you promised," Toby panted before having to pause to get his breath back. "Our eagle. This time, though, we know what we're looking for." He pointed to the stone block on which the throne was raised, and the emblems of power at its side.

"'Tis all a Checker-board of Nights and Days,"

the Emperor quoted in a voice of surprising firmness,

*"where Destiny with Men for Pieces plays, Hither
and thither moves and checks and slays."*

He bowed his head.

"A fitting tribute and wise choice. I shall be honored to make the offering to Your Majesty."

Slowly and stiffly, the old man bent to pick up the golden bauble that lay next to his scepter. He put it into Toby's hands as Juno swooped back to perch at his side.

The imperial orb was much lighter than one might expect, and oval-shaped rather than spherical. Not a globe, but an egg.

Toby cupped it in his palms, feeling the cool sheen of metal. Juno gave a gentle caw. Toby dashed the egg against the floor.

The shining shell split cleanly across, and rang against the stone. Inside, there was a miniature gold eagle, as motionless as metal should be, but otherwise a perfect replica of the living one.

Toby reached for the figurine, and the world changed.

Everything had turned to black and white. He was standing alone at the edge of a marble floor that was also a chessboard. Through its squares he thought he could see the model battleground from his bedroom, come to shadowy life. Or maybe it was the board Mia had shown him in the Chariot, the landscape and its inhabitants shaken into yet more disarray. It was as if the entire world of the Arcanum was contained on these checkers of black and white.

How had the oracle put it?

You must renew their first offerings on the Game's board. . . .

Unsteadily, Toby bent to place the gold eagle on the black corner-square. As he did so, the board seemed to shudder.

And when he straightened up, he was back in the Emperor's move. His hand was empty, but otherwise it was as if he had never left.

KNIGHT OF WANDS

CHAPTER NINETEEN

THE MINOTAUR WAS TOO quick for Cat.

Without even turning around, let alone breaking his stride, he jabbed his elbow into her chest with enough force to send her flying. Cat lay winded on the sandy floor of the arena, dark spirals floating at the edge of her vision. The roar of the spectators seemed very far away, and small, like the buzz of flies. Dimly, she was aware that something, or someone, was coming for her and she should probably try to get up. But her limbs were limp as string.

Meanwhile, yelling and cursing, Blaine jabbed electric shock after shock at the Minotaur. It succeeded in getting the Minotaur's attention back to him. Suddenly, a huge, brawny arm shot out and grabbed the cattle prod, twisting hard. As a tug-of-war, there was no contest: Blaine had to choose between being pulled into the beast's crushing embrace or giving up his one defense. He could only watch as the Minotaur snatched the slim metal wand and snapped it contemptuously in two. By now he had been backed toward a corner. The Minotaur planted his feet squarely, and then—snorting and steaming, his eyes flaring red—he lowered his head for the charge.

Blaine had little space, and less time. There was just enough room for a run and a leap. Before he could think through what he was doing, Blaine raced forward and grasped the bull's horns, then half hauled, half flung his body upward, so that his legs scrambled and kicked over the Minotaur's head. His feet found a ledge on the creature's shoulders, and he took advantage of the bull's temporary confusion to scrabble around so that he was riding on the Minotaur's back. For several long, hideous moments Blaine hung there like a monkey, his legs crossed under the bull's dewlap, hands grasping the horns, as the beast tossed his head and bellowed with fury. The crowd groaned.

Blaine's grip was slippery, his hands blistered. He could smell a hot animal stink and his face was flecked with foam from the beast's muzzle. Vast, calloused hands clawed at his legs, which felt absurdly thin and snappable. He leaned all his weight forward on the bull's head, hoping to topple him over before the bucking of his body could throw Blaine off. It felt as if his bones were humming, his teeth rattling in his jaw. At any second Blaine would be sent tumbling through the air. . . . Any moment now he and Cat would both be lying on the sand, their guts gored out in bloody heaps for flies to feast on. . . . Until suddenly Cat was there, too, flinging her arms around the Minotaur's knees, dragging the creature down.

All three of them crashed to the earth. Somehow Blaine was still on top, still clinging to the horns. As the monster thrashed and roared below him, he and Cat, swaying, breathless, scarlet-faced, looped the collar over the bull's horns and around his thick neck.

Instantly, the Minotaur's body went limp. There was an electrified silence: no movement or sound from the people in the arena or the surrounding streets. Blaine and Cat began to back away, breathing hard. They didn't have the energy to run.

With the wrenching, tormented groan Cat remembered from before, the Minotaur dragged himself up to his knees, putting his hands down on the ground for balance. Although the collar was only a thin loop of leather, the creature seemed to stagger under its weight. On all fours, he roared and heaved, and beat his animal head up and down, grunting, as the colossal body began to thicken and grow dark fur.

The crowd murmured.

Even as the bull-form grew more distinct, the shadow of a human body was still there, thinly visible both around and within the creature that—just—anchored it. Like a snake casting its skin, and groaning all the while, the animal stretched and twisted and rubbed himself against the ground, so that the shadow-flesh rippled into new substance and solidity. Until at last the beast was neither man-bull nor bull-man, but two separate beings entirely.

The bull was thick-bodied and short-legged, with a coarse black pelt and sharp, curved horns.

The man was dark and curly-haired. When Cat had last seen him, he had been convulsed with the savagery of his metamorphosis. This time his face showed liveliness as well as strength, and was lit by the dazzle of his smile.

For the marching band had begun to play again, and the arena was once more ringing with cheers.

Meanwhile, the bull blinked sleepily in the sun. Its tail twitched at the flies.

The man turned to Cat and Blaine. "I am Asterion," he said, "and I owe you thanks for my deliverance. Now and for always, I shall be whole again."

"Marvelous show! Splendidly played! Well done, well done."

The mayor had bustled up, grinning from ear to ear. The girl in the pink fairy dress pranced after him, holding the ax. With a flourish, the mayor took it from her and presented it to Blaine.

"The animal will go consenting to its sacrifice. An offering fit for a king!"

The iron blade of the ax shone dully in the sun. Blaine tested its weight, frowning.

"Perhaps," said Asterion, "you will allow me...." He looked at their doubtful faces. "Do not fear," he said quietly. "I know what you seek."

Trying not to look too obviously relieved, Blaine passed him the ax. The man stood beside the beast and placed a hand on his curly brow, murmuring something no one else could hear. The bull snuffled softly. Asterion braced his feet apart.

He swung up the ax, and struck it boldly down. The bull did not cry out, but choked a little, as scarlet spurted from the cleft in his neck and his great head lolled. The carcass twitched, and was still. So, too, was the crowd.

Asterion bent to pluck something out of the river of blood that was already soaking into the sand. A little bull carved from horn lay in the center of his palm.

He handed it to Blaine. As Blaine took it, the world reeled. He found he was looking down at a square of white marble in Temple House. Except that the hall was also a chessboard, and he was standing at its corner.

Blaine was not alarmed, nor even surprised. He understood that this was how their offering was to be made.

He put the bull down on the white square, and the ground quaked. And before his vision could adjust to the checkered paving that stretched around him, and the muddle of mountains and cities and plains that was somehow both above and beneath, he was back in the arena, smiling at Cat.

CHAPTER TWENTY

"ALL HAIL MISTRESS CYBELE, Queen of Cats!" a disembodied voice boomed.

The woman pranced forward to the edge of the stage, hips swinging and head held high. She was covered in gold body paint, and wearing spiky boots with a leopard-print leotard, slashed to the waist. A ringmaster's top hat was tilted provocatively on her head. As she swaggered back and forth along the footlights, she cracked a long leather whip to whoops from the stalls.

From their vantage point in the wings, Toby and Flora watched Cybele sashay over to where a cage, partially covered by purple drapes, had been wheeled onto center stage. A drumroll sounded, followed by a cymbal clash from the orchestra pit, as the woman whipped off the cloth. The cage contained a huge lion: the King of Beasts, and Toby and Flora's next offering.

The lion opened its red throat and roared.

The audience roared back, delighted.

The Triumph of Strength could not have been more of a contrast to the windswept desolation of the Emperor. Flora and Toby looked through the proscenium arch into a grand theater, its tiers undulating with gilded balconies. Everywhere was so festooned with chandeliers, velvet, and plump plaster cherubs that it was like being in the middle of a giant's jewelry box.

Meanwhile, the wings seethed with activity as stagehands and technicians checked props, and performers limbered up. The show itself appeared to be a hybrid of a zoo and a cabaret, and nobody seemed the least bit concerned that a lion had just been let loose onstage.

Toby and Flora watched as a succession of metal hoops was lowered from the flies. The rings varied in size and hung at different levels from the ground. Although the stage was large, the arrangement looked dangerously cramped—much more so when, at a flick of Cybele's whip, the hoops burst into flame. The lion growled and shook its head, but at a command from its mistress, it began to leap and twist through the fiery circles, weaving its way around the stage in a kind of graceful dance.

It came to a halt in front of the footlights, and roared again. The hoops had burned themselves out and were hoisted back up into the stage loft. Advancing toward the woman, the lion snarled and lashed its tail, aiming a swipe of its paw at her legs.

But Mistress Cybele cracked her whip and the beast at once crouched low, all aggression gone. Her own face was powerfully catlike, with its wide cheekbones, snub nose and slanting eyes. She tossed back her mane of tawny orange hair. Then she gave a gentlemanly bow, one hand on her hip, the other offered to the lion. Tenderly, it nuzzled her palm before rearing up onto its hind legs to join her for a stately waltz, paw in hand, its shaggy head resting on her shoulder.

The curtain fell to a standing ovation.

Toby and Flora shrank back to allow the lion tamer to stalk offstage, leaving a trio of stagehands to shepherd the great cat back into its cage.

"What are you?" she growled, baring sharp white teeth. Her body paint was smeary with heat. She slunk closer, sniffing them up and down. "Not knights . . . Nor knaves . . . Hmm . . . No, a different kind of animal entirely."

"I'm the King of Wands and this is the Queen of Cups," Toby replied, though not quite as boldly as he had announced himself to the Emperor. He had seen how the woman's muscles rippled as she cracked her whip.

Cybele's lip curled. "Well, a cat may look at a king, as the proverb goes, and *I* am Queen of Cats. And mistress of ceremonies at the Triumph Cabaret, what's more. If you're not here to play my card, you're wasting my time."

"As a matter of fact, we came for your lion," said Flora.

"The Emperor's already given us his eagle," added Toby.

"Did he indeed? Yes, I thought I felt a tremor on the

board. . . . Hmm." Her sneer softened somewhat and she clapped Toby on the shoulder; he could feel the prick of her sharpened nails through his shirt. "Very well. If you wish to make a play for Androcles, I won't stop you."

"Androcles?"

"My partner there." She gestured to the cage in which the lion was prowling restively. It was not the only big cat waiting in the wings: a panther and a tiger were dozing in cramped crates against the wall. "The Lion's Den is a thrilling climax for the show. After me, it's the most popular act." Her green eyes glinted. "But that only involves players who have failed to entertain. I'm sure royalty such as yourselves will have no trouble impressing the crowd."

Toby beamed. "You want us to join in the show? Excellent."

"What kind of entertainment?" Flora asked suspiciously.

"Well, you could test your nerve on the Wheel of Death." Cybele pointed to a pockmarked circular target board painted with Fortune's Wheel, and with ankle and wrist straps fastened to the spokes. "It's very simple: one of you spins while the other one throws the knives. Then there's the Iron Maiden." She indicated a glass box pierced with metal spikes. "Our contortionist can get in and out in under two minutes. But if confined spaces don't appeal, maybe you'd like to improve on the Starlight Sisters' aerial display."

They looked behind her onto the stage, where two trapeze artists were skimming through the air at dizzying heights.

Toby gulped. "Uh . . ."

"It's only fair to warn you that my patrons are accustomed to the *very* best," Cybele purred. "The most daring, the most beautiful, the most exotic . . . It will not be easy to win their applause. So whatever you decide on for your act, I hope for your sake that it'll be a crowd-pleaser." She shrugged sleekly. "Otherwise, you might have to try your luck in the Lion's Den, after all."

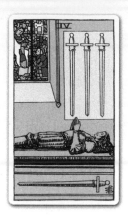

CHAPTER TWENTY-ONE

"I'VE BEEN HERE BEFORE" was the first thing Blaine said once they'd arrived in the Four of Swords and begun to look around them.

They were in a graveyard that was so large, with tombs so grand, it was almost a marble city. Cypress trees soared into the soft blue night, and torchlight warmed the white stone. Tiny lizards darted through the shadows.

"Was it when you first joined the Game?" Cat asked.

"No. When Misrule gave me the Knight of Wands, this was the move my so-called prize took me to. Should've guessed when I saw your card."

The Arcanum never created the same setting twice, and the first time Blaine had seen these effigies, they had been in the sculpture gallery of a dilapidated museum. The life-sized monuments were lavishly adorned with decorative pentacles, swords, cups and wands, and they all had carved figures on them, lamenting over urns, kneeling in prayer or lying in stately rest.

"There're knights sleeping in tombs as far as the eye can see," said Cat. "How are we to know which one is the man we need for our offering?"

She moved to look more closely at the effigies. Though they were uniformly dressed in flowing robes or chain mail, the statues were otherwise individual portraits, depicting men and women of all ages and physical types. Their faces were very peaceful. Although the memorials didn't bear any names, they did have epitaphs: DEARLY BELOVED. MUCH LA-MENTED. SADLY MOURNED.

Cat looked at Blaine hesitantly. "I s'pose you must have, uh, checked them before, in case you recognized your step-dad."

"Yeah. Took hours. I'd know his ugly mug anywhere but there was no sign of him—alive or dead." Blaine remembered the long, lonely wander among the galleries, examining each carved face for Arthur's features, regarding each shadow with suspicion in case his stepfather should suddenly spring out from the gloom.

His face hardened at the memory.

"I wonder what's the point of this move," Cat speculated, partly to distract him. "What a player has to do to win it, I mean."

"*We* don't have to win anything. We just have to find the right stone bloke."

After wandering around for a while, they reached one of

the tree-lined paths that quartered the cemetery. In the center of the junction where the four paths met, there was a block of white marble with an iron sword thrust in the center, so that half its blade was buried. Cat thought it might be a war memorial, but instead of a list of fallen soldiers, there was a single line inscribed on the marble:

UNSHEATHE THE SWORD, SUMMON THE SLEEPERS.

Blaine raised his brows. "DIY instructions—the Arcanum must be going soft."

"Was the sword here the last time?"

"Might've been. I wouldn't have paid much attention to it if it was. Arthur was the only thing I was bothered about." He reached toward the platform. Then he stopped. "Sorry. It's not for me to go grabbing. You're sword royalty, after all."

Cat smiled and shook back her hair. She jumped lightly up onto the block and grasped the hilt. The iron was bitingly cold, but when she tugged it, she felt the blade shift, deep within the stone. She was Queen of Swords indeed. "Whew. Here goes...."

As she began to pull out the sword, the cypress trees shivered, and torch flames danced. Blaine was seized by a sudden foreboding.

"No, Cat, wait—"

Too late. The sword slid cleanly out of its marble sheath. And the city of the dead awoke.

It began with a grating, grumbling sound, faint at first, and very slow. Stone lethargically scraped on stone. The effigies were stirring on their monuments.

Blaine and Cat watched with a fascination that turned to horror as the moving statues began to crumble at the edges and turn to dust. As the powder blew away, it revealed the bodies encased beneath. The memorial closest to them was of a woman holding a rosary; the figure's stony curls and smooth cheeks disintegrated to expose a skull, which turned and stared with empty sockets and a moldy-toothed grin.

"This," said Blaine, snatching up one of the flaming torches, "is not good."

Cat tasted a bubble of nausea. "God. It's like being in a zombie flick. Only with *really* special effects."

At that moment, one of the little lizards scuttled past the skeleton-woman's crumbling skirts. She stabbed at it, clumsily. Although her bone finger brushed only the end of the lizard's tail, the creature froze. In the blink of an eye it was covered in fine dust. Seconds later, this had solidified into stone.

"Not your average zombies, then," Blaine managed to say.

Cat's grip tightened around her sword.

"Look—there." She pointed down the eastern avenue. It led to a mausoleum even grander than any of the other memorials they'd seen: a black marble temple that had previously been shrouded in darkness. Now the building was lit up from the inside, and all the stained-glass windows were ablaze.

Could it be a refuge? Or was it a trap?

It didn't matter: there was nowhere else to go. One touch from a dead hand, and they would be rotting inside stone themselves. And so they began to run.

The sleepers' awakening was gradual and started from the head. When Blaine and Cat began their flight, nearly all of the dead were free of their stone casing only from the shoulders up. The frames underneath were mostly skeletons of brittle yellow bones. However, not all the relics were so ancient.

Corpses shrugged off dust from shriveled sinews to which scraps of skin and garments still clung. Even more hideous were those in states of recent decomposition. A few bodies were almost intact, though exuding a green clamminess and gusts of mold. Others were bloated and black and crawling with maggots. The smell of putrefied flesh hung sick and sweet in the air.

Yet as Blaine and Cat flung themselves down the avenue, their weariness almost overwhelmed the fear. I'm worn out, Cat thought resentfully. It isn't *fair.* Then one of the cadavers lunged out, sweeping an emaciated hand so close to her arm that she could almost feel the breeze of its passing. Suddenly it was as if she had been the one sleeping. Beside her, she heard Blaine's breath rasp.

Many of the dead had worked free from their monuments by now, and were joined in a shambling pursuit. As Cat and Blaine reached the last ten feet or so before the mausoleum's doors, they were close to being surrounded by a ring of cadavers who advanced slowly but persistently, oozing foulness. Some even had the power of speech. More recent corpses, who were still in possession of their tongues, gave soggy cries of rage and threat. Others gibbered with blackened gums.

Blaine lashed out with his torch. Cat, meanwhile, brandished her sword in a series of clumsy thrusts.

The sudden attack seemed to disconcert their pursuers. More by luck than skill, a shove of Cat's sword and a flaming swipe of Blaine's torch managed to fell two of the corpses at the same time. Their fellows drew back a little.

"Quick," Blaine panted. "Now's our chance. *Run*."

CHAPTER TWENTY-TWO

A STAGEHAND SHOWED TOBY and Flora to a cramped dressing room along the corridor, and informed them that their curtain call would be in fifteen minutes. The room was stuffy, and smelled of sweat and cigarettes. A froth of discarded costumes—chiffon, tulle and lace—littered the floor.

Toby tried on a feathered hat. "I can juggle a bit. At any rate, I don't usually drop the balls more than a couple of times."

"I doubt that and my collection of dumb-blonde jokes are really going to cut it," said Flora crisply.

"What about a vanishing act? One of us could disappear through a threshold."

"It would be rather an anticlimax when that person failed to appear again. Besides, we've already lost Cat and Blaine; I don't think we should risk splitting up."

"You're probably right." Toby turned to finger a set of

silver-and-blue pom-poms. "Flora . . . Don't you think it's strange we haven't seen any sign of Misrule since the Tower?"

She sighed. "If Eternity's the Great Triumph, and the only one he can't meddle with, it's quite possible he can't interfere with our search for it, either. His trick with the threshold coins didn't work, did it? Not now that we're kings and queens."

"I suppose. I just thought he'd put up more of a fight."

"Don't speak too soon. There's still time for him to appear in a puff of smoke and start throwing thunderbolts." Flora sat down in front of the mirror. The dressing table was littered with garish cosmetics; automatically, she began to sweep a cleansing wipe over her face. "Right now, though, worrying about what Misrule is up to is a distraction we can't afford."

"The Show Must Go On."

"Yes. And we have to find a way of starring in it."

Toby snapped his fingers. "I've got it."

Flora waited.

"And?"

"Seems obvious, really. It'll be a risk, of course. It has to be. That's what makes a performance exciting. But if we can pull it off . . ."

"*Toby.* What are you talking about?"

He doffed the feather hat. "A card trick."

Flora drummed a hairbrush against the table in exasperation. "Are you being deliberately stupid? Do you honestly think Catwoman is going to be impressed by a bit of fancy shuffling? We need magic and spectacle and—"

"Exactly. That's why it'll need to be an *Arcanum* card trick."

Toby drew up his cards, skimming expertly through the deck. "I was remembering what the High Priestess said in the Tower, about the boundaries between the moves breaking down. How characters from one card can now stray into another."

"So?"

"So how about we bring something exciting from another card into this one? Something magical and spectacular, like you said."

"Can we do that?" Flora asked, trying not to sound too hopeful. "How would it work?"

"I'm not entirely sure," he confessed. "But I think we could raise a threshold, draw a card ready for the next move and . . . tear it? That's how you play an ace. Of course, there's a risk that it won't work and we'll have destroyed a card with nothing to show for it."

"Or else we unleash something much worse than a few lions." Flora frowned. "I don't know. It's a clever idea, Toby, but . . ."

"It's our *only* idea. We're nearly out of time, let alone options."

There was a sharp rap on the door. "Two minutes, please," said a voice outside.

"There you go." Toby rubbed his hands. "Let's pick a card. And, Flora, don't take this the wrong way, but maybe you should put on a bit of lipstick or something. You're looking awfully washed out."

The stage was even larger than they remembered: acres and acres of empty space. High above them was a bewildering web of furled-up backdrops, grids and pulleys. Immediately in front, the glare of the lights made it difficult to view their audience. Toby found this a relief, but for Flora, the fact that she couldn't properly see the hundreds—thousands—of eyes fixed on her only made her feel more exposed.

Toby cleared his throat and heard his microphone crackle.

"I'm the King of Pentacles," he announced.

"And I'm the Queen of Cups," said Flora.

There was a stirring in the stalls. Somebody coughed. Several people laughed.

Toby's face burned. "Ladies and gentlemen, erm, honored guests, tonight is your lucky night. Yes. Because we've got something very special for you. In fact, we're going to perform a card trick."

The audience rustled and hummed, discontentedly. He pressed on.

"First off, my beautiful assistant will prepare the Magic Rites and Incantations. . . ."

Flora gritted her teeth but decided that now was not the time to dispute job titles. Instead, she shone her best party smile over the footlights, and bobbed a curtsy.

Her hand shook as she rolled the die along the stage. For added effect, Toby waved his arms in what he imagined were mystic gestures as a threshold wheel appeared on the floor, its patterns cast by a spotlight's lens. "Abracadabra! Hocus-pocus! Supercalifragilistic*arcanum*alidocius!"

Watched by the faceless, murmuring crowd, Flora held up the card they'd selected.

The Magician would have been the obvious choice, but neither she nor Toby possessed the triumph. Instead, Flora had taken her idea from the Eight of Cups; much as she had loathed the marsh and its treacherous mists, it occurred to her that now was the time to turn the Arcanum's trickery to their own advantage. And so she had suggested the card immediately preceding it. The Seven of Cups showed a figure watching a billowing cloud in which fantastical visions appeared: a serpent and dragon, a castle, a ghost . . . an angelic head and wreath of laurels . . . a chalice spilling jewels. Its formal title was "Reign of Illusionary Success." They would just have to hope that their own chance of victory wasn't about to vanish into thin air.

"With this card," Toby was saying, "we are going to conjure marvels for you. A world of mystery and miracles! Prepare yourselves to be amazed!"

At his signal, Flora tore the Seven of Cups.

Nothing happened.

Toby licked his lips nervously. "Any moment now."

Nothing.

"Sometimes the, er, magic needs a while to take effect. . . ."

The silence of the waiting, watching spectators was stifling.

"L-ladies and gentle—gentlemen," Toby tried. "Ladies and—ladies—"

Laughter now. And grumblings. Far back, somebody booed. Then somebody else did, much closer.

"If you'll just be patient, I'm sure . . ."

He shot an agonized glance at Flora.

Flora didn't return it. Her eyes were fixed on the threshold, where, at last, something was happening.

The threshold was growing. The flat patterning of the wheel—bright white light on shadowed ground—stretched out, from a circle the size of a bicycle wheel to a disc wide enough to encompass the whole stage. Dry ice began to rise from each long spoke.

Flora and Toby retreated to the side of the stage, their backs against a length of velvet curtain.

In the wheel's axis, where the four spokes of light met, something was thrusting and wriggling. Out of the center of the threshold, a knot of smoke-snakes began to coil and uncoil across the stage. The reptiles' bodies were almost transparent, their skins as thin as a soap bubble. Gasps of consternation rose from the stalls as the reptiles squirmed toward the footlights.

"Remember," Flora had told Toby as they left the dressing room, "whatever happens, this time we know that nothing's to be trusted. Whatever or whomever we see, none of it's real." Now it was Toby's turn for instructions. "Don't look so startled," he told her through the side of his mouth. "We're supposed to be in control of this show. Keep smiling."

Multicolored sparks were shooting from the wheel's axis, followed by puffs of much denser smoke. And suddenly there was a new creature onstage, its ghostly body scaly and horned, with wide, hooked wings: a smoke-dragon that pounced on the smoke-snakes and gobbled them whole, beating its wings in triumph before taking to the air and swooping into the auditorium.

The theater heaved with excitement and alarm.

Back onstage, the misty turrets and pinnacles of a fairy-tale castle had risen out of the threshold. The dragon swooped back toward the stage—where Flora and Toby ducked, clutching at each other for support in spite of themselves—and blew a plume of its breath at the battlements. More sparks flared from its mouth, and the hazy towers began to crumble, then melt away. So did the dragon.

Out of the dry-ice swirls of the ruined castle, a ghost emerged. It led a host of featureless fog-specters, wringing their hands and wailing piteously, who swept across the stage to float upward and outward into the theater. Their lamentation was so loud that Flora had to put her hands over her ears; the audience, too, cowered from the howling advance.

It was another vision that came to their rescue: an angel crowned with a garland of leaves, and with wings nearly as large as the dragon's. As the whirling ghosts ranted and sobbed, loud enough to make the chandeliers shake, the angel drew a cloudy sword and cut through the throng.

Ghosts and angel alike then dissolved into a shower of jewels, their sparkles falling thickly as confetti through the air. People leaped to catch the gemstones, clambering over their seats and scuffling in the aisles. But all they grasped was handfuls of smoke.

The dry ice ebbed away. The spotlight wheel switched off. The stage was once again bare. Silence fell.

Shakily, Flora and Toby walked to the footlights to take their bow. The entire building seemed to be holding its breath.

Then, from far away, high in the back of the upper circle, somebody started to clap. Three slow, deliberate smacks that echoed around the theater like the shots of a gun.

As abruptly as a switch being flicked, the theater erupted into applause.

THE MAGICIAN

CHAPTER TWENTY-THREE

THE DOORS TO THE MAUSOLEUM were closed. Cat and Blaine both hurled themselves against them at the same time, hardly daring to hope they would open. But the two of them got inside and bolted the doors behind them, shutting out the horror.

A knight's tomb lay in the center of the mausoleum's black-and-white checkered floor. This effigy was lifeless. His body was carved from gray marble and he bore a shield emblazoned with four swords. Candles burned at the windows, which were high and arched and filled with jewel-bright glass.

"Crap. The only Sleeping Beauty who the sword won't summon," said Cat. "Of *course* he'll be the one we want."

"At least we're near a threshold."

Blaine pointed to the base of the memorial, where the sign of the wheel had been worked into a marble wreath.

Then he gave the base a kick. "C'mon, mate. Time to rise and shine."

They tried shouting at the knight. Tugging his arms. Prodding him with the sword. Drawing the sign of the wheel, commanding him to Rise in the Name of the Game . . . They would have felt ridiculous if the situation wasn't so desperate. At one point Cat caught Blaine's eye and almost giggled.

A moment later, there was a scraping, clinking noise at the window. They froze. The clinks and chinks continued, followed by a crash. One of the stained-glass panes had been broken, and a wizened black arm was stretching in.

"It's no good," said Blaine tersely. "We can't wake him. Maybe it's the wrong knight or the wrong card. Either way, we should use that threshold and get out of here."

"None of it's wrong. You know that as well as I do. There's *got* to be a way."

More tinkling glass as another window broke. More withered hands clawed at its frame. The openings were too narrow for a normal body to squeeze through, but skeleton shoulders were a different matter.

"If we wait much longer, there'll be two new statues in the graveyard."

"If we give up on this, we're lost anyway."

They glared at each other helplessly. A scabbed skull, still trailing wisps of hair and flakes of skin, chattered its teeth at them from behind broken glass.

"All right," said Blaine suddenly. "All right. I see it now. This here is our last chance."

He seized Cat by the arm and roughly pulled her toward him.

"Kiss him."

Cat drew back.

"That's how it works in the fairy tales, right? Sleeping Beauty, you called him. Yeah, the conventions are screwed up, but so is everything. He's a knight; you're a queen. Wake him up with a kiss."

"This isn't—what if—" What if the statue's mouth turned to dust, and then decay, that sucked her into a last, festering embrace? But the alternatives were no better. She took refuge in insouciance. "OK. Whatever. Guess there's nothing to lose."

Cat stood by the knight's head, and lightly put her finger to the curve of his lips. As she did so, she forgot about the throng of horrors outside, and the bone shoulders already wriggling through the window behind. The carved stone face was strong and serene, as a prince's should be. She bent low and, very gently, put her mouth on his.

Blaine tensed as the girl's warm lips met the man's cold marble ones. His own breath was quick and light. Cat looked up; her hair tumbled and fell across the fearful brightness of her eyes.

The air shivered, and candle flames danced. Stone lethargically scraped on stone, and there was a long, soft sigh.

The sleeper was waking.

Unlike the effigies in the graveyard, he did not shake off his marble casing, but moved in it. The living statue blinked his stone eyes, flexed his stone hands and slowly swung his stone legs over the side of his platform. Then he knelt on the floor in front of Cat. "My Queen," he said.

Though she hardly knew how or why she did so, Cat touched the tip of her blade to his shoulders.

"Arise, Sir Knight," she said, and handed him the sword.

It was not a moment too soon. A skeleton had just sprung from the window onto the checkered floor, with a clatter of yellow bones. Its grasping fingers were only an inch from Blaine's neck when the knight lunged at it with his blade. The intruder disintegrated into a brittle ivory heap.

Cat and Blaine climbed onto the deserted tombstone for safety as their defender cleared the besieged mausoleum. Just as the dead lumbered at a stilted, unsteady pace, the man of stone did not move quite as quickly as a man of flesh and blood. But there was a heavy grace to his motion and a relentless precision to every stab and slice of his blade.

Less than a minute later, all the invaders had been dispatched, and calm had been restored. The knight strode toward the doors and crashed them open.

The rest of the dead were waiting outside in the torch-light, a ghastly army of the damned. Some of the corpses murmured, others called out and stretched their shriveled arms, but none of them made any further advance on the mausoleum.

The knight held up his shield, and struck his sword against it four times. The iron clanged on the stone and the ground seemed to tremble.

A fine, pale dust began to swirl off the bare slabs and empty pedestals of the abandoned tombs. The breeze blew it around emaciated flesh and bones, where it settled in a thin layer. As the dead stiffened where they stood, the layers grew thicker, softening angles, restoring weight and covering the rot with marble smoothness.

"Come," said the knight, striding forward. Cat and Blaine found themselves following him down the avenue, toward the sword's original platform. Both tried to avert their eyes from the frozen throng of half specters, half statues that crowded their path.

Cat felt another wave of tiredness. After the struggle with the Minotaur and the flight to the mausoleum, her limbs were heavy and sore, and about halfway down the avenue she began to fall behind. She had just started to catch up with Blaine when she heard a human voice. One of the stone-corpses was speaking to her.

"P-please," it stammered.

Under a film of dust, the thing—person—looked intact, with no evidence of decay. The stone powdering had not yet obscured his hooked face and silvery hair. She thought it must be a player who had only very recently failed this move.

"I b-beg—" the man croaked grittily. The marble had already hardened as far as his waist and more dust was swirling into his mouth and eyes.

Cat couldn't bear to watch. She hurried on to where Blaine and the knight were waiting by the sword's plinth. "There's a man back there, a player, who's still alive. His body's whole, anyhow."

"So?"

"So we can't leave him to rot away inside a statue. We can still save him." She turned to the knight in appeal. "Can't we?"

He regarded her gravely. "As long as the dust has not settled."

"What do I need to do?"

"It is breath that gives life, even to a stone heart. And it is breath that may blow the dust away."

"I'll come with you," said Blaine.

"No, stay here. I'll do it myself."

It was hard to explain, but Cat felt, as Queen of Swords, that this was her responsibility. The Four of Swords was a card from her suit, and it was her predecessor who had dealt it to this poor man—and all the other people beyond her help. Before Cat could suppress it, she saw the image of another card, the Ten of Swords, showing a different kind of corpse: a man with a cluster of swords in his back. That had been the first card to draw her into the Game, and the first player she had failed to save.

When she returned to the statue, she thought it was already too late. Every part of him appeared solid marble. Yet when she looked closely, she saw that faint traces of powder still swirled over the figure's carved surfaces. After a moment's hesitation she leaned and blew softly into his face. Her breath stirred the dust, which started to float away again, almost imperceptibly at first, then in pale, thick drifts. "You'll find a threshold in the mausoleum," she told the player as his fingers began to twitch and eyelids flicker. "Good luck."

Cat didn't wait to see the whole process of transformation. Surrounded on all sides by statues, she felt isolated and exposed. In her eagerness to finish the move, she hastened away and didn't look back.

Blaine was waiting for her. "Everything OK?" he asked anxiously. "Are you all right?"

The shadows under his eyes were like bruises. He was exhausted. So was she. But he looked at her with an intensity that made her heart stammer.

Before he could say anything else, she came up to him and kissed him. It seemed to happen of itself, like blinking against dust. They clutched at each other, wordlessly. In this world of chill marble and dead flesh, their own warmth had never felt so powerful or so fragile, so fearfully alive.

Afterward, Cat drew away, and smiled at him through her tumbled hair, as she had by the knight's tomb. The rest of the graveyard and its effigies were motionless. The flames were bright, the marble smooth, the night air free from any taint of corruption. From the plinth, the gray knight was watching over his kingdom.

"Now," he said, "I am free to offer myself to you. This time, my sacrifice shall be a willing one."

He knelt down and turned the sword so that the point of its blade was aimed at his stone breast.

"No!" Cat exclaimed.

She started forward, but Blaine held her back. "He knows what he's doing."

The knight bowed his head. "Farewell, my Queen."

Then he thrust the weight of his body down on the blade. His face remained as serene as ever.

There was a deafening crack. The stone around the sword's piercing began to crumble and turn to dust. Yet when the sandy powder blew away, no underlying body was revealed. Instead, all that remained was a stone chess piece. A gray knight.

The applause rang on and on.

It pounded at Flora and Toby's ears. It rattled their heads long after the curtain had fallen; it tingled through their veins.

"Not bad," pronounced Mistress Cybele. She sauntered over with the lion, Androcles, on a leash. "The act needs polish, of course, but on the whole, yes, quite an amusing little piece."

"You're too kind," said Flora dryly.

Cybele flung back her tawny head and laughed. "I expect I am."

She led them through the back of the theater to the stage door. It opened onto a savanna of silvery grasses under a midnight sky. Cybele sniffed the air appreciatively, then handed Flora the lion's leash.

"Sacrifice is not always about payment or suffering, however ritualized. Sometimes it is simply a release."

Flora nodded to show she understood. The lion waited quietly as she reached into its coarse, warm fur to unclip the leash.

Free at last, the King of the Beasts shook out its mane and, in one great bound, leaped away from the theater, into the wild grasses. Its former mistress watched impassively.

Flora was left holding the leash. Now that she could look closely at the clasp, she saw that the fastening was decorated with a polished yellow gemstone, carved in a lion's form.

Jewel lion, stone man.

Black and white.

Large and small.

The empty board, the marble hall, the teeming landscape . . .

As Flora took the lion and placed it on her black corner-square, and Cat took the knight, placing it on her white, the chessboard violently heaved. It was as if someone had picked it up and shaken it. In their separate moves, Toby and Blaine felt the world shudder, jerking them to the ground. For a brief moment the kings and queens faced each other from the four corners of the board.

There was another thunderous crack and rumble, like breaking rocks, and the print of the wheel on their palms glowed silver-bright. It was the only light in a void of darkness. There was a rushing sound, like the beating of mighty wings.

The cherubim had been summoned.

But when the quake and crashing stilled, and light returned, each of them was alone, and outside the Arcanum. The chessboard had thrown them off.

THE DEVIL

CHAPTER TWENTY-FOUR

WHEN THE COMMOTION SETTLED, Blaine found himself standing in a run-down shopping street. The scene was shocking in its ordinariness.

Perhaps they had failed, then, and the earthshaking tumult that had brought him here had expelled him from the Game. Or maybe it was some trick of Misrule's. . . . Blaine rubbed his hands over his face, trying to steady his thoughts.

How long had he been in the Arcanum anyway? Hours? Days? Longer?

He turned to a grandmotherly type who was just coming out of a launderette. "I'm sorry," he said blearily, "but I . . . er . . . What day is it?"

She looked at him curiously. "The thirty-first, dearie. New Year's Eve." Curiosity turned to nervousness as she took in his strained face and disheveled appearance. After the Arcanum treatment, the clothes he'd borrowed from Flora didn't look that different from his castoffs.

Blaine had to lean against the wall to collect himself. He didn't know what to think. He was sure he was back in his own time and place. This was the London of the every-day world. And yet . . . something wasn't quite right. Off-kilter.

"You've dropped your postcard, dearie."

Blaine looked down. There was a playing card at his feet: an enthroned goat-god with black horns and jagged wings. Dumbly, Blaine picked it up.

The Devil.

The most fallen angel of them all.

But an angel nonetheless, he realized. One of the cheru-bim. One of the fallen gods of the Game's city. Like an echo of memory, the High Priestess's prophecy came back to him: *Only you can release them: outside the Arcanum, where the Game's play meets the play of your other world.*

So Blaine's last move in the Game of Triumphs would not take place in the Arcanum. He had summoned the Devil and now he must play his card. The other three must be facing their own final moves, too, somewhere else in the city. Though how releasing the Devil into the world would bring about the Triumph of Eternity and defeat of Misrule was anyone's guess. . . . I hope the High Priestess knows her stuff, he thought grimly.

Meanwhile, the old lady peered at the card. Her face sharpened with alarm. Blaine had grown used to people taking a second look at him and backing away, but her fearfulness shook him, all the same. He had a futile impulse to call after her, tell her it was OK. That he wasn't whatever she was afraid of.

The wheel on his palm began to glow steadily. He sensed the essence of the Arcanum underneath every surface, as close and secret as a second skin.

And ahead of him, a shadow was oozing slickly along the ground: a shadow of something that wasn't there. It was already dusk, but the shadow was a deeper black than shadows usually are, with two long, curving horns and a jagged spread of something that might have been wings.

Blaine followed the Devil along the road.

The shopping street fed into a nondescript housing estate. Most people appeared to be indoors, preparing for the approaching New Year's festivities. The yellow windows and blue flicker of television screens felt as distant to Blaine as the lights of an airplane winking overhead.

Soon the shadow had drawn him into a grid of increasingly lifeless streets. At the end of one, however, he could see people and movement, and a different kind of blue flicker. This one belonged to the flashing lights of a police car. It was parked outside a corner house with boarded-up windows and a tumbledown roof. The two houses next to it were similarly dilapidated. The patchy garden at the back was quietly teeming with activity, which had drawn a knot of spectators onto the road.

The oily black shadow poured itself into a gutter and disappeared.

Blaine stood at a distance from the other onlookers. The low garden wall gave them a good view of the mounds of earth inside, and the comings and goings of the police officers and forensic team. In spite of the bystanders' mutters of dismay, their excitement was obvious as they watched a lumpy thing in a zip-up bag being put onto a stretcher.

Since the Arcanum, Blaine knew what death smelled like. He could smell it here, too. The faint, sweet stink of corruption . . .

"They say it was a dog, digging, that found the body," somebody behind him was saying. "It's been buried for nearly a year."

"Shocking," murmured somebody else.

"That's modern life for you," agreed their friend. "Country's going to hell in a handbasket."

"The neighbors can't b–believe their luck," the man nearest to Blaine observed. He was tall, wearing an expensive-looking coat, with a bony, hooked face and silver hair. "It's even better entertainment than TV."

Blaine looked closer. "I know you," he said. "It was before last Christmas. You came looking for Arthur White. My stepdad." He paused. "I'm looking for him, too."

"Then," the man replied, "it seems you've f–found him."

Blaine swallowed hard. His eyes flinched away from the thing on the stretcher, though it seemed to him that he had already known what it meant. A dull inevitability closed around him. "But—we're not in the Arcanum . . . are we?" He knew, instinctively, that the man would understand his question, just as he also sensed that no one else would pay them any attention at all. For all intents and purposes, the two of them were alone.

"Not quite. But then, the unfortunate Mr. White never got as f-far as the Arcanum. I went instead, you see." The man gave a thin smile. "And I was doing very well, until my misadventure in the Four of Swords."

It was then that Blaine realized that the smell of rot wasn't blowing over from the sad, huddled body in the bag, or the freshly turned earth. It came from the man next to him. Glittering particles of dust still clung to his hair. He was the player whom Cat had freed from the statue in the graveyard.

You have brought a new player into the Game, and a new knight for my court. . . . That was what the King of Wands had told him. But the new knight wasn't Arthur. It was this man. It was this man, too, who had been lost in the Arcanum. All this time, Blaine had been chasing a ghost.

The scar along his arm began to ache and he pushed up his sleeve to trace its familiar line. The oily black shadow pooled at their feet and stretched out again. Arthur was dead. Arthur was *dead*. He didn't yet know what this meant or even what he thought about it. He felt light-headed and hollow. Nothing felt real—not yet.

"Tell me what happened."

"Your stepfather had arranged to sell me his invitation to the G-Game. He'd stumbled on something he didn't understand and had no use for, whereas I had been waiting for such an opportunity to c-come on the market for a long, long time. . . . And when it did, I took c-care to ensure mine was the highest bid."

The Knight of Wands began to walk leisurely down the road. The black shadow followed him and so did Blaine. The damp in the air had begun to condense, forming small drifts of mist.

"When Mr. White failed to k-keep our appointment for the sale," the knight continued, his voice gentle as ever, "I became concerned. That was when I went to his home and you were so k-kind as to inform me that the police were after him. My concern grew. The police and I . . . Hmm, let's just s-say they have an ongoing interest in me.

"However, thanks to our enc-counter, I did have a lead. Or rather a line: Temple House, Mercury Square."

With a rush of sickness, Blaine remembered the quiet suburban street and the bench at the bus stop. Arthur's notebook, casually open to the sketch of his invitation card.

"It was not much to g-go on, but luck was on my side. I took a chance that Mr. White had g-gone to London, and managed to intercept him on his way to the square in question.

"I brought him to this place. I reminded him of our deal and requested my card. Unfortunately, your stepfather refused to listen to r-reason. He appeared to be in various kinds of t-trouble, and believed the Game was his only w-way out of it. His behavior was—well, unhinged. I regret to say that our subsequent d-disagreement grew violent."

"You mean murderous."

"Indeed. But you must understand that my search for an invitation to the Game has been long and d–difficult. It began with a card I won in a bet, and which was subsequently stolen from me. That was nearly t–twelve years ago."

Blaine clenched and unclenched his fists. For the first time, he understood the true nature of his intervention in the Game. He had set in motion the train of events that led to this man killing Arthur and joining the Game in his place. But there was something more. Twelve years . . . a missing card . . . and a man who murdered for the Arcanum.

He was struck by a new and terrible inevitability. It took all his strength to ask the next question. "That first invitation card. Did you—" The words clogged in his throat. "Did you get it back?"

"No. But an eye for an eye, a tooth for a tooth . . . and two bullets for a stolen c–card."

Two bullets . . . a stuttering man . . . was this the killer of Cat's parents? Blaine stifled a gasp.

"Mind you, when I finally obtained a new invitation, it was worth it," the Knight of Wands continued. "Even though I wasted months in my first move, l–lost in one of the Arcanum's labyrinths. The second move was more easily won; the next was the Four of Swords. But here, too, Fortune f–favored me."

He leaned closer, so that Blaine tasted a gust of rot. "I would offer c–condolences for the loss of your stepfather, but I doubt you need them. A 'vicious maniac,' I think you called him. . . . Would you like to hear how he died?"

Blaine backed away. "I—I—I don't know."

"Of course, it may be that you would have preferred to do the job yourself. But I can still tell you how he whimpered and sniveled and begged for m-mercy."

"I didn't want to kill him. . . ."

Or only in dreams, thought Blaine, like when I was lost in the fog. No, I wanted to drag Arthur back to face what he'd done. I wanted him to suffer and be shamed and for the whole world to see. I wanted Helen to look him in the face and call him a monster.

The hollowness inside had filled itself, grown heavy and scorching. "I'm not some psychopath," he said hotly. "Not like you. Christ—what's so great about the Game that you're ready to butcher all these people just for a way into it? Once you're there, everything's a nightmare and a swindle anyway. You'd still be rotting in that graveyard if it wasn't for Cat. The girl *you* orphaned. But she's a Game Master now, she's a queen, she—"

Then he stopped. Appalled, he listened to the echo of his words.

"Cat, you say? Well, well. Perhaps I should have known, however brief our encounter. The family resemblance was s-striking."

The Knight of Wands laughed a little. "Life's rich irony! So many tangled webs . . . and all their threads seem to l-lead back to this Game of ours." His voice grew brisk. "But now's the time to t-tie them up. Or cut them off, rather. I don't like to leave loose ends."

Fog rolled down the street, swallowing up all shapes and

shadows, including the silver-haired man. Perhaps the Devil had spirited him away; perhaps he was the Devil himself. But Blaine no longer cared about the High Priestess's prophecy or the fallen angel he was supposed to release. Leaving his final move unfinished, and its angel unreleased, he blundered off in the direction he thought the knight had gone, thinking only of Cat: the loose end in a murderer's web.

CHAPTER TWENTY-FIVE

"OI, MATE, SHOVING WON'T get you nowhere, all right?" said somebody ahead as they moved another inch toward the foot of the escalator. Two escalators were down at Piccadilly Circus, and late afternoon on New Year's Eve the Underground station was at a rowdy, jostling standstill.

As Cat trudged up the motionless staircase, the moving panels along the wall flashed with glittering blue wheels on a black ground. TAKE YOUR CHANCE TONIGHT! they invited. PRIZES FOR ALL! The silver heads from Misrule's coins seemed to wink at her, and she had to pause, suddenly breathless. "Please . . . ," she heard herself wheeze to no one in particular. Her abrupt halt nearly tripped up the woman behind. Cat began to mumble something—an apology or appeal—but the woman turned away, her expression blank and impenetrable.

Outside the station, Cat's disorientation only increased.

She was out of the Arcanum, yet she felt she was moving through the landscapes of dream. Illuminated billboards shimmered under a leaden sky, flashing words of promise: HEADS YOU WIN, TAILS YOU LOSE.

In front of her, winged Eros hovered, forever drawing back his bow. His body was slick from rain. The trickling of the fountain below the statue should have been a soothing noise, yet it set Cat's teeth on edge. Her eyes smarted at the neon signs. Every nerve was jangling.

She half expected to see two men and a woman, in dark clothes, lean and purposeful, emerge from the station's east exit. The card she was looking at should have been the Ten of Swords; it would have been fitting for her Game to end in the same way as it had begun. But when she had reached for her travel pass at the barriers, she had found a different kind of card in her pocket. An angel card. Her next, and final, move.

The Triumph of Temperance showed an angel with one foot on a rock and the other in a river, measuring liquid between two chalices. The landscape was bathed in the light of a setting sun. Her wings were red, and white lilies grew in the shade by the river's edge.

It struck Cat that the angel's face was similar to Justice's, though not so stern. Whatever was being balanced between her vessels, it involved a judgment of sorts. But how was such an angel to be released?

The trickling of Eros's fountain grew louder; Cat looked up from her card to see that his wings had grown, their aluminum feathers rippling with life. He—or possibly she—

held out two vessels toward her. Cat blinked, and the statue was the boy aiming his bow again. He seemed to be aiming it at Lower Regent Street. The smell of lilies, a heavy, somber sweetness, and the sound of running water drew her down the road.

Cat followed Eros's arrow, but she did not know what to think when she reached the discreet black-and-green awnings of Alliette's. As she hovered on the pavement, a long silver car drew up to the entrance and a doddery old gent heaved himself out, followed by a younger woman whose luxurious mink stole failed to soften her gaunt frame.

Cat trailed after them, all too aware of what a guttersnipe she must appear. But when the couple went through the doors, the perfume of lilies grew stronger, and the concierge's eyes passed over her with perfect indifference.

It was the same once she was inside. People looked at her without really seeing her. She drifted through the club lounge and the champagne bar, the first-floor gaming hall and up to the second-floor suites, listening to the click of chips and shuffle of cards, the politely social hum. There was none of the seedy exhaustion that permeated the Palais Luxe, and very little obvious excitement, either.

There was a fountain in the lobby, and Cat could still hear its gentle splashing behind the background noise. The collective glister of all the mirrors and gilding and cut glass reminded her of Temple House. She looked through a door and saw four people playing cards around a green baize table. There were two men, one of them black, a woman dressed in white and a darker one in furs. But the woman in white turned to reveal a tanned, bony profile, and when the younger man laughed, Cat saw he was Chinese. None of them were people she knew.

The sweetness of lilies and murmur of water increased until she reached the stairs at the end of the hall. They led up to a private gaming salon that was closed for refurbishment. Paper had been stripped raggedly from the walls, and the floor was littered with builders' and decorators' tools. The only light came from a cheap desk lamp.

Bel was sitting on a chair by the fireplace, staring listlessly at something in her hand. She looked up as the door opened.

"Cat . . . ?" Her aunt blinked at her, bewildered.

She should have been more than bewildered, of course. Tearing hair and spitting nails, in fact. It had only just dawned on Cat that she had been gone overnight, without a word. But Bel's manner was like that of a sleepwalker who hasn't quite woken up.

"I wasn't feeling right so my manager sent me home," she explained vaguely. "I had a funny turn, they said."

"But we're not at the flat. We're at the casino."

Bel looked around in bemusement. "Oh . . . I see. So we are. I could've sworn . . ."

Cat drew nearer to the chair. Bel was wearing her croupier's uniform of tight black skirt and low-necked satin blouse, but she was in nearly as much disarray as her niece. Mascara had smudged down one side of her face, and there was mud on her skirt. The same mud was on Cat's jeans. Mud from the Eight of Cups.

Cat looked closer. Bel was holding something in her hands, stroking it over and over. It was a gilt-trimmed card, thick and richly colored. The Triumph of Eternity was pictured on the front.

"Where did you get that card?"

Bel didn't answer.

"Do you know what it is?" Cat's voice was harsh with fear. "Do you?"

But Bel shook her head and shivered and did not speak, her eyes glassy with unshed tears.

"Where did you get that card?"

"I dreamed it," said Bel at last. "And when I woke up, it was in my hand. I dream of it all the time, Cat. Every night it goes dancing through my sleep, in a shower of dark coins. At least . . . it used to. Not so much anymore. I thought it was going to leave me be. I thought . . ."

And this time the tears did fall.

Shudders of dread were running up and down Cat's spine. She was shaking so hard that she could barely speak. "In the swamp . . . you begged me for forgiveness. Why?"

"What?"

"You were in the swamp with me. You remember. I know you do."

For just as the boundaries between moves in the Game were breaking down, so were the boundaries between the Arcanum and the ordinary world. Cat understood that now.

"I had . . . I had a funny turn. . . ."

Cat crouched by her feet. "Please, Bel," she said softly, helplessly. "Tell me how you found the card."

The invitation to the Arcanum turned this way and that, flashing through Bel's quick croupier's fingers.

"It's not mine," she whispered. "It never was. I stole it from him."

After a long, echoing silence, Bel got up and stood by the window. Her shivers had stopped. When she began to talk again, her voice was tired but calm. There may even have been relief in it.

"I was eighteen. That's not an excuse, course it's not, because in lots of ways I was older than my years. Those ways were mostly the wrong ones, though.

"So I left for the city and didn't look back. My mum had died the year before; my sister Caroline was twenty-six and had her own family. Age gaps don't count for much when you're adults, but growing up, it felt like a world apart. Dad scarpered when I was little and Mum and Caro had done their best with me, but I ran rings round them like it was an Olympic sport.

"When I got to London, I had enough confidence for ten people. I'd come to find my fortune, see. And I got a job pretty quick, cocktail-waitressing at a West End bar. They had these uniforms: silver lamé, the skirts split up the thigh. . . . I thought I was the bee's knees.

"Anyway, there was a casino attached to the hotel next door, and sometimes the gamblers came round to us to toast their success or drown their sorrows, as may be. I'd only been working there a couple of months when I met Alec. Alec Crawley. He came in with a gang of bankers one afternoon. And the next night he asked me over to the casino, to help him win.

"Alec was always very charming, with this stammer that made everything he said sound gentle, somehow. He used to call me Red. Although he wasn't the obviously dashing sort, he had a way of looking at a girl like she'd melt quick as butter. He'd made his money in Russia, so the gossip went, and owned a club in Chelsea. The waiting list for membership was a mile long and it was only ever open three nights a week. The other nights he used it for business. I didn't ask what this business was.

"I wasn't his only girl, I knew that, but he saw more of me than the rest, and thought more of me, too, so I flattered myself.

"When Alec wasn't at his club or the casino, he spent a fair amount of time in these crusty old antique shops and libraries. Treasure hunting, he said. Occasionally, he'd drop everything to follow a lead, and dash off for a day or so, though he always came back bad-tempered.

"The other thing he did was Tarot cards. Time and again, I'd find him spreading them out on his desk, poring over them like a treasure map. They gave me the shivers, to be honest. Once I told him that fortune-telling was for old women and little girls. Afterward, I was afraid. He looked at me so coldly I felt as if someone had shoved ice down my throat. Then he laughed, and he said he'd already made his fortune, and was on the hunt for a new kind of gamble. The biggest wins were yet to come.

"I thought he meant poker. He took it seriously as any cardsharp.

"Anyhow, one night I was meant to be meeting him at his club, and he was late. When he finally arrived, he'd been out drinking with his buddies and had forgotten I was supposed to be there.

"However, he said he was celebrating because that day he'd found something he'd been searching for for a long time. He patted his coat pocket and smiled. It was a lucky day, he said. Then he gave me a kiss. *You're the second of my treasures, Red.*

"He told me to stick around to mix the drinks and so on for their poker game. I wasn't keen. I didn't much care for his friends and there was one who really gave me the creeps: this big, swarthy chap with fat hands. I didn't like the way he looked at me.

"So they drank and they smoked and they played their cards. Toward the end of one round, the swarthy man— Mathers, I think he was called—said he wanted to mix things up a little. Make the stakes more interesting, he said. 'Fine,' said Alec. 'What do you want to play for?' 'The Queen of Hearts,' Mathers said. And he leered toward me. 'I'll raise you my flashy new sports car. My car for your girl.'

"'All right,' said Alec. And off they went.

"I couldn't move. I couldn't speak. Nothing. I just waited, this silly smile stuck on my face like it'd been chiseled there. I didn't know who I was anymore. It was as if some other poor chump sat at the bar and the real Bel was watching her from far, far away.

"Alec won in the end. Mathers chucked over his car keys like it was one big joke, though everyone could see he was sore about it. There was a lot of laughter. Old Alec winked at me. Ha-ha, no hard feelings.... And then they started another hand.

"When I brought him his next drink, I made it a double. He'd been drinking for a while, and was far too pleased with his winnings to notice. And I brought him another couple after that. Then I said I was going to bed. Alec stayed in hotels mostly, but he had an apartment over the club, too. When I said good night, I even managed to smile.

"It was near daylight when he came up. He was drunker than I'd ever seen him. Hardly able to stumble into bed. And when I was sure he was out cold, I reached into his coat. Just to see. I don't know what I was expecting: the key to a safe, a portrait of his dear dead mum.... God knows. What I found was a funny kind of card. There was a picture of a wheel on the front, and an invitation on the back. Something about a house and a temple, cards and coins. And I thought of Alec talking about his treasures, and how I was the second one, so I took the card, and left a poker chip instead. That's what I was worth to him.

"Then I walked out of the club and all the way to the station, still in my party dress and my sparkly heels. And I left the city and I didn't look back."

"But he . . . Alec . . . he came after you."

"Yes."

"He came after *us*. My mum and dad. He—"

"Yes."

"He came after the card."

Bel hung her head low. "Yes," she said. "God forgive me, he did."

"I turned up on your parents' doorstep with no warning, no luggage, nothing. I said I'd split with my boyfriend and lost my job, and didn't know where else to go. Straight off, Caro made a bed up for me on the sofa and told me not to worry, everything would work out for the best. Adam said their home was mine, for as long as I wanted.

"I told myself I'd put all the other crap behind me. I looked into taking some courses—maybe even going back to college—and helped Caro out with you, and around the house. I wanted to prove myself like I never had before.

"I kept finding different hiding places for Alec's card. I couldn't imagine why the invitation was valuable, and yet something kept drawing me to it. It was so beautiful, you know? It was in my pocket for a while, then tucked in my bedclothes, behind the fridge, under your parents' bed. . . . I wanted to forget about it, but I couldn't let it go. Finally, I tore it up.

"A couple of weeks went by. I had my birthday and we celebrated together, the four of us. A family. And the next Saturday, I offered to take you on a visit across town, to stay overnight with an old friend of our mum's. I thought it'd be nice for Caro and Adam to have the place to themselves for once. I thought it would be nice to give them a night off.

"And that was the night . . . that was the night . . . the night . . ."

Cat watched stonily as her aunt fought to compose herself. After a while, Bel was able to speak again.

"As soon as I came back the next morning and saw the police car in the street, I knew what must've happened. I knew that Alec had caught up with me, I knew what he'd done. What *I* had done.

"The house was trashed. Some druggie, the police thought, looking for a fix. A burglary gone wrong. I knew better, of course.

"I was the only person who could connect Alec Crawley to the crime. Maybe his revenge on me had only just started. So as soon as I could, I got some bits and pieces together, took you and began the first of our disappearing acts.

"From then on, it was just the two of us. I changed my name. I changed my hair. I changed as much about me as I could manage. Those first years, I moved us every couple of months, and never stopped looking over my shoulder.

"Then I started to put some feelers out. On the sly, and in secret, I took the risk of getting in touch with people who knew people who knew Alec. And I heard that only a couple of days after your parents died, the police came looking for Alec on account of something else entirely. He'd had to leave the country in a hurry. Rumor had it he'd gone to ground somewhere in the Far East.

"As time went by, I felt safer. We stayed put in places for longer. I didn't start and quit quite so many jobs. I went back to being a redhead and a loudmouth. I started to relax.

"Then last year, I heard a whisper that Alec Crawley was dead. He'd got on the wrong side of some powerful people, and his crimes had caught up with him. We were safe, both of us. So I came back to London to start again."

Bel's voice had been steady enough, but now her face crumpled and she began to gasp and gulp dryly, like someone starved of air.

"You have to believe me, Cat. I knew Alec was dodgy, a bit of a crook perhaps, but I never dreamed . . . It's not like I'd talked to him about my family, or where I came from, but if I'd known what he was, what he was capable of . . . God's truth, I swear I'd never've—I swear—I—"

Cat swallowed. Her fists were clenched so hard that the whites of her knuckles poked through the skin. "OK. Your part in my parents' deaths was an accident. You weren't that much older than me and you'd stumbled into something you didn't understand, not until it was too late. And I know . . . that is, I can see how one wrong turn can change your life." She drew a wavering breath. "So, yeah, maybe I can understand how it happened. But not how you could lie to me about it. About *everything*."

"I—I lied to protect you."

"And yourself."

"How could I face you with the truth? I couldn't even face it myself."

"But I found the truth out anyway. Or half of it: how there was no car crash, only murder. I confronted you, and you apologized and you cried. We both did. And then you *kept on lying*. And *lying*. It was Alec you were thinking of, not Mum, when you found my Tarot card book, wasn't it?"

Bel looked away.

"Don't you see what you've done?" Hot tears sparked from Cat's eyes. "It was supposed to be me and you against the world, together, always. And now—"

"You once said that nothing could change what we have," Bel whispered. "You told me you wouldn't let us be changed, not by anything."

At that, Cat felt the violence of her grief take hold. "Don't you *dare*. Don't you dare throw that back at me. Christ! I've spent most of my life on the run without even knowing it."

All those years! A long, colorless blur of new places, new faces, new starts. She wasn't just an orphan, but a fugitive. Self-sufficient and solitary, the Cat who walked by herself. Until, that is, she found the Game. Or it found her.

"My whole life . . . ," she echoed.

"Yes. And my whole life is about trying to give back just a little of what you lost. God knows, Cat, I haven't been much good at it. But I have tried. Not just because I had to, but because trying to keep you safe, to make you happy, is the best thing in my world. And I will keep on trying as long as there's breath in my body."

Bel put out her hand, and Cat saw instead her mother, opening her arms. She closed her eyes and saw her father, swinging her up onto his shoulders. *Where's my kitty-cat?* The memories returned to her by the Arcanum had always had an otherworldly brightness, but now she could trust them again. Neither her mum nor her dad had known about the Arcanum or the Game or the card that killed them. Their stolen happiness had been real. The enormity of her loss flooded over her as if for the first time: she was drowning in it.

Bel's voice seemed to come from very far away.

"Don't you see? I lied partly to protect you, and partly because I was ashamed, but most of all because I couldn't bear it, Cat. I couldn't bear to think of you looking at me like you are now."

Cat met Bel's wide gray eyes, the eyes that were also her own, and her mother's. "Because," Bel finished quietly, "you are my everything."

A long silence fell. Cat walked back and forth, arms wrapped tightly around her chest. The perfume of lilies was nauseatingly strong, wound through with the trickle of water. She shook her head furiously to clear away the scent and sound.

"That book you found in my room," she said at last. "*The Wondrous World of Tarot.* Did you look inside?"

"I . . . Yes, a little."

"There's an illustration of Justice, you see, holding her sword and scales. I used to look at it and think about my parents, how it was the only thing I could ever hope to give them.

"And then there's this other picture: Temperance.

There's a note saying she's the spirit who guides the dead down into the underworld. But first she weighs their souls in her cups. First she makes her judgment.

"I don't want to judge. I want justice to be *done*. But how can it?" Cat looked at Bel with hard, cold eyes. "I don't know what justice means anymore. I don't know what any of this means. I have no certainties, *nothing*, because you've taken all of them away from me."

"Once a thief, always a thief," said a voice in the doorway. "H-hello, Red."

CHAPTER TWENTY-SIX

THERE WAS SOMETHING FAMILIAR about the art gallery and coffee shop across the road, but it was only when Flora looked to the right of the bus stop, toward the tree-lined green and tennis courts, that she realized the Arcanum had taken her to the neighborhood of Grace's clinic.

She frowned at the card in her hands. Surely this represented the angel she'd summoned and must now set free. The Triumph of Love had a gentle face, but it still put her on edge. Love was the prize Grace had played for. But it was Flora who must win it, so the cherubim would come swooping in in a blaze of glory and save the day. That way she would save her sister along with everyone else.

And now somebody was hurrying toward her, calling her name.

"Thank God!" Charlie exclaimed. "I wasn't sure if you'd

got my voice mails. I'm sorry they were so garbled. Your parents are already with Grace—"

Flora clutched his arm. Unthinkingly, she shoved the card away into her pocket. "My parents are here? What's happened?"

Charlie put a hand over hers. "Flora . . . I'm so sorry. Your sister has had some kind of seizure, they think. No one's sure what's going on. She's stable now, and the doctors are doing all they can, but they don't think she should be moved. We've all been leaving messages for you. People were looking . . ."

He glanced at her stricken face. "Never mind that. Doesn't matter. Between the three of us—me and Tilly; Mina, too—we got you covered."

As they walked together, Charlie talked on, quickly and nervously. He told her how the doctor had phoned the Seatons' house yesterday evening, when only Mina was there, and then got hold of her parents in France. How her mother and father had caught the first flight back and gone straight to the clinic. How he'd helped concoct a story to explain Flora's absence (a mislaid note, a sleepover, a dead phone), and how—well, like he said, that stuff didn't matter now.

"Because I think you should know . . . at least . . . I think you should be prepared. They . . . the doctors . . . they think this could be . . . the end."

"The end," Flora echoed softly. "The end of everything."

In his distress, Charlie was flushed and wide-eyed. She

noticed the mark of a bruise on his cheek. There was something odd about this, something she felt vaguely responsible for, but it was hard to stay focused with the Arcanum so near. She was feverish, distrustful of the ground beneath her feet, as if it might suddenly shrug and once more send her crashing through darkness.

When they finally turned into the clinic's stone entrance gates, the wheel-scar on her palm glowed so noticeably she had to thrust her hand under her jacket. She realized the last time she had seen these walls and windows, she had been stumbling across snow, a woolen doll in her hands.

Flora was only dimly aware of reaching the reception; of being surrounded by the grave, hushed faces of the staff; of being hurriedly escorted along familiar corridors. At some point Charlie had tactfully withdrawn. And then, suddenly, she was in Grace's room, in her parents' arms, all three of them pressed tight together, holding and rocking, holding and rocking. . . . She closed her eyes.

"Flora," said Grace's voice.

Her sister was standing outside the window, but no one else seemed able to see her presence. She was holding a line of red silk. A warm summer breeze blew into the sterile hospital room.

Flora looked at the bed, where Grace's body was stretched out, more waxen and empty-looking than ever before. Machines pulsed, lights blinked.

"Join me," said the other Grace.

"Flora—where are you going?" asked her mother through her tears.

"Into the garden," Flora replied, dazzled by her sister's smile, her beckoning hand. "I need . . . I need to go alone. . . ."

Outside, the clinic's gardens overflowed with the abundance of summer. It was different from the summers here that Flora remembered from before, for even in the height of the season, there was always something clipped and functional about the neat flowerbeds and trim lawns. Today, everything was luxuriantly overgrown. The grass was high and meadow-sweet; blossoms unraveled from briars and arbors; fruit swelled on the trees.

Grace, however, was the Grace from the hospital bed, no longer in the scarlet ball gown but dressed in the plain, clean clothes Flora knew from her visits. Her skin looked thin and sickly, and when Flora—tentative, distrustful, hardly daring to hope—moved to embrace her, she could feel the frailty of her bones, the slackness of the muscle. A faint medicinal smell clung to her.

For a long while the two sisters didn't say anything, just held each other's hands, drinking in each other's faces.

Finally, Grace reached to touch a strand of Flora's hair. "You've grown up," she said wonderingly. "You're so pretty. I knew you would be."

Flora smiled through her tears, and touched the curve of Grace's cheek in return.

"You've been looking for me, haven't you? All this while."

"For—for five years."

"So long . . ." Grace linked her arm with her sister's, and

began to walk along one of the mossy paths, following the thread she still held in one hand. Her movements were slow and uncertain, her voice weak. "I could hear you calling me, sometimes. I knew you were coming."

They went deeper into the garden, among the bees and butterflies and birdsong, through tangled grasses and under flickering leaves. As they did so, the unhealthy pallor began to disappear from Grace's skin, the bloom returned to her face and the gold burnish to her hair. She grew sleek and sure-footed.

At last they came to a grove of apple trees where honeysuckle tumbled over an ancient wall. They sat down together, their backs against the sun-warmed stone. The clinic's rooftops and chimneys, which had been dimly visible through the trees, had disappeared from view.

Flora took the card from her pocket. The Triumph of Love. Two figures in a garden, apples and roses and rainbows, an angel with burning wings.

"This is what you were playing for, wasn't it?"

Grace took the card, tracing the image lightly with her fingertip. "It was how I began, yes."

"I know it was because of Will. You were in love with him."

"I thought I was in love with him. I badly wanted to be in love, you see." She gave a rueful laugh. "Of course, poor Will was hopelessly unsuitable."

Flora stared. "*Poor* Will? If it wasn't for him, you wouldn't ever have got mixed up with the Game, you wouldn't have been dealt that awful Eight of Swords, or taken those risks. It was because of Will that we lost you to the Arcanum."

"If it hadn't been Will, it would have been someone else. Or something else."

"But . . . But, Grace, you were—you had—everything. . . ."

Grace sighed, narrowing her eyes as she looked up through the shivers of light on apple leaves.

"So people kept telling me. The perfect girl in her perfect world . . . All my life, Flo, things have come easily. Too easily, perhaps. I don't think I ever had to work for anything, not properly. Sometimes I'd look around at all the pleasant people I knew, the nice things I had and the plans I'd made, and all I could think was: *Is this it?*

"When I realized that I liked Will and he didn't like me, it was . . . excruciating . . . humiliating . . . but invigorating, too. I convinced myself that I was in love. I had never felt so desperately, thrillingly alive.

"Then I found the Game, and realized I could win Will's heart, just like the knights of old. The heroes who charged off to slay demons and hunt treasure, all for the love of a fair lady. Or gentleman, in my case.

"I was a good knight, too. I played my round successfully. And I won the right to claim the Triumph of Love."

Flora frowned. "If you won, then why . . . ? I don't understand."

"Don't you?" Grace was twirling a daisy in her fingers, and had begun to pluck its petals. "'She loves him, she loves him not. . . .'" The singsong was playful, but there was nothing lighthearted in her expression as she watched the

313

little white flecks float away. "As soon as I knew Will could be mine, I realized it—he—didn't matter anymore. Of course Will wasn't worth the trials I'd undergone for his sake. No one was. I entered the Game to find love, but the Game itself had seduced me.

"So although I never claimed my prize, I decided to play on anyway. Gambling on the cards and capturing triumphs."

Flora felt a chill breeze blow through the sunshine. "Grace, do you mean you wanted to be . . . to be a queen? A Game Master?"

"No, not really. I didn't think that far ahead. For the first time in my life, I was living in the moment. As long as I was in the Arcanum, I didn't have to be this perfect person. This *mannequin*. Instead, I could be someone else entirely: reckless and fierce, untamed. It's ironic, I know, but until that maze in the Eight of Swords, I felt I had never been so free."

Flora had to turn away, into the shade, so that Grace would not see her face. But her sister took her hand again, and pulled her gently round.

"I know what you're thinking. You're thinking how stupid I've been, and how selfish. You're wondering how I could be so careless, not just with my own life but with the lives of the people who loved me. And you are right."

Flora swallowed hard. "I understand about the freedom," she whispered. "I know the Arcanum has temptations."

"So do many things. I have no defense except this: I never imagined that I would fail. The risks I took only made me feel more invincible. Isn't that absurd? Yet in my vanity, I had decided I was the heroine of my own epic, and that my story would always come right in the end." She smiled sadly. "You have reason to be angry with me, Flo. But there are some things you only learn through loss."

They were quiet together after that. Grace sighed. "You will help them, won't you, Flora?"

"Who?"

"Our parents. You're stronger than me and now you'll have to be stronger than all of us."

"They don't need me." The chill breeze blowing through the sunshine breathed on Flora's heart. "They need you," she said with a stubbornness that failed to stifle her unease. "And now that you're back, we'll be a family again and everything will be all right."

"There is no going back."

"Of course there is." Flora scrambled to her feet, looking for the clinic's rooftops through the trees. "Because you're coming with me."

She had abandoned all thoughts of her angel, or Misrule, or the end of the world.

But Grace remained where she was, eyes fixed on the daisies.

Flora seized her sister by the wrists, pulling her up after her.

"What's *wrong* with you?" she cried, just as she had in the Eight of Swords. "I'm here to take you home, out of this. I'm saving you."

"I know." Grace put the card and the line of red silk in

her hand. "That's why you have to follow this again. One last time."

"W-will you come with me?"

Grace was dappled with sunshine and shadow; if there was sadness on her face, the giddy light danced it away. She nodded. "I'll be with you to the end."

FAME

CHAPTER TWENTY-SEVEN

TOBY HAD ONLY EVER seen the crypt below Temple House silent and empty. On this occasion, the stone vaults were filled with people. Some were talking discontentedly in huddles; others kept to themselves, staring into space. Many looked exhausted and unkempt, like refugees.

The illustration on his card, of a radiant winged figure blowing a trumpet, cheered him a little. He'd summoned the angel of Fame itself! For a moment, he thought he could hear the echo of an angelic fanfare.

"Toby, is that you?"

"Mia!" he exclaimed. "What are you doing here?"

"The same as these other knights and knaves: waiting for the Game to be restored."

"Oh." Mia looked more solid than the vision in the Eight of Cups, but she was still tense and brittle, and thinner than he remembered. "Have you been here awhile, then?"

"Hard to say. It feels like ages, but you know how oddly time works in the Game. We were all in the Arcanum, trying out our alleged new freedoms—though, as it turns out, it's not much of a freedom to wander through the cards with no purpose and no end in sight. . . . Anyway, suddenly there was an almighty crash and everyone got dumped down here." She smiled humorlessly. "Misrule must be playing at snakes and ladders."

Toby shifted his feet. So the kings and queens weren't the only players sent tumbling off the Arcanum's board. But whatever force had caused the quake, he was pretty sure it wasn't Misrule who'd triggered it.

"Can't you get out? There should be stairs up to the main house. Over there, through that arch."

"I know. Some people have already left that way. Others think that if you leave, you won't be able to get back into the Game ever again. Not that there's much of a Game left to gamble on."

"Oh," said Toby inadequately. He paused. "Do you mind telling me, now, what you wanted to win?"

"Time."

This only made Toby more curious. The triumph's reward was the chance for someone to change an aspect of their past. "To do what?"

"I had a boyfriend who died. It was a car accident in bad weather, late at night." Her voice was flat. "We quarreled before he left. So I wanted to go back to that night and make things right between us." She sighed. "I don't think turning back time would prevent Peter's accident—that was his fate, not mine. But I would do anything, *anything,* for another chance to tell him I loved him."

Toby hung his head. It was his fault Mia hadn't been given her rightful prize. His fault that all these other people—full of desires and dreams, desperate ambitions—had been cheated of their reward. "Mia . . . I . . ."

"It's all right, Toby. When you crossed paths with Misrule, you were subject to forces beyond your control. I don't blame you for what's happened, not anymore."

He flushed in mingled gratitude and embarrassment. "When it's played properly," he said, "the Game can be a force for good. I see that now. I just wish the others—the other, er, chancers—could understand. Obviously, they want to win their prizes; everyone in the Game does. But they still hate it."

"And you don't?"

"No. Not entirely."

She looked at him searchingly. "Then have you found a way to stop Misrule?"

"I think so. The High Priest told me and the other chancers to find the Triumph of Eternity. It's the triumph that's supposed to control all the others, even Misrule. We each have to play another move to win it."

"I hope you're right. But I'm beginning to fear that in order to destroy Misrule, you will have to destroy everything that's good about the Game as well as the bad. What if playing Eternity is the end of everything?"

He squared his jaw. "I suppose that's a risk we have to take."

Mia pulled him into a swift embrace. "Good luck, Toby. I know you'll do the right thing. For our Game, for everyone." She stood back and gestured to the weary figures slumped under the vaults. "We're all counting on you."

"So why don't you come with me? You can help. The two of us."

She shook her head. "Fortune's chosen you, not me. This has to be your quest."

Toby knew she was right. The weight of destiny was upon him, his burden and privilege. He only wished he knew where this final card was leading him and what he must do to release its angel. As he walked away from Mia and the other players, into the flicker of ancient shadows, he felt he had never been so alone.

He had a final look through his deck before he started up the stairs. Each card was so strange, and so beautiful. In addition to the court cards of the Pentacles suit, he still had three triumphs: the Star, the Sun and Time. He wasn't able to give Mia the latter as a prize, but now he wondered what else such a powerful card could do.

Toby thought back to how he and Flora had won their last move, by playing her Seven of Cups within his Triumph of Strength. They might not have the same control over their decks as the old Game Masters had, but there must be all kinds of wonderful things he could learn to do with the cards—if only he had the chance. He looked back at the card he must play, Fame, and sighed. Victory was almost as hard to imagine as defeat. Everything and everyone before the Game seemed meaningless, so once the four of them had destroyed it, what would be left?

As Toby climbed the stairs up to the ballroom of Temple House, his feet struck the steps in time to his thoughts. Onward, upward, alone. One thing was certain: he could not go back to being the old Toby, that small, needy person always hovering at the edge of things. He had changed inside the Game; outside of it, this change must be recognized, too.

The Arcanum seemed to agree with him, for when he reached the panel at the top of the stairs, it sprang open to the sound of distant music. Bugles blew triumphantly. At the same time, he had to blink his eyes against the brightness. It appeared all the mirrors had been restored, for the flood of sun through the windows lit up the whole room, so that the blaze of light and music felt like one and the same. Yet when the splendor cleared, he saw he was back in the wrecked ballroom, in evening gloom.

Toby paused uncertainly. He looked at the card in his hands, and then at the window. The square outside was filling with people, and even from inside the building, he could hear their excited hum. Was this on the Arcanum or the home side of the threshold? He wasn't sure.

"Hello, squirt," a familiar voice drawled from the doorway.

Toby whirled around. No, he thought. Not here, not now. I can't bear it. But it wasn't Seth. It was the Master of Misrule.

"What have you done to the others?" Toby demanded.

The man laughed softly. "Nothing. I haven't so much as set eyes on them."

"So why me?"

Misrule gave a wide, sweet smile. "Because you are the only one of the four who understands the true nature of the Game."

"Flattery won't get you anywhere. I'm not an idiot."

"On the contrary, you are my greatest adversary."

Toby snorted.

"You think I mock you! No, and I will tell you why. For you alone did not fritter away the power of the ace you were dealt, but used your own wits to win the Seven of Swords. When I lured all four Game Masters to the Tower, only you, therefore, could conjure shelter from the inferno there."

"So Cat was right! You did mean for that card to kill us—"

"The Tower was merely a wager, which the four of you won. That does not mean I failed."

"How d'you mean?"

"I mean that when you raised the stakes, I raised my Game. If I truly wanted to end your run in the Arcanum, I would have done so long ago. But a good gambler can turn any hand to his advantage.... Besides," he continued, his expression brightening, "your triumph over the Tower was not the only proof of your talents. You displayed your authority when you divined the secret of the Emperor's orb. You showed the strength of your mind in Cybele's circus. When your comrades were downcast, you heartened them. When they faltered, you led the way. You—"

"Stop twisting things to make them all about me," Toby muttered. "Everyone did their bit."

"Ah, but not for the same reasons. The other three stumbled into the Game through mischance. You found it while in pursuit of another kind of game and another kind of challenge—one of your own creation, which had been stolen from you. Just like the Game was once stolen from me. . . .

"Shall I tell you why your friends will never understand you? Why you will always be separate to them? Those other three set out to win their prizes because they were desperate, driven by needs and passions beyond their control. But when you gambled on the Chariot, it was not the triumph you wanted but the thrill of its chase. For you, Toby, play only for the joy of playing. And that is why you are the only Game Master worthy of the name."

Cat's angry words came back to him. *You don't understand what it's like for me, for any of us. . . .* Toby began to back away. "You're wrong. I'm not that kind of person. I don't want to play with people's lives. I'm not interested in cruelty for kicks."

"But we both know the best of what the Game bestows. Liberation! Transformation! Hope!" The man's blue eyes shone ardently. "Think what you will destroy if the Game falls with me. Think what you will deny yourself. Think of a future of drab mornings and dusty corridors, of meaningless conversations and empty gestures, where desperation is measured in inches and escape is called fantasy."

"That's . . . how . . . that's—"

"That is life. Yet whatever you do with yours, nothing can ever compare to what you have known in the Arcanum. Do you imagine that if you prevail against me, anything will change? No one will know what you have accomplished. No one will acknowledge your sacrifice. No one will care."

"I don't want to be famous."

I just don't want to be irrelevant, said Toby's inner voice. And that was the voice Misrule answered.

"It doesn't matter how many ideas you had or have," he said in Seth's hateful drawl, "or even how good they are."

"Shut up."

Misrule's smile slanted. "The fact is," he continued, still speaking in Seth's voice, "you're not the kind of person who will ever be able to make anything of them. Because other people won't be interested, so long as the ideas come from you."

Then he said, very gently, "You are worth more than that."

Toby made his fingers into claws, scrunched them up and then opened his fists. "This is pointless. Whatever I might be worth, whatever I might want, you're not going to stop me. I've seen what you plan to do with my city, my world, and all the people in it. There's no way in hell I'll let that happen."

"Brave words. But whether my Lottery stands or falls, Fortune is mistress of us both," said the Master of Misrule. He spread out his hands invitingly. "Though you may reject Luck, can you escape Destiny?"

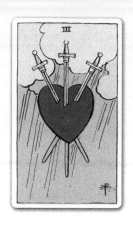

CHAPTER TWENTY-EIGHT

ALEC CRAWLEY SHUT THE DOOR behind him. He was holding a black and blue scratchcard. Misrule's face laughed from its silver coin.

"Long time no see." His gaze moved leisurely from Bel to Cat. "Your niece, I gather. Looks a chip off the family b-block."

Bel sprang in front of Cat. She seemed to gain in height; heat rolled off her body. Her hair flamed and eyes glittered against the deathly white of her skin.

"Get away from us."

"Hmm . . . Is she as much t-trouble as you, I wonder?"

The man moved closer, dusting pale powder from his hands as he nodded a greeting at Cat. "You did me a good turn in the graveyard. A pity you'll soon be g-going there yourself."

His hand moved toward the inside of his jacket, but before it got there, Bel bared her teeth and lunged at him, giving a strangled cry. He struck her across the face, a crashing blow that sent her hurtling off balance. The second smacked her head against the wall. Her body slid downward in a limp heap.

Alec Crawley pulled out a gun.

Cat didn't cry out. She didn't rush to Bel. She stayed exactly as she was, mesmerized. Here he was at last. The murderer. The monster. The man of her darkest dreams.

"So what are you playing for?" she asked.

"Tough kid, aren't you?" he remarked, not unappreciatively, before swinging the gun around from Bel's head to her own.

"You killed my mum and dad to get into the Game. I'd like to know what prize they died for."

"Justice, as it h-happens."

How apt. How pitiless. Cat bit her lip until she tasted blood.

"B-bribery and corruption don't go as far as they used to," he explained. "With Justice in my pocket and the law on my side, I'd be unt-touchable. Crime without fear of punishment. Not that you're doing so b-badly yourself. . . . Queen of something, I heard."

"Queen of Swords." She fixed him with her cool gray stare. "Orphans tend to be high-achieving. We're used to making our own way."

"So what happened to your predecessor?"

"He came to a bad end."

"He won't b-be the only one."

On the floor, Bel twitched and moaned. Cat didn't even glance toward her. All her energies were fixed on proving herself a Game Master to be reckoned with. A Queen of Swords, as chill as any blade.

For she had one sliver of hope: Alec didn't know what had happened to the past kings and queens. That meant he must have been trapped in the Four of Swords for some time, perhaps long enough to have missed the Hanged Man's resurrection as the Master of Misrule. He did not know that the old ways of doing things were gone. Maybe, just maybe, she could turn this to her advantage.

Meanwhile, he surveyed her approvingly. "The Game brought me to you," he said. "After you released me from the graveyard, it l-led me to a grave of my own making, where I found a scratchcard on the g-ground. It is luck that delivered you to me, the p-power of the Game."

He smiled. "And now we are g-going to Temple House, where you will award me every triumph you possess."

Cat could almost have laughed. Temple House was indeed the place of prizegiving: a triumph came into effect only once its winner carried the amulet of their court through its door. So, yes, the power of the Game was at work—but not in the way Alec Crawley imagined. He had captured a queen with no prizes to bestow. Except for Misrule's gift of Justice, that is. Cat looked from her aunt to Alec Crawley and felt the bitterness burn through her, like acid.

❧

Bel was still unconscious when they left. The rest of the people in the casino might have been unconscious, too, for all the attention paid to them. Cat and her family's murderer walked out of the door together and through the West End.

She half expected to see Death riding his white horse up Regent Street. Her nightmare had proved a better prophecy than the High Priestess's oracle. She felt the card edges of the angel that was supposed to wheel out Eternity, but it was only a piece of colored paper. Just like that other card, the Triumph of Justice, which she had carried so far and so pointlessly. The scent of lilies and sound of water had gone. The farther they walked, the more she began to give up hope of escape, let alone punishment, or any kind of resolution.

Mercury Square was often curiously elusive, and hard to locate. This time, however, as Cat and Alec Crawley wended their way through Soho and toward Bloomsbury, they were moving as part of a general crowd. There was a steady drift of people clutching silvery-blue-and-black flyers, laughing and talking self-consciously, like guests on the way to a party they weren't quite sure about.

The Arcanum was very near. Its closeness was not like the natural overlap at Temple House: there was an almost physical sense of tension. It made Cat think of the transformation of the Minotaur into two separate beings, how the struggle of a human body could be seen both within and outside the bulk of the animal one. She could hardly believe how the people around her remained oblivious.

"What's going on?" said Alec Crawley in her ear. The gun barrel ground between her ribs, and she caught the

smell of decay. Close to, his skin was clammy and pallid. The
rot from the Four of Swords had already set in.

"I don't know."

"You're a Game M–Master."

"The Game has changed."

Cat had been part of several gatherings at Mercury Square,
but tonight's crowd looked too disunited and individual for
an Arcanum throng. Locals and tourists of all ages and de-
scriptions were flocking in, while a few stray policemen and
a TV crew wandered about, looking as if they couldn't quite
think how they'd got here or what they were supposed to be
doing. A fairground jingle added to the party atmosphere. It
was New Year's Eve, after all: a night for gatherings and fes-
tivity, and happy-go-lucky adventuring. Most of the anticipation was focused on a Ferris wheel that towered in front
of Temple House.

Cat's mind swarmed with the visions from the High
Priest's mirrors, of blue fire and whirling cards, yet they
seemed curiously flat and far away. Even the image of Bel
slumped on the floor seemed barely real to her. I'm so tired,
she thought. I can't think or do anything, not anymore.

Dumbly, because there was nothing else to do, she began
to work her way across the square. Alec Crawley was close
on her heels, the gun pressed hard in her back. They went
behind the wheel and through the broken door of Temple
House before she was ready for it, or anything.

The wreckage left by Misrule's revels had been cleared
from the hall, and the black-and-white marble was as smooth

and polished as it had ever been. Knight and queen faced each other from their separate squares.

"Now," said Alec, "you will give me my p-prize."

As Flora held the thread in her unwilling hands, the breeze cascaded through the sun-drenched trees, so that their glade became a prism of leaf-light. Her sister was bathed in its rainbows.

"Follow the thread. Please, Flora. It's my only chance."

"Where will it take me?"

"I don't know. But we are near its end."

And so Flora followed the line of red silk along the wall, through blossom and birdsong, dewy ferns and lacy petals, until she came to a weather-beaten door. Grace walked with her.

Flora pushed the door open, and found herself in a marble hallway.

Blaine was lost in the mists again. The Arcanum was reaching out for him: its air in his lungs, its haze in his eyes. The sharp edges of the playing card dug into his hand. It would lead him to his quarry, he was sure of it. And although he was hunting a different man than before, as the damp fog-shapes coiled and billowed, it seemed this was what he had been doing, always. Chasing phantoms through mist.

And then the mist cleared, and he found himself at the north corner of Mercury Square.

Blaine shouldered his way through the crowd, ignoring the indignant protests of those around him. Just as he reached the other side of the garden, the fairground music crackled into static. It returned at an ear-popping pitch of competing melodies that were both jarring and piercingly sweet. At the same moment, the rim of the Ferris wheel burst into flame. The crowd gave a collective jump.

He pressed on through the confusion, and into Temple House.

Blaine saw Cat and the Knight of Wands face to face in front of him. He saw Toby at the foot of the stairs. He saw Flora emerge from the door to their right. He saw a dazzle of blue sparks, and Misrule appear in the center of the hall.

The Master of Misrule's face was joyous and welcoming. His motley robes shook and shimmered as he clapped his hands in delight.

"Ah, my angels! I knew you'd bring them to me."

They moved together, instinctively, even Alec Crawley. All were dazed and bewildered, as unprepared for their sudden reunion as for the intervention of Misrule. Before anyone could react further, Misrule snapped his fingers. At once, the four playing cards released themselves from clothes and hands, and flew through the air to their new master: Temperance, Love, Fame and the Devil.

"I don't understand," Toby croaked. "Does this mean you—you wanted us to get Eternity all along?"

Misrule smiled radiantly. "The Game is already mine; I have no need for the Great Triumph. When you summoned the angels, you brought them out of the Arcanum. Yet you failed to finish your moves, and failed to release them into the world. And since they are still part of my Game, I shall take their powers for myself. Behold—"

He ripped all four cards in half.

> *The glory of the Lord went up from the cherub,*
> *and stood over the threshold of the house; and the*
> *house was filled with the cloud, and the court was*
> *full of the brightness of the Lord's glory.*

Cloud billowed, light blazed, as the noise of beating wings and rushing wind roared through Temple House. Kings, queens and knight reeled from the onslaught.

Misrule, meanwhile, stood tall and proud. In a commanding movement, he brought the thumb and forefinger of his left hand together, holding them up to make a circle in the air. The writhing, rushing, feathery cloud was sucked into it, like thread being pulled through the eye of a needle. There was a sound like the clash of cymbals and the crack of rocks as the space ringed by Misrule's thumb and finger glimmered and solidified.

Now he was holding a silver coin. He tossed it into the air, where it hung, suspended, and did not fall. As the coin began to spin, sparks shot out of the Ferris wheel's spokes. Misrule himself grew taller, brighter, more terrifying than before. Blue fire glittered in his eyes, flashed at his fingertips.

> *For I will fill mine hand with coals of fire from*
> *between the cherubim, and scatter them over the*
> *city.*

He lifted up his arms, and the wheel outside rose at his bidding, until it hung high above the square, huge and whirling and burning bright, like the eye of God.

Beneath it, the unwary crowd oohed and aahed as if at any normal fireworks display.

The Master of Misrule laughed to hear them. "They cannot yet see all the wonders I have worked, but they will not be in ignorance for long. . . ."

He turned from the doorway to look at the four kings and queens. The coin still hung in the air above his head, tumbling over and over yet never falling. Laughing heads and serpents' tails flashed in and out of view.

Misrule put his excitement aside; he was as solemn and peaceful as when they had first met. "You have had a fine run, but the Wheel has turned and your hand is played out. Will you renounce your mastery?"

The four of them had faced loss and defeat before, but this was different. This was everyone's defeat: a whole world's worth of it. Yet the disaster was too huge and too sudden to comprehend. Misrule's triumph had not shaken them out of their individual crises. All Flora could think of was Grace, Cat of Bel, Blaine of men with knives and guns.

Only Toby kept his focus. His hand grasped the card he had kept back for a final gamble, the moment of last resort.

"You should be so lucky," he said to Misrule. "Hold on to me," he told the others. Then he took out the Triumph of Time.

The triumph that Mia and so many others had struggled to win was one of the most potent, and unpredictable, cards in the deck. Toby had once been in its move, and barely escaped with his life. Now he was going to play it the same way he and Flora had played the Seven of Cups, by bringing its powers out of its own move and into Temple House.

He tore the card across. There was the sound of chiming clocks, breaking glass, and running sand. And everything revolved backward.

IX

TIME

CHAPTER TWENTY-NINE

MERCURY SQUARE WAS SILENT and empty, the rustling shadows behind the garden rails illuminated only by the glow of the streetlamps. Wind gusted, driving sleet into Cat's face, and she looked down at the damp pavement, imagining her old self shivering on the corner. She had returned to the first night she had come to Temple House.

Cat had no idea where the Triumph of Time had taken Blaine, Flora and Toby. She was not, however, alone.

"I d-don't understand." Alec Crawley was swaying on his feet. His voice was unsteady, too. "Who—? What—?"

Cat briefly closed her eyes. It wasn't over, not yet. She supposed she should feel relieved.

"Toby tried to turn back the clock," she said at last. "At least, I think that's what he meant to do. To go back in time so everything could be put right... Only it didn't quite work out. We've gone back in time, but not real time in the real world. Instead, we've gone back in time in the Arcanum."

"How do you know? How do you know this isn't real?"

Cat looked at her parents' murderer, sweating and twitching at her elbow, and realized she was no longer afraid of him. The golden curtain hung across the entrance to Temple House, just as it had on her first visit, though there was no concierge waiting to take her invitation, and no sounds of revelry behind the stiff brocade.

"This is only a dim copy of the night I joined the Game. If we'd really gone back in time," she said flatly, "there'd be a party under way inside, with the High Priest guarding the entrance, and the old kings and queens calling the shots." And Cat could make a different choice: not to give her invitation to the old man, not to enter the Arcanum—above all, not to release the Hanged Man. But she knew it was too late for that.

She drew back the curtain. The other end of the building was a near mirror image of their own. It was the same composition of black-and-white marble, golden drapes, open door. The doorway opposite, however, framed a different view of Mercury Square, lit by the flame of a blue wheel and seething with people. In the center of the doorway, a silver coin danced in the air. *Heads. Tails. Heads. Tails . . .*

"There," said Cat. "That's the real and present world, on the other side of the coin."

"What's happening t-to it?"

"Misrule's moving his own mad version of the Game across the thresholds, and soon everyone will be a player.

They won't have any choice. They'll all be enslaved to his Lottery."

Alec wiped his damp forehead. "Very well, so maybe we're not in the p-past. Maybe we're in something better. Maybe this is an alternative present—one we can make our own."

An alternate reality . . . another chance . . . If she turned and walked away, could she go back to some Arcanum equivalent of Greg's flat and find Bel and her old life, just as it had always been? And if she stayed in it long enough, would she be able to forget there had ever been anything else? "Same world, different view" was how Toby had once described the Arcanum to her. But that wasn't quite right. One view was smoke and mirrors. The mirrors might be real mirrors, the smoke real smoke, but what you saw in them was still illusion.

The graveyard smell intensified as Alec sidled closer. "You're still a queen, aren't you? You have the Game's powers. You have your t-triumphs. And you can put them to good use, whether we're in the Arcanum or a p-parallel universe or Hell itself. Together we can—"

Cat thrust her last card into his hand. "Here's Justice, like you wanted. Do your worst with it."

"Where are you g-going?"

"Back to reality—back to the present. If I hurry, there's still time."

"For what?"

"To find Bel, and make things right. To ask her to forgive me."

"*Forgive* you?" Alec laughed shrilly. "She b-betrayed you just like she did me. You don't owe her anything."

"Fool." The scent of her angel's lilies had returned, blowing away the graveyard stench, the taste of bitterness. "I wanted justice, but not at any price. Yes, you murdered my parents; yes, Bel lied. But what does that matter now? Life as we know it is ending."

"You can't s-save the world," he said, clutching at her arm, a whine in his voice. "You can't stop Misrule. But here you're a queen. You can r-rule this place. We both can."

Cat barely heard him. She was thinking of how she had looked at Bel that last time, so hard and so cold, when she said she had no certainties, *nothing,* because Bel had taken all of them away.

But of course Cat had certainties. She had twelve years' worth of them. Twelve years of a love that was lived in but not looked at, because it was so solid, so all-encompassing, that whatever happened outside of it couldn't touch the sureness of what was within. There was no alternative to that truth.

"I'm sorry," she whispered to Bel. Card or no card, she finally understood what her angel needed, if it was to be released. Temperance weighed and measured, but in search of balance, not judgment. The words came to her like those from a remembered dream: *Yet I shall temper justice with mercy. . . .*

She stepped into the house.

"Wait. Come b-back."

Cat walked past the curtain, her eyes fixed on the

dancing coin. It was the emblem of Misrule's power, she was sure of it. His power, and that of the angels still imprisoned in his Game.

She walked back to her own time, back toward Bel, and forgiveness. She walked into the perfume of lilies and the sound of running water, the rush of wings.

"I'm w-warning you—"

But Alec's warning came too late. The first of the cherubim was released.

The first evening Blaine came to Temple House was three days after he had arrived in London. At that point, he was sleeping on the floor of a friend's brother's flat. He wasn't a good houseguest: brooding and jittery, ready to snap at the slightest thing. The brother's girlfriend didn't like him being there; she kept looking at his bandaged arm and pursing her lips. He could see he'd have to move on. That afternoon, he had phoned Helen and, for once, she'd actually come to the phone, her voice quavering with hope. "Hello?" she said. "Hello? Is that you?"

He had put the phone down before Helen could name whom she was hoping for. It would be Arthur, not him; that was for sure. For the rest of the afternoon, he trudged relentlessly through the streets, gripping the card in his pocket. Nobody he asked had ever heard of a Mercury Square. Yet he found it in the end.

Or it found him, he thought, looking at how the tree branches blurred into the bronze dusk, just as they had on his first visit. Somehow, the Triumph of Time's chiming clocks and running sand had taken him back to the start. The start of everything. This time, though, he must call his mother. Tell her that there was danger ahead, that bad things were happening, that he would look after her—

He must tell her he was coming.

Then he heard a gunshot from within the house.

The bullet grazed Cat's arm; she felt the sting and shock of it, and the warmth of blood. Alec's eyes bulged and his arm shook as he waved the gun. "No!" he cried. "You can't go. You have to give me your t-triumphs—"

Cat didn't even look at him. She was gazing at Misrule's coin, whose spinning had begun to slow, to grow heavy and languid.

But when Blaine burst through the golden curtain, he only had eyes for the Knight of Wands, and the jagged black shadow beneath him.

Blaine slammed into Alec Crawley's back.

They both went skidding across the floor, snarling and grappling. The gun fell, too, and was scrabbled for by Alec and snatched away by Blaine. He drove his fist into the man's face and a flash of joy sparked through him. As the Knight of Wands flailed and writhed beneath him, Blaine gripped him by his hair and smashed his head against the floor.

"Don't you dare hurt her," he shouted. "Don't you *dare*. You're dead. You should be a ghost—just like the other monster I've been chasing. All this time—this *useless* time!"

He wanted to bury his fists and knees into every soft part of the man's body, grinding him into bone dust, blood paste.

Something plucked at his shirt. He twitched his shoulders impatiently. Then he heard his name.

"It's all right, Blaine," said Cat. "You've saved me. You've won."

She was standing there, drained but resolute, clutching her bloodied arm.

Blaine's own arm ached. The Knight of Wands stirred and groaned as the shadow pooled around him, thick as oil. Blaine felt soiled by it. All that anger and hate, all that fear . . . Blaine took the gun from the waistband of his jeans and got to his feet. He motioned Alec to get up as well, his breath rasping harshly.

"I should have stayed, I know that now. I should have seen it through. When I abandoned my mother, I let Arthur win. I abandoned myself, too. I gave up everything. I let the Game take me over. I let it trick me and—"

A sob forced its way out of his throat. He shuddered all over. But when he was able to speak again, his voice was calm.

"Arthur White was a bad man, and you're far worse. In fact, you belong to Hell itself. But I'm no killer. Here."

He passed the gun to Cat.

"Blaine . . . no. This isn't what I—" She paused. "We might not have our cards, but I think we're in your move now. So whatever happens next, it's got to be your call." Cat had come to realize that whatever strange angels or demons needed to be released, they were as much a part of her, Blaine's, Flora's and Toby's personal history as the Arcanum's. To win these last moves, and unleash the powers the cards represented, would depend on the choices they made for their lives outside the Game.

"I understand." He glanced at Misrule's slow-turning coin. "It's all right. Just keep the gun pointed at his head and make sure he doesn't pull any tricks."

Cat stood between Alec Crawley and the curtain to the false past. Blaine stood before the doorway to the true present.

"Here's your choice," he announced.

Blaine pointed to where the burning wheel whirled in the sky. Fireworks were flying from its spokes in a rainbow explosion of wands, cups, swords and pentacles as the reckless crowd cheered below.

"Either you're going to go out into our city and face what's coming, along with the rest of humanity, or you can take your chance in the Arcanum, starting with a card from my deck."

"You're d-dealing me a new move?"

"It'll be a lucky dip. I have seven cards from my Suit of Wands and two triumphs for you to pick from. Here's the threshold."

He rolled his die along the checkered floor. The print of a silver wheel appeared on a black square.

Alec Crawley looked at Cat, and the curtain behind her. Her face was white, her arm bloody, but her aim was steady.

"I have a t-triumph of my own now. Justice."

Blaine shrugged. "You think Justice will count for anything in Misrule's world? Then stay here to find out."

"All right." Alec Crawley licked his cracked lips. "All

right." He touched the blood on his face and laughed a little. "I'll hazard another card."

The King of Wands held out his deck. The illustrated sides were blank. Cards dealt by Game Masters to players always were, until they were taken into the Arcanum. The knight fumbled through them with shaking hands. Even so, his eyes gleamed with excitement at the moment of choice. He was a gambler, after all.

Alec Crawley bent to the threshold's sign, and traced the pattern of its wheel. A coin appeared in his palm. He fingered it, and the card, with a final hesitancy. He grinned crookedly at Cat. "Time to t-take what's due to me."

In a flip and flash of metal, he was gone. With a feathery rustle, the thick shadow that followed him was gone, too. The second angel had been released.

Misrule's coin faltered, and began to sink.

Cat and Blaine looked at each other.

"What—what card did he get?"

Blaine flicked through the remainder of his deck. He raised his brows.

"Death."

As soon as Flora realized where she was, she was sure that everything was going to be all right. Misrule's cataclysms faded into insignificance. Here and now was what mattered. Dirty traces of snow rimmed the grass within the railings, pavement and road alike were churned with icy black sludge and brown grit, but all Flora's attention was fixed on the red thread she still held. The end of it was tied across the threshold of Temple House, and Grace was on the other side, framed in the doorway. Beyond her was the garden: golden-green, luminous.

"It's my first night," said Flora, exultant. "The first night I came to Temple House and joined the Game. It means we can go back to how we were. I've brought you home."

She waited for Grace to step out of the doorway, under the thread.

Grace, however, remained where she was. "This isn't home."

"It must be. Time's gone into reverse. At last, the Game has given us our very own miracle. Come here. Come to me."

But her sister shook her head. "I can't, Flo," she said very quietly. "I took a gamble and my gamble failed. The Arcanum has held me for five years. I am too much a part of it now to come home."

"I can still save you—"

"You have already saved me. How else could I have escaped the Spinners and got here?" She indicated the garden behind her, with its roses and rainbows and shining leaves. "Only Love could bring me this far."

"Yes," said Flora, crying, "because Love conquers all."

"No," said Grace with a great and terrible tenderness, "it doesn't."

She reached out and stroked Flora's hair, as she had before. "Listen to me. You must be the one to cut the thread. Not to banish me, but to set me free. From the Arcanum, from everything."

Flora screwed up her face against the drowsy murmur of the bees, the warm scent of honeysuckle. "I won't do it. I won't." Her voice cracked. "You said you'd be with me to the end."

"This *is* the end. And you have to reverse it. For our mother and father, for Will and Charlie, for everyone you've ever known, and a world of strangers besides."

"We already failed—"

"It's not too late. The cherubim can still be released. There is still time for another sacrifice." She held Flora's hands across the thin red silk. "Please," she said softly. "Let me go."

The leaves whispered, the sunshine welled.

"I love you," said Flora.

"I love you," said Grace.

"Forever." Flora wept as she snapped the thread that tied her to her sister, and the angel to the Arcanum.

Across the threshold, Grace smiled. She bloomed with even greater life and beauty, but it was the beauty of the garden, glowing through her, growing ever richer, brighter. Everything was caught in its prism of leaf-light, leaf-shade; the curve of its flowers and honey of its breath; the dew and the dazzle; the dazzle of her—dancing, loosening, losing itself in a last uncontainable loveliness.

ETERNITY

CHAPTER THIRTY

CAT, BLAINE AND FLORA stood together in the hall at Temple House.

Toby stood in the doorway to the square, staring up at Misrule's wheel. Although they were used to the building's shifting interiors, they had never seen the place look so large or so empty.

The three of them felt emptied out also, but this came with a sense of freedom, not hollowness. Blaine felt the lifting of a dark shadow; Cat felt cleansed by sweet waters. Flora felt sun on her face, drying her tears. She could still hear a silvery note ringing in her ears: the chime of Misrule's coin as it fell to the ground.

She turned to the other two. "Did we do it, after all?" she asked. "Are the angels . . . are they . . . free?"

"Not quite," Blaine answered. He pointed to the floor. "Look."

The silver coin was rolling steadily, purposefully, toward where Toby was standing.

"What's he doing?" Cat looked again, and frowned. "And who's he with?"

The disappointment of the Triumph of Time had been crushing, especially since at first glance, Toby thought he'd pulled it off. The wilted brown grass in the garden . . . the traffic fumes and summer heat . . . Everything was how it had been the first evening he'd found Mercury Square. Then, like Cat, he had looked through the door and seen the other side of the coin, and realized that the world was doomed just the same. Even so, he hadn't hesitated. He had raced across the hall in desperate haste to do something, anything. A final gesture. A last stand.

Outside in Toby's city, people were dancing in the streets, under the glare of the wheel. Midnight was not far away. Men, women and children, friends and strangers, were singing and laughing together, feverishly happy. There was a lurid blue light in their eyes. Helplessly, Toby tried to warn them. To tell them to wake up, to get away before the chaos started, before everything changed. Nobody listened. Nobody cared.

In the end, he came back to the steps of Temple House. There was nowhere else to go. It seemed like fate to find that Mia was there, too.

"I had to come," she said eagerly, turning to greet him. "I couldn't wait on the sidelines any longer. Now I see how wrong I was before. Oh, Toby, I didn't know it would be so beautiful!"

Then he, too, looked up at the wheel, properly this time, and as it whirled and flamed, the light seemed to burn through his eyes and into his skull. At once, the nightmares conjured in the High Priest's mirror were exposed as the lies they were. The center of Misrule's wheel glittered with visions of every move ever played in the Game, and every move still to come, in all their beauty and madness. He had reached the heart of the mystery itself.

If this was defeat, then Toby couldn't think of anything more glorious.

Blaine, Flora and Cat hurried to the door. Toby was holding Misrule's coin clamped in his fist.

"Toby," Cat exclaimed breathlessly, "we've still got a chance of winning Eternity. There's just one more angel that needs to be released. Then we'll be able to destroy Misrule and the Game—"

"Destroy it?" A spark of blue flickered within his eyes. "Why would we want to do that?"

"You know why. Because it's mad, it's out of control, it's—"

"That's what *you* say." Toby's voice was cold.

"They don't understand," Mia put in. "They still don't see what's at stake." She turned to the other three, and they saw that her gaze held the same strange glint of blue. "I used to be like you: afraid of the Game, even more afraid of Misrule. All that's changed."

Blaine stared. "Is that a fact?"

"Success and failure are the same to me now. I don't

care, so long as I can keep playing. I don't care about any-thing. Even Toby spoiling my plans for the Ace of Pentacles—it was meant to be."

Toby blinked. "*Your* plans?"

"Oh yes." Mia laughed. "I'm afraid you got our duel the wrong way around: Mr. Marlow was the player you saved by your intervention, not me. *I* ambushed *him*. It was me, too, who played the ace. But I wasn't as angry with you as I should have been. In some ways, you see, it was a relief. I hadn't ever tried to kill someone before." She squeezed his arm affectionately. "Not that it matters anyway. We're all in Fortune's hands."

He frowned.

"There," said Cat disgustedly. "You see what your pre-cious Game does? It creates madmen and murderers. For God's sake, Toby! Don't you under—"

"No," Toby shot back. "*You* don't understand *me*. None of you do. You've always laughed at and patronized me, right from the start. None of you understand what this means to me, how much I—"

"Hush," said Mia, lips parted and eyes bright. "It's beginning."

The Master of Misrule appeared on a platform in the axle of his wheel. He lifted up his arms, and his voice rang jubi-lantly around the square.

"My friends, I know how uncertain this world is. I my-self have suffered imprisonment and torment. I have been called a traitor and charlatan, condemned by false laws. Yet my luck turned, and now I want to share the fruits of my victory with you.

"This is not my city yet, but I know its heart like I know my own. Every city is sacred to the fortune hunters, those who hope against hope to turn a corner and find a pavement of gold. These are my people.

"Some of you have played the cards in my Lottery of Luck. Some of you have lost; many more have won. Those of you dealt adversity by the serpent's tail, do not despair, for Lady Fortune's Wheel turns in the blink of an eye.

"My new Lottery will be free, and open to everyone, for I guarantee prizes for all. Prizes more potent, more exhilarating and strange than you could imagine. But every one will enrich your lives.

"All of you with hopes and dreams, fears and follies, ambitions and tragedies . . . bring them to me, and I will transform them with my Game."

As the wheel spun and the music played, cards began to float out from between its spokes. The crowd leaped to catch them.

"I'm going to join in," Mia cried. "I want to be in the heart of it, always."

She ran down the steps and into the center of the square.

Toby looked after her, dazed. The blue spark in his eyes trembled. Flora came forward.

"The Game isn't real, Toby. It's what we do outside of it that matters."

He shook his head groggily. "Not what I do." Resentment strengthened his voice. "You don't know what it's like."

"I know the freedom and thrill of the Arcanum. My sister did, too. That's why we lost her. We lost her because she began to love the Game more than she did us, or reality, or even herself."

Flora took his hand. "I don't know what our lives will be like, what we will do with them or the sort of people we will become. Sometimes this excites me, sometimes it frightens me. But that's because even the most ordinary life is a gamble. Its possibilities are infinite."

Toby stared down at the silver coin. Misrule's head laughed up at him. "So . . . so are his."

"Misrule offers prizes, and with them possibilities," said Blaine. "But they're his dreams, not yours. Don't let them take you. Don't give us up."

Toby looked up and met Cat's eyes. She nodded.

"You're worth too much."

Gently, Flora uncurled his fingers from around Misrule's coin. "Let it go, Toby. Let it go."

And, as all over the city its clocks struck midnight, Toby let the coin fall. With it, he released his hopes of heroism, his dreams of fame and the last of the four cherubim.

There was a sound of trumpets. Sad and sweet: the Last Post. The doorway of Temple House filled with cloud once more. When it cleared, its frame enclosed a life-sized playing card. Fame, the angel with the golden horn. The illustration melted away, revealing the Devil enthroned. Love, with the burning wings. Temperance and her chalices.

The angels who stepped out of them were nothing like

their cards. They were huge and winged, only vaguely human in form. Their movements were sinuous as smoke and their bodies were covered in shimmering scales of every color and none.

They spoke as one, in the same lofty, cold tone as the High Priestess's voice of prophecy.

"The offerings are complete. You have summoned us, and you have released us. What would you bid us do?"

"We want—we want the Triumph of Eternity," said Toby, though his voice shook.

"Which of you claims final mastery of the Game?"

"None of us," said Cat. The words came easily, although they did not feel like her own. "The Game has been fought and won, and now it is finished. The board must be put away."

The gods of the Game's city bowed their heads.

"Then you must throw the last coin to turn the last card."

The lost card, and the last: Eternity.

Humbly, Toby faced his fellow king and queens. "May I?"

They nodded. What had once been Misrule's coin lay where it had fallen, its metal now blank and dull.

The King of Pentacles grasped the coin and tossed it up into the heavens.

The walls of Temple House began to soar upward at the same time as the floor stretched out on every side. Soon the building had grown to twice, three times its original size. It was a great temple indeed.

Outside the enlarged doorway, there was nothing but sky. An endless indigo night, in which the stars were concentrated so brightly that the constellations looked ready to burn through Heaven itself. Misrule's wheel outshone them all. He was spread-eagled in the center of it, his white hair streaming, his blue eyes blazing, his mouth open in an anguished howl as the cherubim surged toward the wheel, rolling hoops of fire before them. Strange creatures gleamed within.

> *As for the wheels, it was cried unto them in my hearing, O wheel.*
> *And every one had four faces: the first face was the face of a bull, and the second face was the face of a man, and the third the face of a lion, and the fourth the face of an eagle.*
> *O wheel.*
> *O wheel—*

The four rolling wheels spun into the greater blue one. The moment of impact was a mighty starburst, its explosion soundless, though the sky itself seemed to rock, sending a deep crack ripping through the floor of Temple House. The tangle of wheels and cherubim churned and whirled, faster and faster, a spinning globe.

Finally, it stilled.

Now there was only one wheel, or only the rim of it: a

circle that moved and writhed, its shifting scales like a serpent's, shimmering with every color and none.

A naked dancer was in the center. Neither man nor woman, neither flesh nor spirit, and moving joyfully to the music of the spheres.

The music had no melody, no phrase or rhythm, nor anything else that its human listeners could understand. The senses it spoke to were different from the ones they knew, for its harmony was somehow beyond sound. But just as it became almost too beautiful to bear, both music and dancer faded into the stars.

Only a ring of silver light remained. It now held a woman in the shadow at its heart.

The four kings and queens stood on the edge of the temple's cleft floor. They were pawns on a giant's chessboard. And yet they were also overlooking a confusion of landscapes, and a jostling crowd.

The High Priest and the High Priestess. The Emperor and Asterion and Cybele, the robed Inquisitors, the hatchet-faced nurse, the beaming mayor ... A magician in a top hat and a soldier in camouflage, three sisters winding a thread ... A man with a cluster of swords in his back, another one hanging from a tree ... Each king and queen saw every being they had ever encountered in the Arcanum, and countless others that were strange to them, yet familiar, too. For every face bore the mark of the woman within the Wheel of silver light.

Fors Fortuna, Imperatrix Mundi.

Her eyes were blindfolded. Her smile was knowing.

She beckoned lovingly.

At her summoning, a dark wind thundered through the sky and swept the board clean. Cards flew upward from the tear in the marble, twisting and lifting across the threshold of the temple, and into the Wheel's axle.

The last kings and queens of the Game of Triumphs stood and watched its end. As the cards blew away forever, they ached for their loveliness. Some floated past slowly, reluctantly; some rushed forward; others swooped in intricate spirals around the door. One was caught by a splinter in its frame. Toby saw it but looked away. The card was fluttering like a trapped bird. He reached to free it, faltered and—

Fortune lifted up a hand and spun her Wheel.

The scars on their palms glowed silver-white. Pain flashed through the wheel's mark, so bright and searing it felt as if their own hearts had been branded by the flame. And the four of them were falling, then flying—through solid earth and marble floor, through black and white, among images that cascaded like a stack of cards. Love and loss . . . hope and sorrow . . . beauty . . . fear . . . triumph . . .

All their possibilities, all of them infinite.

FORTUNE

Epilogue

DOGS FRISKED THROUGH the mud as their owners called and cajoled; a group of boys milled around a football. Their scuffles kicked up the remains of a flyer among the leaves, but its glister was long gone. If people did remember flashy coins and a fiery wheel, it was in terms of a craze that had fizzled out as quickly as it had begun. A practical joke or elaborate scam—who knew, who cared? The Lottery of Luck's promises were as dead as the old year.

Charlie and Flora were idling on the steps of a summerhouse that had once borne a threshold wheel. Across the park, the trees' bare branches shone wetly in the brightening afternoon.

"It was a nice evening," he was saying. "I thought your parents looked well."

"Yes. They're . . . doing better, actually," Flora replied.

"My mother in particular. Which is strange. I always thought she'd take Grace's death the hardest."

It was only a month since the end of the world. The end of *a* world, rather. The shock of its fall was still with her.

Flora tilted her head toward the sky, thinking of her sister's final moments.

"Mummy's convinced the angels came for Grace."

"Perhaps they did," Charlie said seriously. "How does that line go? 'There are more things in heaven and earth . . .'"

He touched his cheek, feeling for a bruise that was no longer there. Both of them remembered the blow that couldn't have been dealt, in a place that never existed.

Their eyes met, asking their different questions. An indefinite kind of acknowledgment passed between them.

"Look," said Flora, in mingled embarrassment and pleasure and relief. "Look, there's Toby."

Toby's face broke into a grin as he returned her wave. He began to jog toward them.

"Apparently, he's got some secret project he wants to talk about." Flora lifted her brows mischievously. "I'm rather afraid he's writing a novel. . . . Come on, let's go."

They went to meet Toby, across the sunlit park.

At the same time, in a different part of the city, Cat was sitting on a bench, watching pigeons squabble over crumbs. The back of her seat was engraved with a couplet:

ONE DAY I'LL BE WAITING THERE
NO EMPTY BENCH IN SOHO SQUARE

The words kept running through her head; she was so absorbed in trying to fit a tune to them that she didn't see Blaine until he was standing over her.

"Sorry," he said. "Stupid bus. It's always late."

"Doesn't matter."

Blaine put his bag down and pulled her toward him. Cat put her fingertips to the shadows under his eyes, as she had once wanted to long before. They looked at each other searchingly and a little shyly. They were still getting used to these reunions, adjusting to togetherness after weekdays apart.

"How's Helen?"

"She's started playing the piano again. And she and Liz are going out tonight."

"That's good."

The Game had ended with Flora at her sister's clinic and Cat at her aunt's casino. Toby was back with Mia in Mercury Square, in the dazed aftermath of a party that no one could quite remember. But Blaine had found himself outside Arthur's house.

Helen had opened the door as if she was expecting him. She said she always knew he would come back to her. Afterward, he broke the news that Arthur wouldn't, and she said she knew that, too. When she cried, he thought it was from relief.

"We're getting there." Blaine settled next to Cat on the bench. "There's a lot of stuff we don't talk about. We haven't really talked about that night in the study. Not yet. Still . . . I dunno. Being without me, being without Arthur, perhaps it was good for her. Helen will never be strong. But she's trying. In our different ways, we're both moving on."

Cat nodded. She knew there was no going back. She and Bel would never be quite the same. They had both been stripped down to their rawest, most wounded selves, and although the closeness that had grown out of this was healing, it was different from the old. But they would be the stronger for it.

"Speaking of moving," she said, "we're supposed to be meeting Toby and Flora in a minute."

"They'll wait." Blaine took her hand in his again, drawing her close. "I missed you," he murmured into her neck. "All the time."

Their smiles moved, met, opened; their individual warmth enfolded into one.

Afterward they sat and watched the square, in the intimacy of shared silence.

"I miss it sometimes," Cat said quietly. No need to name names. Through trees, a couple of tourists were photographing the gardener's half-timbered cottage: a fairy-tale fantasy in the heart of London. "I never thought I would. But I do."

"It will always be a part of who we are." Blaine circled his finger around her palm, tracing the line of a vanished scar. "And that's OK. But it won't be part of what we do next. Whatever happens, we're free."

There are many cities with a quiet square, an ancient house, a door that is just ajar.

At the same time, in a different city, a piece of paper was

blowing down a street. It bore no mark from its long journey, or from the splinter on which it had once been caught. It had been saved from banishment and now it danced in freedom on the breeze.

The gilt edges glinted. The card was thick and richly colored, designed to catch the eye. Its movements were not as haphazard as they might first appear. It would find a resting place.

The Arcanum
Temple House, Mercury Square

Admits One

Throw the coin, turn the card.
What will you play for?

AUTHOR'S NOTE

The cards played in the Game of Triumphs are based on the classic Rider-Waite Tarot designs. However, Tarot imagery is full of variations, and my conception of some of the cards in the Greater Arcana also draws on the Visconti-Sforza deck, the Tarocchi del Mantegna and the Tarot de Marseilles.

I have made one small amendment to the excerpts from the Vision of Ezekiel. The rolling wheels, and the four creatures within them, are described in two passages, the first in Ezekiel 1 and the second—which is the one quoted by the High Priestess—in Ezekiel 10. The latter replaces the bull with a cherub's face. No biblical scholars have come up with a satisfactory explanation for this discrepancy, and since the bull featured on the Triumph of Eternity (the World, in the Rider-Waite deck) is a reference to both Ezekiel 1 and Revelation 4:7, I have substituted *bull* for *cherub* in my quotation of Ezekiel 10.

The lines of poetry quoted by the Emperor on pages 248 and 249 are from stanza 69 of *The Rubáiyát of Omar Khayyám,* translated by Edward FitzGerald (1879 edition).

Acknowledgments

A lot of people put a lot of time and effort into this book. Huge thanks are due to Sarah Lilly at Orchard Books, but for this edition, I'd like to give a big cheer to Nancy Siscoe and Katherine Harrison at Knopf. Their insightful and encouraging editing has been truly inspirational.

May Lady Luck smile on them all!